M000316858

Getting Dirty
Sapphire Falls, book three

Erin Nicholas

Copyright 2014 by Erin Nicholas

All Rights Reserved.

No part of this book, with the exception of brief quotations for book reviews or critical articles, may be reproduced or transmitted in any form or by an means, electronic or mechanical, including photocopying, recording, or by any information storage and retrieval system without express written permission from the author.

This is a work of fiction. Names, characters, places, and incidents are the product of the author's imagination or are used fictitiously, and any resemblance to actual persons, living or dead, business establishments, events, or locales is entirely coincidental.

ISBN: 978-0-9915579-7-4

Editor: Heidi Moore
Cover artist: Laron Glover
Copy edits: Fedora Chen
Digital formatting: Author E.M.S.

DEDICATION

This is to "my girls".

Every author needs a team behind her that she can count on
no matter what. Mine includes my family and many, many
people who cheer me on, keep me going, and make this the
best job ever. But then there are those special ones who I
can call on for absolutely anything and who are there over
and over again...
my girls, Kim B, Brenda M, and Crystal S.

CHAPTER ONE

A chicken crossed the road in front of her.

Presumably to get to the other side. There didn't seem to be any other reason.

Not that she thought she really understood why a chicken would do anything.

Lauren Davis stared at the bird as it started to peck the ground on the other side of the path. A chicken. She was in the middle of a place where chickens roamed free.

"*Mmmaaaaaa!*"

She jumped and spun.

And cows. Chickens and cows.

Technically, it was a calf. But it was roaming free. And looking up at her with big brown eyes.

"*Mmmaaaaaa!*"

She did not like cows.

"No," she told it. "I don't know what you're asking, but, no."

It continued to stare up at her with what she would have described as either affection...or predatory intent.

Lauren gave it a frown and propped her hands on her hips. "No."

The calf moved forward and bumped its head against her leg.

So maybe it was affection. It didn't matter. She did not like cows.

"Listen, where I work, you're food. You might want to keep that in mind." She took a step back. The calf followed her.

She wasn't sure what it was about cows that she didn't like, but she didn't. It wasn't a fear or a phobia exactly. But they were big lumbering things. That didn't smell very good. And that attracted flies. And that turned into steaks.

She was a part of an organization that had a mission to

feed the poor, specifically by teaching them to farm. Her company, Innovative Agricultural Solutions, specialized in crops, but they also partnered with a group that provided livestock. Sometimes that meant chickens and cows for egg and milk production, but sometimes it was for their meat.

That freaked Lauren out. In her mind, the food she liked was completely separate from the animals they supplied to the villages. She worked hard to keep it that way. It was silly but necessary. She wouldn't make it long as a vegetarian.

"Stop it," she admonished the calf. "I can't look at you and think about filet mignon at the same time. That's creepy. And I like filet mignon so don't think you're going to talk me out of that. Just knock it off."

The calf stretched its neck and lapped at the hem of her skirt. Its tongue grazed the skin at the side of her knee and she shuddered.

"I don't think so." She stepped back again.

The calf took a step forward, took a hold of the edge of the skirt and sucked on it.

"No fucking way." She pulled the material from the thing's mouth.

"*Mmmaaaaaa!*"

"Forget it," Lauren said. "You can't suck on my skirt. I draw the line there. And we can't be friends. Go find your mom or something."

It just blinked its big eyes at her.

"Whatever." She was leaving. What the hell she was doing in the midst of chickens and cows, she didn't know. This was Sapphire Falls and it was the annual town festival—most of both of those things didn't make sense to her.

She turned her back on the calf…and ran directly into a hard chest.

And something cold and wet.

"Ah!" She jumped back and shook her hands free of the

icy liquid that cascaded down the front of her. It soaked into her shirt and froze her skin.

It was a warm June afternoon so she was quickly more concerned about the fact that the liquid was purple. On her white shirt. Because of course it was.

She looked up into the grinning face of the man whose grape slushy had just soaked her.

Travis Bennett. Because of course it was.

She sighed. Mud, cornstalks, manure…she'd had all of that *on* her at various times in Sapphire Falls, and Travis Bennett was always the cause.

"*Why* am I always getting dirty when you're around?" she demanded, grasping the front of her blouse and pulling the wet stickiness away from her stomach.

He chuckled—the bastard. And it was a low rumbling sound that made her realize her nipples weren't perky just because of the cold slushy all over them. The bastard.

"Oh, darlin', that ain't *dirty.*"

No apology, no reaching for a napkin, no sheepish look. All she got was *darlin'* and the word *ain't*. In a drawl that was like fingernails on a chalkboard. Oh, and a big fat cocky grin.

"I'm soaking wet!"

His grin pulled up more on one side. "Now *that* I have some theories about."

Lauren narrowed her eyes and planted a hand on one hip. "Theories about what exactly?" She knew where he was going with this, but she wanted him to say it so she could shoot him down. Like every other time he'd made any kind of sexual innuendo.

"You being soaking wet when I'm around."

She gestured to her clothes. "Clearly, you need carnival food to get me wet, Farmer Boy."

"No kiddin'. I woulda pegged you for a fancy schmancy wine-and-caviar girl."

Liquor actually. She loved a good martini.

"But hey, a girl who likes meat on a stick and funnel cakes is my kinda lady."

Meat on a stick. Yeah, right. Though funnel cakes weren't *horrible*. They involved powdered sugar after all.

She blew out an exasperated breath. Travis talked like a hick. *Why* did she want to put her hand down the front of the blue jeans that had been covered in who-knew-what in the course of the *years* he'd owned them?

Travis was a farmer. A small-town farmer. A small-town farmer who had never traveled outside of the county in which he'd been born—and his father had been born and his grandfather had been born. She knew the type. Too well. She'd been surrounded by the type, involved with the type, in *love* with the type, until she'd escaped to the *city*. Where she'd found real life. Real culture. Real *coffee*.

And it didn't matter what city. She loved them all. Traffic, people, action...*life*. And not a cornfield or haystack for miles.

She was a city snob, small-town-phobic. She knew it. She owned it.

And no good-looking, suntanned, slow-talking, cheap-beer-guzzling small-town *farmer* was going to change her opinion.

"Clearly, the slushy needs to be applied externally for it to get me wet," she told the cheap-beer-guzzling small-town farmer she wanted to lick from head to toe. In a cornfield.

She hated him.

"You city chicks are into some weird stuff," Travis said. "But darlin', I'll apply anything you want *anywhere* you want."

Stupid tingles all over her body.

She put on an unaffected expression. "And I suppose it would be some sexy setup like the bed of your truck with mosquitos buzzing around and maybe some straw poking me in the ass while we're at it?"

He gave her a slow grin. "You, me, the bed of my truck...I'll put twenty bucks on soaking wet in five minutes."

The bed of his truck. Of course.

But it wouldn't take five minutes and he knew it. Somehow.

Damn him.

She was hard to read. She worked at being hard to read. She'd practiced it for years. And yet this guy...

Either he was really insightful—she almost snorted out loud at that—or he was really, *really* full of himself.

Lauren looked him up and down, from his well-worn seed-corn cap to the brilliant blue eyes, past the day's growth of scruff on his chin, the red wrinkled T-shirt and the worn-and-washed-over-and-over blue jeans all the way to the scuffed work boots.

He was really, really full of himself.

She reached into her purse, pulled out a fifty and handed it to him. "It's pretty clear you need this way more than I do. I'd feel so bad taking that twenty off of you."

Travis grinned, took the fifty and tucked it into his jeans. "I don't care what they say, Dr. D. You're not all bad."

She wanted to smack him.

She hated when he acted like he didn't care a bit what she thought of him. She had yet—in the almost two years of running into him on and off in Sapphire Falls—to really feel like she'd gotten the best of him.

And she also hated when he called her Dr. D.

And said stuff like, "I don't care what they say." They who? What did they say?

Dammit.

"Well, you can tone down the country-boy charm, because I don't do farmers."

His grin hadn't faded a bit. He leaned in. "Is it the penises?"

9

She narrowed her eyes and leaned in as well. "Actually, it's the smell. Eau de Barnyard doesn't really do it for me." But that wasn't the problem with Travis. At all. He smelled like man and laundry that had been hung outside to dry. And sunshine. He smelled like sunshine. For God's sake.

Travis wasn't bothered by her comment. He chuckled. "Well, glad to know I don't smell like all those pretty girls you usually go for."

No, he sure didn't. He smelled better. And that was saying something since she really liked how those girls smelled.

She wasn't a lesbian. But she'd had relationships with women. She had embraced her bisexuality during her sophomore year of college. But on the spectrum of sexuality, she still went for men more often than women. She hadn't been with a woman in over a year. She hadn't been with *anyone* in almost seven months.

But Travis Bennett did not need to know that. He didn't need to know anything about her sex life. Like that he was totally her type. Totally.

She loved men like Travis. Men's men. Guys who used their hands to get things done and had muscles sculpted by hard work rather than by a gym. Men who were comfortable in their own skin without any hair products or a daily moisturizing regimen.

Country boys.

But country boys made her stupid.

And she was *not* going to live in the country. Never again.

So she steered clear. Really clear. She dated men who knew wine and theater and spa treatments. And there was nothing wrong with any of those things. She was attracted to them, she enjoyed spending time with them and they were okay in bed. Some had been better than okay. A couple had been damned good.

It still took more than a smile and a *darlin'* from them to get her going though.

Which was good. She didn't want to be falling for anyone. She had important stuff to do.

"So you could move back a few feet," she said, giving him a little push. "Or across the sidewalk. Or across the square completely." He always stood so damned close.

Of course, she noticed how hot and hard his chest was when she pushed him.

He chuckled again and the sound washed over her, making all the body parts she didn't want to think about when Travis was around say, *"Well, hello, Travis."*

"Aw, I'm not goin' anywhere, darlin'," he said in that irritatingly sexy slow way he had. "This is my town, remember? You'll never get away from me entirely."

It seemed to be true. She ran into him every day. All. The. Time. Of course, Sapphire Falls was a small town with only twelve hundred and six other people besides Travis. The odds were against her. Especially when she figured in the facts that there were only two places in town with coffee, and she and Travis were both devoted morning-coffee drinkers, that there was only one bank, one post office and one gas station—and they both used all of those places regularly—and that Travis was one of the farmers working with Lauren's company, Innovative Agricultural Solutions, also known as IAS. They were bound to run into each other. Like it or not.

"You could at least try to keep your stuff off of me."

He grinned at that. "You mean my stuff that's making you wet and sticky?"

She *really* didn't like him. Or the way he got to her.

"Well, I'm nothin' if not a gentleman," he said.

And he stripped off his T-shirt.

He handed it to her. "You can use this to dry off."

She was vaguely aware of a scattering of gasps and a wolf whistle from the people wandering through the square, but there was no way she was going to glance at any of them. Not when she had *this* view. Her mouth never went dry when seeing a man's chest for the first time. Then again, it had been a long time since she'd seen a chest like Travis's. Toned, tanned and completely lickable.

Muscles rippled under smooth skin with just the right amount of light hair dusted over defined pecs. It trailed down between the ridges of his abs and dove into his waistband. There was a tattoo that curved from the top of his shoulder down over the biceps that she attempted not to stare at. It was an elaborate letter B, she assumed for Bennett, that bunched and stretched as he moved his arm.

And speaking of arms…he didn't even have a farmer's tan.

The jerk.

Her synapses stopped sending *lick-him, lick-him* signals and finally switched over to *quit standing here like an idiot.*

She dragged her gaze from his chest to his face. She gave him a little half smile. Then she began unbuttoning.

She was gratified to see his gaze riveted on her fingers as her shirt parted. She shrugged out of it—briefly noting more gasps and an ego-stroking, "Holy shit," of appreciation—and handed it to Travis. He didn't take it. He was too busy studying the white lace she'd revealed.

"Thanks, Farmer Boy." She draped her shirt over his arm and pulled his T-shirt on. "I'm completely *dry* now, thanks to you."

His shirt was warm. And smelled like fricking sunshine.

It was big on her. The bottom hung past her butt and the sleeves fell to her elbows.

Still enjoying his stunned expression, she tied a knot in the bottom of the shirt to keep it at her waist.

His gaze roamed over her and she cursed the tingles again.

"White lace and chicken poop," Travis said thoughtfully. He shrugged. "I don't get it, but I'm sure you know more about this fashion stuff than I do."

"Chicken poop?"

He pointed at her right shoe.

No, please, not my Jimmy Choos. She looked down with trepidation. But sure enough, there was a glop of something on the toe of her right shoe. She wasn't sure she'd ever seen chicken poop up close, but she trusted Travis in this. She was grateful the shoes weren't open-toed.

"Dammit."

The man had distracted her to the point of not noticing an animal *pooping* on her shoe?

She looked from side to side, trying to locate the culprit. She loved chicken marsala. And cordon bleu. And fajitas. But there were at least six chickens and over a dozen chicks running around on the grass. "What the hell is going on here? Chickens and cows just running loose all over the square?"

"They'll be corralled in a minute. They're putting the fence up now." He pointed toward the cluster of trees in the north corner of the town square.

There were three men and two little girls putting up a temporary fence, setting out hay bales, and feed and water buckets.

"Petting zoo," Travis filled in.

A petting zoo. Full of barn animals.

"And they just let the animals wander while they set up?" Lauren looked at her shoe again. How was she going to get chicken poop off of it? And would she really ever want to wear it again once she did?

"Someone will catch them and shoo them back in that direction." As he spoke, he flapped her shirt at two of the chickens, sending them running in a northerly direction.

"What if someone wanted to steal one?" Lauren asked. She couldn't just wipe her shoe on the grass. She could use her shirt, she supposed. It was stained with grape syrup and ruined anyway. But it rubbed her wrong to clean chicken poop with silk.

Travis chuckled. "Everyone around here has their own chickens. And cows, rabbits, goats and sheep."

Sure enough, all of those other animals were also present, though sticking closer to where they belonged.

"So what's the point of a petting zoo in a town where everyone has their own animals to pet?" Lauren wanted to know. A paper napkin probably wouldn't work. She was just not going to be able to salvage the shoes. Or her shirt. *Why* had she agreed to help out at her friend's booth during the festival today? This was so not her thing.

But the scent of cotton candy hit her at the same moment a shriek of laughter came from the Ferris wheel and she sighed. This actually was kind of her thing. She was a sucker for sweet, charming little towns. And Sapphire Falls was nothing if not sweet and charming. All the damned time. Everywhere she turned. Their annual festival, their Fourth of July street dance and barbecue, their community theater production of *Alice in Wonderland*, their Thanksgiving reenactment—it was all sweet and charming. She freaking loved it all.

Unfortunately.

She couldn't afford to get sucked into Small Town USA. She had important stuff to do. Stuff that took her around the world. Some of her time was spent in fancy offices and conference rooms and ballrooms with politicians and other VIPs. Some of her time was spent in the poorest, saddest, most worn-down areas of the world.

But none of it involved cotton candy and Ferris wheels.

So rather than tempt herself with the idea of turning her life upside town and buying a house with a wraparound porch and a couple of rocking chairs, she spent as little time in Sapphire Falls as possible.

If her best friend, Mason, hadn't fallen in love with a woman who loved Sapphire Falls, Lauren would have never set foot in the quaint little town in the first place. And she wouldn't know that their Knights of Columbus made the best pancakes she'd ever eaten or that the town's Christmas pageant made her want to believe in Santa again.

Travis chuckled at her question about the petting zoo. "All I know is that there's always been a petting zoo at the festival. Just like there's always been a haunted house."

She shook her head. She knew *of* the festival and the traditional haunted house, but she'd never attended. Because it just seemed wrong somehow to binge on cotton candy when there were people literally starving in other countries. "A haunted house at a summer festival is weird."

He shrugged. "The city council talked about saving it for Halloween only, but the whole town protested."

"Why?"

He gave her a wink. "Lots of good memories made inside that house at festival time."

She could imagine what those memories consisted of. And she would guess just as many were made at Halloween too. Teenagers in the dark. That's all anyone needed to say.

"Got it." With a sigh, she stepped out of her shoes and hung on to them by their heels. The sidewalk was warm under her bare feet and she wondered briefly when she'd last gone barefoot.

"So, stimulating as always, Dr. D, but I've gotta get to the kissing booth."

There was a kissing booth? The festival just got cuter and cuter. Dammit.

Lauren raised an eyebrow. "You've got to pay to get kissed? That's sad."

He gave her a slow grin that curled only half his mouth. "I'm *in* the kissing booth, baby doll. We're gonna get the money for the new welcome sign in a couple of days."

Baby doll? Really? And it actually made her a little tingly too. *Really?*

The biggest damned problem with this sweet, charming

15

town wasn't the cotton candy or the Pies and Ties event where everyone dressed in formal wear to eat pie—she still wasn't sure *why* they did it, but it was cute—or the local band that covered John Denver and Elvis—*only* John Denver and Elvis—and whose youngest member was seventy-one.

The problem was the hot farmer boys.

And there were several. Whatever the mothers in Sapphire Falls fed their baby boys, it turned them into hot, charming men almost across the board. Someone should really patent it.

"Who else is in the booth?" she asked. Heck, she could contribute to the new welcome sign.

Which would probably be really, really cute.

Travis cocked an eyebrow. "Drew and Tucker during this shift. Why?"

Drew was a sweet guy who also farmed locally. He was a great dancer. She lifted a shoulder. "I'd pay a buck to kiss Drew for a good cause."

"You'd come to the booth for Drew?"

"I didn't say that. But if I was already there, I'd give Drew a dollar too."

Travis indicated his naked torso. As if Lauren could have forgotten.

"I think this is gonna cost you more than a dollar, City."

Did he seem interested? Had he leaned in slightly? Had his pupils dilated a little?

"Well, let's put it this way," she said, tipping her head and wetting her lips. "I might need that fifty back."

Sapphire Falls wasn't stupid. Manning the kissing booth with Travis and Tucker Bennett would ensure the funds in a few hours, not to mention a couple of days.

Tucker was Travis's brother. He was equally hot and significantly nicer to Lauren. In fact, she was pretty sure Tucker had a little crush on her. And every time they flirted, it seemed to annoy Travis. Which made it even more fun.

"Might have to come up with somethin' special for fifty," Travis said. He definitely leaned in.

"Special," she repeated. "I like the sound of that."

"In fact, maybe you get to pick *where* you get kissed if you hand over fifty."

She tapped her finger against her chin, pretending to ponder that...and ignoring the damned tingles. "Okay, I think I want Tucker to kiss me...on the bridge over the pond in the park."

The park was adorable, the pond had adorable ducks, adorable weeping willows surrounded it and an adorable white wooden bridge arched over the water.

"That's not really what I meant by *where*... Wait, Tuck—" Then realization dawned and he leaned back. "Okay, you got me, City."

"It's just that Tucker is so..." She trailed off with a sigh, as if she just couldn't think of the right word. And she couldn't. Tucker was a great guy. Hot. Sweet. Absolutely worthy of big money in a kissing booth. But he didn't give her tingles like Travis did.

Which was fine. She wasn't going near Tucker Bennett for real. Tucker was looking for a wife. To live on his farm. He probably wanted someone who would hang the laundry on the clothesline and take care of a bunch of chickens and can things. So the right word for Tucker was *forbidden*.

Travis pulled the fifty she'd given him from his pocket and handed it to her. "Tell you what, baby doll. You take this back. I wouldn't feel right taking money from my sister-in-law."

She took the money. It was her fifty dollars after all. "Maybe Tucker's not the best choice for a kissing booth if he's going to propose to every girl who lines up."

Travis shook his head. "Not every girl. But you? I hear wedding bells by the time the leaves change."

She grimaced and he laughed.

"Yeah," he said, pointing his index finger at her nose. "You remember that."

She slid the money into her pocket. She wasn't going to kiss Tucker Bennett. Not even for a good cause.

She could, however, stuff herself on cotton candy and funnel cakes. Fifty bucks would go a long way in junk food.

"And I'm thinkin' that a fifty-dollar kiss from you might just kill Drew," Travis added.

"How sweet of you to look out for your friends," she said dryly. But she wasn't so sure he wasn't right. Drew was a nice guy, but...he was a *nice* guy. She, unfortunately, needed a little cocky to get her going.

"Aw gee, Dr. D, it's what we do 'round here. So, you be nice to the chickens and cows now, 'kay? I'd better be gettin' to my post."

She watched him walk away in spite of herself. The view of his naked back was every bit as nice as the view from the front.

'Round. 'Kay. Gettin'. The guy dropped letters all over the place. And he said *gee* and *aw*. *Why* did she want to ride him in the front seat of his truck? And not ride *with* him in his truck. No, she very much wanted to ride *him*.

He'd be thinking *aw gee* then.

God, even the *cows* liked her.

Travis shook his head as he started toward the kissing booth. He'd seen Dr. D crossing the town square and had been so startled it had taken him a minute to realize she was talking to the cow that was trying to suck on her skirt.

But wow.

Lauren Davis was impossible to *not* notice anywhere she went. She was gorgeous and haughty and always dressed to kill. But in the Sapphire Falls town square, surrounded by the festival activities that included things like a merry-go-round and little kids getting their faces painted to look like cats and princesses, she definitely stood out. When he'd seen her in the short black skirt, nearly see-through white blouse and crazy high heels that wrapped around her feet in some weird criss-cross pattern and hoisted her at least three additional inches off the ground, he'd stopped mid-stride and simply stared. Exactly as he would have if he'd suddenly come upon the most beautiful sunset of his life. Or an alien space ship.

She was as out of place as anyone could be. Who wore high heels to a carnival? Who wore high heels like *that* anywhere?

Lauren Davis didn't fit in in Sapphire Falls. She was not the kind of girl who should be turning his head. But he'd made a beeline for her anyway.

And as he'd drawn closer, he'd heard her talking to the calf about filet mignon rather than acting squeamish or running away, and Travis had felt something even more worrisome than the attraction he'd felt since he'd first seen her at the edge of his cornfield—he'd felt intrigued.

"Why do you do that with her?"

Travis turned to find Tucker leaning against a tree.

"Do what?"

"Act stupid."

Travis grinned. "Maybe I'm not acting."

Tucker fell into step beside him, also on his way to the kissing booth. "You are. You're saying *ain't* and drawling."

Travis shrugged. "It's what Lauren expects."

"She seems to distinctly *hate* when you say *ain't*."

"I know." Travis loved that. "Have you ever met a woman more full of herself? She thinks she's better than the rest of us. Especially me."

"Why is that?"

"Because she's from the big city where guys wear suits

and ties and pronounce everything perfectly and never burp or fart."

"Did you fart in front of her? Because *lots* of women don't like that."

Travis chuckled. "Nothing so simple. Though I'll keep that idea in mind."

"I think Dr. D is nice," Tucker said. "I don't know why you're always irritating her."

Travis knew that Tucker thought she was nice. Tuck liked the stuck-up city girl. Which was no good. Tucker would think he could win her over, charm her with the country life, talk her out onto the farm...because he'd never met a girl who *didn't* want the life he had to offer.

But there was no way Miss Spray Tan Salon Highlights would want to live on Tucker's one-thousand acres. She liked the word *gourmet* where Tucker liked *homemade*. She liked *designer* while Tucker liked *practical*. Wearing high-assed sexy heels to a small-town festival was anything but practical.

"Because irritating her is so easy. And fun." Travis thought about the way Lauren's cheeks flushed and her eyes flashed when they talked. It was fun pushing her buttons. She was polished and sophisticated. She clearly took a lot of pride in looking all put together and out of reach. She wore her stylishness like armor. No one else seemed to notice, but nothing riled her up like something messing up her clothes, shoes, hair or makeup.

Like when he'd accidentally swiped a dirty glove across her cheek, leaving a streak of mud and she'd about bitten his head off. Or when he'd accidentally caught the fancy twist in her hair with a cornstalk and her hair had fallen in sexy waves to her shoulders and she'd leveled him with a glare that would have made a less confident man's knees shake. Or when he'd not-as-accidentally dumped a bucket of mud and manure on her shoes and she'd called him an ignorant, insensitive lumbering boor. She probably thought he didn't know any of those words.

Some of those had truly been accidents.

The way he talked to her was completely on purpose.

She'd arrived on day one of his partnership with her company, IAS, at *his* field, in thigh-high red leather boots, a short black fitted skirt and enough attitude to fill his barn from floor to ceiling. Twice.

What was a simple country boy supposed to do when confronted with a prissy girl in red leather? Admire her, of course.

He'd even included a long low whistle and said, "Well, Dorothy, those aren't quite how I imagined the ruby slippers lookin', and this sure ain't Oz, but I'd be happy to play the wizard and grant you a wish or two."

That drawl and grin always worked on women.

Lauren hadn't been amused. In fact, in the course of multiple interactions, Travis had come to the conclusion that amused was something Dr. Lauren Davis simply didn't feel.

She'd given him a look that said, "Yeah, right," and then proceeded to talk to him like he was a kindergartner.

He'd had her number right then.

She thought small-town farmers were dumb. They didn't go to college because they couldn't cut it. They didn't do big important things because staying home and taking over Daddy's farm was easier.

And Sapphire Falls was small because no one wanted to live here.

The vibe from her had been strong and clear. She didn't want to be in Sapphire Falls and they needed her more than she needed them.

Everyone knew that her partner and friend, Mason Riley, was the reason their company had relocated their growing projects to Sapphire Falls. It was true that they had been successfully growing and testing various crops for years before Mason had fallen in love with Adrianne and decided to live full time in his tiny hometown. It was also true that the influx of money and people to Sapphire Falls had helped the town's economy and had put them on the map for some significant agricultural and scientific contributions.

But Sapphire Falls had been very good to IAS. The employees were welcomed with open arms, the grocery store had started ordering things like tofu, and the Stop, the gas station/convenience store/pizza place/ice cream shop in town, had started making a spinach-and-mushroom pizza and serving chai tea.

He could take her looking at him like he wasn't worthy, but she also disparaged his home town and insulted his friends and family by assuming they were making their lives in Sapphire Falls because they couldn't do any better.

He didn't put up with people looking down on the things and people he loved best about his life.

He could be in her face about it. But instead, he was biding his time.

For one, she was a diversion in a town where things were always pretty routine. Not that he minded routine. He loved it in fact. The routine and comfort were two reasons he lived here, after all. But it wasn't bad to shake things up once in a while.

For another, the more she ticked him off—and the more times he ran into her, the more she ticked him off—the more fun it was going to be to take her down a peg. Or two. Or three.

"So you're really okay with her thinking you're a dumb country bumpkin?" Tucker asked.

Travis chuckled. "No."

They stopped at the tent where the United Methodist Women were displaying their quilts and selling baked goods. They each got a bottle of water and Tucker grabbed a brownie. Travis got one too—you didn't turn down homemade desserts in Sapphire Falls—but he handed it to

Tucker as soon as they were around the corner of the tent. Travis didn't make a habit of turning down brownies, but he'd already had a corn dog, a soft pretzel, a deep-fried Snickers bar and a grape slushy. Well, half a grape slushy.

"But you keep doing things to make her believe you're a dumb country bumpkin," Tucker said, refusing to drop the subject of Lauren, and Travis's tendency to drive her nuts.

"For now."

They arrived at the tiny wooden structure that was painted bright red with *Kissing Booth* in bold white letters across the front. Drew was already there and there was a line.

As he stepped inside for his hour-long shift, Travis glanced in the direction of the Scott's Sweets booth where Lauren's friend, Adrianne, was giving samples and selling her gourmet candies. There was a dunk tank, a display of handmade jewelry and a stand selling fresh-squeezed lemonade between them, but he still felt itchy with her that close.

He *really* wished he didn't know that her bra was made entirely of white lace and was see-through enough that he knew what her nipples looked like. His icy drink had perked them right up—though he liked to think that he'd had a bit of an effect too—and they would have been grape flavored.

He cleared his throat and focused on Tucker again.

"For now?" his brother asked.

"I'm just waiting for the perfect chance to show her how wrong she's been with all of her assumptions," Travis said. He caught the T-shirt Drew tossed to him in one hand.

"You're waiting for the perfect chance to make a fool of her," Tucker clarified.

Travis lifted a shoulder and then pulled the T-shirt over his head. It said *A hug—$1. A kiss—$2. I won't date your daughter—$10.*

"Grandma wouldn't approve of you embarrassing a lady," Tucker said as he pulled his own kissing-booth T-shirt on.

"Grandma wouldn't approve of Dr. High and Mighty's attitude either."

Kendra Bennett was as opposite from Lauren Davis as two women could get. Kendra had farmed right beside her husband every day until the day he'd had a heart attack while harvesting their corn and died with his wife and three of his sons beside him in the dirt he'd loved his whole life.

Her fingernails got dirty, her nose got sunburned and her back ached from the manual work she did. But she did it with a smile and a sense of gratitude for honest work that could support her family, a body that could physically work for the things she needed, and the beautiful land they'd been blessed to have in the Bennett family for five generations.

Travis knew roots. He knew how to appreciate the things he had. He knew hard work.

And he wouldn't trade any of it for anything that Lauren Davis had in that big city of hers.

"That's probably true," Tucker said of their grandmother. "But you can't humiliate the good doctor."

The thing was he probably *could*. But he wouldn't. "Nah, I'll...*surprise* her."

He didn't know how or when it would go down, but one of these days he and Lauren would be in the same place at the same time with the perfect opportunity for her to realize that she was not a bit better than him—and he'd take that opportunity.

"I figured you'd just fuck her and show her who's best," Tuck said and then swigged the rest of his water.

Travis's water went down the wrong pipe.

He hacked and coughed until Tucker beat on his back and Travis could pull in a deep breath again.

Holy crap.

"You okay, man?" Tuck asked.

He was *not* okay. "Why would you say that?" he demanded.

Tucker looked genuinely puzzled. "The two of you have some major heat. And she's…hot. Really, really hot. Are you telling me you *don't* want to sleep with her?"

He didn't.

Well, he didn't want to want to sleep with her. If that counted.

But yeah, okay, so he spent his time around stuck-up, sophisticated Dr. Lauren Davis irritated and turned on. In equal parts.

"I don't think sleeping with Dr. D is a good idea," Travis said causally. At least he tried for casual.

"Why not?"

"I don't like her."

Tucker just looked at him.

Travis frowned. "I don't."

"You don't like the way her company has made our family farm a part of something that will guarantee our stability for the next decade and possibly the rest of our lives?"

Travis shook his head. "That's Mason."

"Mason is the one working with the crops," Tucker said. "He's the one who's come up with what we're doing here."

Travis knew there was a *but* coming.

"But Lauren is the one making sure the reporters are putting our names in their articles too. She makes sure we get paid, and that the government folks know what's going on out here and that we have the supplies and machines we need."

Yeah, yeah.

Tucker was right.

IAS was known world-wide for their innovative farming techniques and their humanitarian efforts in some of the poorest areas in the world.

The money for those programs came from the government and charitable organizations. What paid the bills for IAS were the things they developed for the private sector in the US and other large, wealthy countries. Not all farmers were poor.

It was true that Travis often didn't follow Mason when he explained what he was doing. Mason was a scientist. Travis was a farmer. He knew how to plant and cultivate and harvest crops. But he didn't feel bad about not understanding Mason. The man was a genius. Literally. Something like two percent of the world was at Mason's level of intelligence.

Then there was Lauren.

Mason was the one with the ideas for the actual seeds and the planting techniques and the soil and water adjustments they were working on. The meat and potatoes. The direct, actual product they were creating.

However, without Lauren, the whole thing would have fallen apart a long time ago. She was the brains behind their public and government relations. She didn't do all the work herself, but she was definitely the driving force.

This was the second growing season since IAS had partnered with local farmers around Sapphire Falls and it was even better than the first. They were not only producing successful crops with Mason's seeds, but they were getting attention from both the government and private sector in the form of grants and donations. Multiple companies had lined up to supply everything from the latest tractors to caps and blue jeans. They had been interviewed for farming magazines, had been the subject of a documentary on PBS, and the farmers—three of whom were Bennetts—had posed for a Country Boy calendar. Including Travis.

He remembered Lauren had been at the photo shoot. And she'd seemed mildly amused that day now that he thought about it. Probably because most of the guys had been pretty shy in front of the camera. It had taken the photographer almost thirty minutes to get Drew out of his T-shirt. Lauren had seemed even more entertained when Travis had offered to be Mr. July in Drew's place. The photographer had told him that he'd make a perfect Mr. October and that he should leave his flannel on.

Being the subject of her humor had rubbed him the wrong way. But it had been nice to see the smile.

"Okay, she's not *all* bad," he finally admitted to Tucker. "But she's hoity-toity and doesn't like to get dirty and bitches about the coffee around here constantly."

Tucker shrugged. "Those hoity-toity heels look damned good on her, the coffee around here sucks, except for Adrianne's, of course, and I'm not the only one thinking that Dr. D probably does dirty just fine." He tossed his water bottle and two napkins into a bucket in the corner and then slapped Travis on the back. "Let's do some kissin'."

Travis watched his brother move in front of one of the windows and give the girls in line a big Bennett smile.

The asshole.

The last thing he needed to be thinking about were the high heels that always gave him hard-ons or getting Lauren dirty in any way that didn't involve mud or manure.

But the memory of see-through white lace didn't help. Nor did the idea of grape-flavored nipples.

CHAPTER TWO

"*What* are you wearing?" Phoebe Sherwood demanded as Lauren approached the Scott's Sweets booth.

Phoebe's fiancé, Joe, was there too, cutting Adrianne's locally famous toffee into squares. His eyes also went wide when he took in Lauren's bare feet, her black pencil skirt and the rumpled red T-shirt that said *Slow Pitch Champions 2010*.

"Where's Adrianne?" Lauren asked, letting herself in the little side door to the booth.

"She didn't feel well, so we convinced her to go lie down for a while."

Dammit. Adrianne had to feel well. She was three months pregnant, and doing well according to the doctor, but she'd been plagued with nasty morning sickness. Nasty enough that the only way Lauren had been able to get her business partner—Adrianne's husband, Mason—on the plane to Haiti to take care of a crisis with some of the crops, was for Lauren to promise to stay in Sapphire Falls and look out for Adrianne until he got back in a month.

A *month*.

Mason and Lauren shared the responsibility of traveling to Haiti where their company's primary growing program was active. Haiti was the entire reason they'd started working on the project to grow crops in less than ideal conditions. Mason's love and knowledge of plant science combined with Lauren's passion for water and soil conservation combined to produce pioneering ideas for poor countries like Haiti. And that fulfilled Lauren in a way she had trouble explaining. She'd first visited Haiti as a college student and had been moved by the people, their situation and their desire to rise up.

She'd wanted to rise up too. To get over the things she'd let hold her back, to do more with her life than what had been laid out in front of her, to exceed expectations.

She'd wanted to surprise the people around her. And herself.

She'd felt at home in Haiti and she'd been working ever since to make it better.

But sometimes Mason had to be the one who went to Haiti. The program and their scientists sometimes needed his input. For a while, they'd traveled together, when IAS was just getting started, but now it seemed that it made more sense to have one of them stay back for needs that arose with the company that was now eight times the size of what they'd started with.

Lauren missed the trips with Mason.

She also missed having him in Sapphire Falls when she was here. He was a buffer of sorts. When he was here, they worked. That kept her from partaking of much of the everyday life and social activities in Sapphire Falls.

She always limited her visits to Sapphire Falls to no more than two weeks at a time, and more often to only seven or eight days. More than that and she started thinking crazy thoughts like how much she'd like a dog and how she could really do something with the tour of homes at Christmas if they put her in charge.

She did not want a white picket fence—or a fence of any other color—she did not want a pet, she did not want to take part in chili feeds and cake walks, and she did not want to help plan a parade. Or an Easter egg hunt. Or a Founder's Day picnic. Or any of the other adorable, sweet things this damned little town did.

But if she was stuck here for a month, she wasn't sure she'd be able to resist.

She grabbed a napkin with Adrianne's logo on it and wiped the alleged chicken poop from her shoe as best she could.

"And now back to you. *What* are you wearing?" Phoebe asked.

"Travis Bennett's shirt."

"Why?"

"He spilled grape slushy on mine."

"That's…interesting," Phoebe said.

"Interesting is far too generous a word," Lauren assured her.

Phoebe narrowed one eye. "Then how would *you* describe your little encounter with Travis?"

"Typical."

"You don't *typically* end up half naked." Phoebe paused. "Wait, do you?"

Not so far. Though she had the urge to strip off her clothes and rub herself all over him every time they ran into each other. It was very annoying.

"It's not interesting at all. He spilled on my shirt and offered me his to dry off with. Then he gave me a cocky smile and called me darlin', so I took my shirt off. I've done more than that for a guy who smiled and called me darlin' before."

Phoebe leaned in and Joe raised both eyebrows.

"Tell us more," Phoebe said, propping an elbow on the counter top that ran the length of the big opening at the front of the booth.

Lauren grabbed a bottle of water and took a long drink. "I just need to stay away from Travis," she said after she'd swallowed.

Wearing his shirt was not exactly a good way to get him out of her system, but she could take care of that as soon as she found a book of matches. Tomorrow sometime. Not that she'd do something stupid like sleep in his shirt. Unless she was too tired to change out of it or something. But she wouldn't do it more than once. Or twice.

After all, Hailey might not even have matches. Maybe.

Hailey Conner was the mayor of Sapphire Falls and a total diva. She also had a spare bedroom, an extra bathroom and the best fashion sense of any woman in Sapphire Falls.

Lauren stayed with Hailey whenever she was in town. Lauren could deal with other divas if they let her borrow their Gucci pumps.

Besides, Hailey was regularly out of town, like now, so Lauren had the little house to herself.

"What is with the two of you?" Joe asked. "Travis is a nice guy. No one else growls and sighs about him like you do."

"I guess everyone else is used to his good-ol'-boy ways. They make me want to put a fork in my eye."

That was a little dramatic maybe. And Phoebe thought so too, if her eye roll was any indication.

Phoebe laughed. "Travis is a good ol' boy," she agreed. "But he's a great guy."

Lauren shrugged. "Don't care."

"You don't care about great guys?" Joe asked. "You prefer jerks?"

"I prefer men who know how to use more than one utensil at a meal and who don't think the Zac Brown Band is the best music out there and who know how to use a razor."

"You know the Zac Brown Band?" Phoebe asked, clearly surprised. "Now *that* is interesting."

Lauren ignored her. That was a reckless slip. She wasn't going to admit to liking country music. Not for anything.

"That guy you took to the big dinner in DC last summer had a goatee," Joe pointed out.

Neal. Yes, he had, and she'd taken him to that dinner because he did know how to use more than one fork at a meal and she didn't want to sleep with him. "A very well-trimmed goatee. Not just some scruff he let grow because he's lazy."

Phoebe and Joe both gave her knowing looks that made Lauren shift uncomfortably on her chair.

"You and Travis have chemistry," Phoebe said. "No

matter what you say about his scruff."

Lauren took another sip of her water and then set her bottle down and nodded. "We do. And I have a little crush on him. Just like I have a crush on this entire fricking town."

Phoebe snorted but Joe nodded. Lauren and Joe had talked before about the way Sapphire Falls could suck a person in. Joe's best childhood friend, and the woman he thought he'd marry, had come to Sapphire Falls as a part of IAS and had fallen hard for the town and a local boy. Joe had come to win her back and had fallen for the town and a local girl. Adrianne had been a Chicago city girl until she'd come to Sapphire Falls to escape the fast-paced, stressful lifestyle she'd had in the city. Mason had escaped Sapphire Falls only to be sucked back in when he'd come home for what was supposed to have been a weekend high school class reunion.

"I do," Lauren said. "I don't know what you all put in the water around here, but dang, whenever I'm here I have this stupid urge to chase lightning bugs and drink lemonade and go fishing and get some chickens."

Joe chuckled. "You don't want chickens."

"No. That's my point. I most definitely do not want chickens. And I hate fishing. But when I'm here…I lose my mind."

"I know what you mean." Joe reached for his fiancée, hooked the back of her jeans with his finger and hauled her up against him. "But the insanity here is a hell of a lot of fun."

Phoebe gave him a kiss and then turned a grin on Lauren. "I get the falling in love with Sapphire Falls," she said.

Lauren rolled her eyes. Phoebe loved her hometown and every one of its strange little quirks.

"But I don't really get the crush on Travis."

"Hot country boys are my type," Lauren said with a

shrug.

Phoebe laughed. She looked at Lauren, realized Lauren was serious and said, "I thought *I* was your type."

Lauren smiled at that. "Oh, honey, you are. I love perky redheads."

"Travis isn't...a redhead," Phoebe said, glancing at Joe. Joe was grinning, clearly amused.

"What you really mean is Travis isn't a girl," Lauren said.

"Well, yeah, that too," Phoebe said with the little blush Lauren loved to elicit.

"I'm mostly into guys," Lauren said.

"But you're..." Phoebe looked perplexed.

Someone came to the window and it was obvious that Phoebe was annoyed to have to serve truffles and caramels when they were in the middle of a juicy conversation, but she did it with a smile and even asked the customer how her mother had liked the cruise she'd gone on last month.

"You're bisexual, I know." Phoebe picked up the conversation as the woman moved off with her Scott's Sweets bag in hand. "But you haven't hooked up with one guy in all the time I've known you."

Lauren had just come off of a breakup with one of her girlfriends when she'd met Phoebe. Phoebe was clearly heterosexual, but Lauren loved to tease her and flirt with her because it made Phoebe stammer and blush. Phoebe was from Sapphire Falls. There wasn't much diversity here, and Lauren felt that she was expanding minds a bit by making them face the fact that there were lots of variations in lifestyles in the world.

It was true that Lauren hadn't seriously dated anyone since she'd been coming back and forth between Chicago, DC, Haiti and Sapphire Falls. She hadn't had a lot of time, for one thing. The travel made it hard to make time for socializing, and it was hard to get to know someone when she often needed to be gone for extended periods at a time.

And she hadn't met anyone interesting lately. For a while.
For a long while actually.

She wasn't heartbroken anymore. She'd gotten over
Alex fairly easily considering how upset she'd been when
her girlfriend of four months had told her that she couldn't
deal with Lauren always putting her work first.

Lauren did that. Her work was her main priority, the
thing that would always take precedence. It was who she
was. She'd made several life choices—leaving her
hometown, moving to the city, studying what she had,
putting her tiny life savings into the business with Mason—
specifically to make her life what it was right now.

She was a nationally renowned conservation specialist.
She was the co-founder and co-owner of a company that
was helping feed some of the poorest areas of the planet.
She was called to the White House on a regular basis, was
interviewed by *Newsweek* and the *New York Times*, and
was to be the keynote speaker at conventions in Sweden
and France and Germany this year.

There was only one man who really appreciated—and
put up with—all of that. Mason Riley. When they'd first
met, they'd attempted dating. Lord knew, they were
compatible on almost every level. But they'd never been
able to get past their passion for work and their tendency to
brainstorm whenever they were together long enough to get
romantic.

And then Mason had met Adrianne and Lauren was no
longer the most important woman in his life.

She knew she was never going to find someone else
who could really understand her and her life. And she was
going to do everything she could to avoid falling for
someone who might make her want to give any of that up.

"I love men," Lauren told Phoebe. "*Men*. Like the guys
around here. Guys who work with their hands and have
muscles on their muscles."

Phoebe's eyes had gotten progressively rounder as

Lauren confessed. "Are you sure?"

"Definitely." Lauren looked around, located her favorite thing that Adrianne made…her mini cupcakes…and grabbed three.

"Then what's with the lesbian thing?" Phoebe asked.

"It's not a lesbian *thing*," Lauren said around a bite of red velvet. "I'm bisexual. I'm attracted to women and men. Not *all* women and men, of course, but I am sexually attracted to women at times. More often, I'm attracted to men though. And much more often, it's to guys who look like Travis."

"You don't date guys like Travis," Joe said. "You go for the suave, sophisticated type."

Lauren nodded. "They're safer."

"Safer?" Phoebe asked.

"I won't fall in love with any of them," Lauren said simply. "I'm attracted but I can stay a little detached."

"And you don't think you can with the guys around here?" Phoebe's eyes and body language said she was fascinated.

"Right. It's a stupid…addiction…that I fight whenever I'm here. But I'm *not* falling for a small-town farmer. I'm *not* settling down in a town like Sapphire Falls. I'm *not* spending my weekends barbecuing and going to demo derbies and tractor pulls and drinking *beer* here."

Phoebe shook her head. "You drink when you're here."

She did. The coffee sucked here, but the martinis weren't bad. "It's temporary. Once in a while. It's not a lifestyle choice," Lauren corrected her.

"How do you even know what a demo derby is?" Joe asked.

Joe, the rich kid who'd been raised in casinos, probably didn't know what a demo derby was.

"I just do," Lauren said

Another customer came to the window and Joe moved to fill her order of cupcakes and truffles. Lauren eyed the box of treats he was putting together. It would be a problem if the white-chocolate strawberry cupcakes were all bought. Cupcakes and martinis had gotten her through visits to Sapphire Falls before. And if she was going to be here for a month, she was going to need plenty of sugar and liquor.

"But you're the classy girl," Phoebe said. "You haven't been to a demo derby or a tractor pull. Have you?"

Lauren couldn't resist a glance in the direction of the kissing booth. Was he kissing half naked? Surely not.

"Yes. Travis drives in derbies," Phoebe confirmed, following Lauren's gaze.

Yeah, she'd figured.

"I need a repellent," Lauren said. "I swear I'm going to end up having a fling with one of these guys if I'm here for a month. And then they're going to think I'm ready to settle down and then I'm going to break somebody's heart."

Phoebe shook her head. "Wow. You think Travis is looking to settle down?"

"No, but Tucker is."

Phoebe hesitated and then frowned. "Tucker? I thought you were hot for Travis."

Lauren nodded and stuffed a lemon cream cupcake into her mouth.

"So why would you have a fling with Tucker?"

"Because Tucker likes me." Lauren licked lemon icing from her fingertip.

"And Travis doesn't," Joe said with a grin.

"Tucker Bennett is hot and cocky and sweet and charming," Lauren said. "Travis Bennett is just hot and cocky."

Another customer approached and Lauren quickly hid four of the white-chocolate strawberry cupcakes and then grabbed two of the chocolate mocha fudge for later.

Phoebe and Joe put together the huge order of "two of everything" and Lauren thought about how fat she was going to get over the next twenty-nine days.

This town was just like these cupcakes—sweet, delightful and completely bad for her.

She sat up straighter. That was actually a fantastic analogy.

She needed to get off of the cupcakes that were threatening her pants size. She worked hard to stay in shape and to look good in her black pencil skirts and high heels. She couldn't let some enchanting little cupcakes with their bright colors and sweet centers ruin everything.

And she needed to get off of Sapphire Falls—and the hot guys—that were threatening her lifestyle. She worked hard to keep her company running and to reach the people who needed them. And she worked hard to keep her life full of culture and current events and meaningful activities. She couldn't let a quaint little town and its charming men ruin everything.

Cupcakes were the key. How had she not realized that before?

When the customer left with three Scott's Sweets bags, Phoebe and Joe turned to Lauren.

"So—"

"I think I *do* need to spend more time with Travis."

"Travis," Phoebe repeated. "What about Tucker?"

"Tucker's too nice. He needs a nice country girl."

"And Travis needs…" Joe said, trailing off clearly with the hopes she'd fill in the blank.

"To help make sure I'm on that plane to Haiti in a month wearing the same size pants I'm wearing right now."

Joe frowned. "I'm confused."

"Travis Bennett is the fingernail in my favorite cupcake," Lauren told him.

Joe looked at Phoebe. Phoebe shrugged and shook her head. Joe looked back at Lauren.

"I'm even more confused."

"As long as Travis is around, my silk blouses will keep getting spilled on and chickens will keep pooping on my shoes and I'll still be certain that I do *not* want to settle down in Sapphire Falls." Lauren put the white-chocolate strawberry and chocolate mocha cupcakes back on the display, wiped her hands on the bottom of Travis's shirt and slipped her Jimmy Choos back on.

"Sapphire Falls is a wonderful place," Phoebe protested.

"I agree. It's currently my favorite small town," she told Phoebe. "But even the best cupcakes have a downside. And Travis Bennett is the perfect person to help me find the downside I need."

৩৵৶

"You decide where you wanted that kiss?" Travis asked. "And I'm not talkin' about the bridge. If you want a list of options, I'm happy to oblige."

Lauren had just plunked her fifty-dollar bill down in front of him. Not Drew. Not Tucker. *Him.*

Her gaze went from the front of his shirt and the price list to meet his eyes. "I figured this way you would have twenty-five chances to get this kiss right," she said.

He grinned. Twenty-five kisses. He could handle that. She looked damned good in his shirt. And he bet she still smelled like grape.

He wondered if he was destined to get hard every time he smelled grape from now on.

"Well, come here, darlin'."

She braced her hands on the edge of the window and leaned in.

Travis met her part way.

Their lips touched in a brief kiss just like he'd been giving all the other girls who'd come by. But this time heat exploded in his gut and his hand, almost of its own will, lifted to the back of her head. And very *unlike* all of the other kisses he'd given out, he didn't pull back after the obligatory three seconds.

He tipped her head, pressed against her mouth and urged her lips open. She sighed and obeyed.

It was either the little sigh—that shot straight through him and hardened his entire body—or the simple act of her letting him lead, but either way, this kiss was going to continue for the foreseeable future.

This was Sapphire Falls. He'd spent his whole life here. He knew ninety percent of the people walking by and standing in line. Which meant what he was about to do was going to make headlines.

And he didn't give a shit.

Still cupping the back of her head, he stroked his tongue along hers, absorbing the feel of the slick heat of her mouth and the low moan from the back of her throat. He started walking sideways, pulling her with him, and she also took the four side steps that got them to the corner of the booth. He had to let go of her for a moment to step out of the booth and around the back of the wooden structure, but he gave her no time to rethink their actions. He pressed her up against the back of the booth and resumed the kiss, this time with no wooden divider between them.

Her lips opened immediately this time, and he leaned into her, bracing a hand next to her head, the other on her hip.

The kiss deepened and heated as she wrapped her arms around his neck and arched into him. And it went on for several seconds, until a pounding from inside the booth interrupted them.

Travis pulled back and looked into Lauren's eyes. "One down, twenty-four to go."

She grinned up at him. "Money well spent."

"That's the nicest thing you've ever said to me."

"That's the nicest thing you've ever done to *me*."

"I can be even nicer."

"Me too."

"Not until you finish your shift in here!" Tucker's voice called from inside the booth.

She giggled. Dr. Hoity-Toity Lauren Davis giggled. And Travis wanted her with an intensity that almost buckled his knees.

Travis smiled down at her. "I've got twenty minutes left."

Lauren nudged him back and reached into her pocket to pull out another fifty. She leaned around the corner of the booth and handed it to Tucker. "I've more than paid for the rest of his shift."

They were definitely going to make headlines. His mother was going to hear about this by dinner time.

And he still didn't care.

"I need you," Lauren said.

"I know you do, City."

She rolled her eyes. "I need a *favor*."

He ran his hand up and down her bare arm and thought about the pleasure of stripping her out of his shirt. "You can call it whatever you want. A favor, the best thing to ever happen to you, heaven."

She sighed. "Maybe this is a bad idea."

"I promise you it's not."

"But you don't know what my idea is."

"It doesn't matter. I'm in."

She tipped her head. She had a sly look in her eyes and Travis felt a niggle of trepidation. It was probably a bad idea to mess with a woman as smart as Lauren. Because even though he was a lot smarter than he'd let on, he wasn't anywhere near Lauren's level. He could probably get into a lot of trouble by letting Lauren take the lead in…whatever they were doing.

"So you admit that we have a pretty major attraction going on here?" Lauren said.

"Is that a surprise?" He'd been of the opinion that their chemistry was pretty obvious from minute one.

"But you don't really like me."

He was definitely smart enough to realize that he needed to tread carefully around *this* topic. "I...think we don't...have a lot in common," he managed.

Lauren gave him a big smile. "And I need you to keep reminding me of that."

"Remind you that we don't have a lot in common?" he asked. "Are you going to be forgetting that?" It seemed that the contrasts between them were pretty clear every time they were together.

"Yes. And you have to help remind me that eating my weight in cupcakes and cotton candy is a bad idea, no matter how good it feels while I'm doing it."

"Okay," he said slowly. "Have you been out in the sun a long time today, Doc?"

She shook her head. "I'm not crazy. I need your help. I need you to show me real life in Sapphire Falls. The Sapphire Falls that I *don't* want. Not the cute cupcakes and the sweet festivals and the charming front porches and the sexy guys. I need to experience the boring Tuesdays, the annoying Thursdays, the oh-my-God-I-need-more-than-this Mondays."

Travis was torn between laughing and telling her to fuck off for some reason. "I'm not following you exactly, but I think I'm offended."

"Turn me off of this town. Keep me from wanting to settle down here."

"You want to settle down here?" He started laughing. "Yeah, sure, City. Whatever."

"I wrote up a plan for improving the Christmas tour of homes and I just barely stopped myself from interjecting ideas at the coffee shop when they were talking about doing a Summer of Shakespeare."

Travis stared at her. "There are things about Sapphire Falls that you *like*?"

She huffed out an exasperated breath. "Yes. Several

things actually. Which is annoying as hell."

"Annoying?" He was pretty sure he was offended again.

"Yes. I don't want to live in Sapphire Falls. I don't want your life, Travis. I just need help remembering that while I'm surrounded by all the freaking *charm* for the next month."

"And you want me to…"

"Date me for the month I'm stuck here."

"Date you?" He started laughing again. "Honey, that's not gonna get you over anything."

She rolled her eyes. "That attitude right there is a good start."

He frowned, realizing that she was actually serious. "We'll kill each other."

"Exactly. I need someone who doesn't want me here either. Someone who will drive me crazy. And who won't be won over by *my* charming personality."

Uh huh. That wasn't going to be a problem. He liked nice girls.

"Why me?" Travis asked. He was under no illusion that Lauren had too many soft feelings for him either.

"Because you're not as sweet as the other guys."

He snorted. Well, that was true.

"Seriously, you don't like me and you agree that I don't belong here, so you won't fall for me and no hearts will get broken when I get on the plane at the end of the month."

Well, those were all very good points.

"And what if I can't turn you off of Sapphire Falls? What if you love everything about it?"

This just seemed like a really bad idea. And he was seriously considering it anyway. It wasn't like this would be the first bad idea he'd jumped into whole heartedly. He still had a scar on his shoulder to show for one such bad idea. It had involved a four-wheeler and a major rainstorm rather than a woman, but Lauren had a few things in common with a sudden torrential downpour—they both snuck up on you and could knock you on your ass if you weren't careful.

She was already shaking her head as he finished. "I won't."

"You're so sure?" That also annoyed the hell out of him. Everything about her and this idea annoyed the hell out of him. Except the promise of more kissing.

"I don't want to hang out every weekend in the same place with the same people doing the same thing. I want to meet *new* people, try new things, go new places. I do *not* want your life, Travis Bennett. I do *not* want Sapphire Falls."

"So just keep telling yourself that." He pivoted on the heel of his boot and started walking away. The woman drove him nuts. She was actually insulting him in the midst of asking for his help. Unbelievable.

"Wait!" she called after him, running to catch up with his long strides. "Hang on. I need your help."

"What's in it for me?"

"I…won't hook up with your brother instead."

Travis laughed. "You want to take T.J. on? Go for it. I'd love to see it."

"Not T.J."

Travis stopped walking and turned to face her. He had two other brothers, but the youngest one, Ty, wasn't living in Sapphire Falls. And he already had a lifestyle much like Dr. D's, actually. "Tucker."

She nodded. "Tucker likes me."

He did. Tucker was also looking for a wife. "It wouldn't be casual with Tucker."

"I'd tell him up front that it's nothing serious. I am getting on a plane on July first."

"It won't matter. And Tucker will be romancing you and showing you all the *good* things about Sapphire Falls. You'll be up to your eyeballs in cute and charming."

43

"So help me out."

"This seems like a dumb idea."

"I'm sure it will work. It's like my favorite cupcake place."

"Huh?"

"I loved this gourmet cupcake bakery in Chicago. They have it all—the best tasting cupcakes in the world, the best *looking* cupcakes, the cutest shop, the sweetest staff, the best website...everything."

"Uh huh." He was kind of following. Sapphire Falls was cute, had sweet people and even had a pretty good website.

"I was going there all the time. I gained weight and didn't even care. Those cupcakes were worth going up a pants size. I sent them as gifts, I took out-of-town guests there, I even held a couple of business meetings there. I was completely infatuated," Lauren said, her expression and hand gestures animated.

Travis sighed. "Is there a but coming?"

"But," she said, "one day it all crumbled."

Travis chuckled in spite of himself. "Crumbled. Cute."

She nodded. "It was. Until I found a fake fingernail in one of my cupcakes."

Travis grimaced. "Gross."

"Right. All the cuteness faded. I was over those cupcakes immediately. I lost weight and I started going to a smoothie bar instead. It was a *good* thing really, but I needed that truth to show me that nothing is perfect."

"So you want me to show you something gross about Sapphire Falls."

"Just help me see beyond the cuteness and the shine and the charm. Let me see what real life would be like here."

He studied her face. He loved Sapphire Falls. As far as he was concerned, real life here was damned good. Even great a lot of the time. It was...home. But yeah, this wasn't where Lauren belonged.

"Can't you just *tell* yourself all of that? Tell yourself that there has to be more to life here, that there's got to be stuff behind the scenes that you won't like?"

She shook her head. "I've got a pretty big crush going on this town right now. And the universe is conspiring against me. My best friend loves it here, Adrianne loves it here, Phoebe and Joe love it here, and they're all so happy and relaxed and at peace. I want some of that."

He frowned. Lauren Davis could not settle down in Sapphire Falls. She would do exactly as she'd threatened. She'd make some nice guy from here fall in love with her and then, eventually, when the shine wore off—and she was right, for her it would—she'd realize Sapphire Falls wasn't big enough or fancy enough or fast-paced enough and she'd leave. And break the poor sucker's heart.

Travis couldn't let that happen. The chances of the guy being one of his friends were huge. Maybe even one of his brothers.

Plus, showing Dr. D the less-than-glitzy side, the rough-around-the-edges, downright-dirty side of Sapphire Falls could be kind of fun.

He'd love to see the snooty girl out of her element and not quite so put together. Something about messing her up was very, very tempting.

He studied her for another long moment. "I don't do roses and romance."

"Great. That's the last thing I need."

This was a really dumb idea. "But if you show up at the river party tonight, I'll make out with ya."

She opened her mouth to reply and then snapped it shut and nodded.

Travis grinned. She'd likely been about to tell him that he could go *make out* with himself. But if they were dating for real—like in some alternate universe where snooty rich scientist girls did it for him—he would most definitely get her into the cab of his pickup or on a blanket by the campfire for a good old-fashioned make-out session. If she wanted a real taste of dating a guy from Sapphire Falls, this was a start. They'd see if Miss City was willing to get her heels muddy.

"Fine. Where's the party?" she asked.

"Phoebe's place." He grinned. "I'll be the hot farm boy you want to jump on."

He turned and walked away. And noted that she didn't deny it.

৵৹৻

The smell of wood burning in the summer air hit Lauren as she stepped from Phoebe's truck, and it catapulted her back to the July before her senior year in high school.

She could almost hear the Dixie Chicks and Garth Brooks belting it out into the humid Nebraska night. She could almost taste the cheap beer. She could almost feel the tickle in her stomach thinking about seeing Shawn, dancing with him, feeling his hands running up and down her back, kissing him.

Lauren took a deep breath. Apparently, time didn't dull all memories.

Because, yeah, beer parties at the river were something she knew a little bit about.

She tugged at the hem of her cut-off denim shorts. They were *short*. Phoebe had done the cutting and they hadn't had time to buy a new pair of jeans after the result had been a little bit *less* than Lauren had wanted. Phoebe had assured her they were fine—with a grin that said she had totally intended the length the shorts had turned out to be.

Considering Lauren hadn't worn denim in years, and that she hadn't been to a river in a truck in even longer, she'd given in. This was Phoebe's turf. She knew the rules.

It hadn't, however, escaped Lauren's notice that Phoebe

wasn't wearing cut-off denim shorts.

But this was literally Phoebe's turf. The land they were parked on belonged to the redhead. Her house sat about a mile away. She was the most common hostess of the get-togethers with her group of friends. Her land ended on the edge of a bluff that dropped about a hundred feet to the river, but there was one point with a gentle slope where they could get coolers and firewood to the riverbank.

Lauren had heard all the details on the way out here.

"Travis will definitely be here?" she asked.

Phoebe slid to the ground from the high seat of her truck. She grinned at Lauren across the front seat. "Definitely."

Lauren followed her out of the truck, tamping down the tiniest stomach tickle. She was looking forward to seeing him if only to remind herself of all the reasons this—*he*—was not what she wanted.

Travis was a typical Sapphire Falls guy. Born and raised here, farming his family's land with his brothers, spending his free time with the same people he'd been spending his free time with since he could walk. An evening around a campfire with juvenile jokes and talk about football games that were at least a decade old would definitely help cure her of any farm-boy infatuation.

It hadn't worked with Shawn, but that was a long time ago. She wasn't seventeen anymore. And the big wide world with its excitement and diversity was no longer only in her imagination. She had experienced that big wide world. There was more out there than this little corner. There were important things to do, issues to deal with, problems to solve.

Sitting around a campfire never solved any problems.

Even if making out to Garth Brooks had felt damned good.

She needed to focus here. She was here to *talk* to Travis. She might have to ask him a few questions about

47

the political situation in Ukraine or who his favorite author was, just to be sure she didn't get caught up in how charming and funny he was when he started talking about his latest fishing trip or singing along to Toby Keith, but she could do that. Maybe he only read horror. Or *Sports Illustrated.* That would definitely give them nothing in common.

Lauren grabbed the other handle on the cooler that Phoebe pulled from the back of her truck. Joe hauled a second one off the tailgate.

"After you, ladies," he said, nodding in the direction of the river.

Phoebe gave him a wink and started down the slight hill.

There was already a crowd gathered on the sand.

Everyone greeted Phoebe and Joe with big smiles…while staring at Lauren as if they'd never seen her before.

She self-consciously tugged at the hem of her shorts again. They *hadn't* seen her like this.

"Hey, Phoeb." Tucker Bennett came forward and took the cooler from them, though his eyes didn't leave Lauren. "There better be dip in here."

Apparently, Phoebe was also famous for her taco dip. Lauren had heard all about it on the way to the party site too.

"There's dip. And burgers," Phoebe answered.

"And hard lemonade and beer in here," Joe said, dropping his cooler to the sand next to the fire that was already roaring.

"Dr. D, nice to see you," Tucker said. His gaze traveled from her ponytail over her T-shirt—that belonged to his brother—to the Phoebe-made short shorts and down her bare legs to the black heels. They were her least expensive pair and were only three inches high. "I like the new look."

Lauren waited for his eyes to return to her face. Then

she gave him a small smile. "You think this is okay? Or would this be better?"

She stripped Travis's shirt off, leaving her in only her red bikini top.

Tucker Bennett was definitely one of *those guys*—the ones she was attracted to. He oozed country charm and had the tanned, hardened body of a guy who worked outside. But he was one she could appreciate from a distance and dismiss with a sighed, "Too bad he prefers fried catfish to fresh sushi."

He didn't have *it*—whatever it was that Travis had. The extra *it* that made her not care that he would not only fry the catfish but that he would sit on the river all damned day to catch the stupid thing in the first place.

That alone should make her not want to be with him. Even when she'd been madly in love with Shawn, she'd hated fishing and his eager willingness to give up spending the day with her to sit and catch fish. But it hadn't stopped her from being stupid for him.

Travis had that. Whatever it was.

"I think that's a lot better," Tucker finally said.

She noticed his voice was a little gruffer now. She loved that. When her cool, bitchy façade didn't intimidate, she could always count on her sexuality to give her the upper hand.

"Thanks for returning my shirt."

And suddenly Travis appeared beside his brother. Dressed in boots, jeans, a T-shirt and ball cap. Just like Tucker was. Yet somehow the word *delicious* came to mind when she looked at Travis.

He took his shirt from Lauren's hand, also blatantly studying her remaining attire.

This felt completely different from when Tucker did it.

Having Tucker's eyes on her had made her glad she was religious with her Pilates.

Having Travis's eyes on her made her want to take the

rest of her clothes off and climb up on him.

"Well, I had no reason to keep it," she said with a shrug.

Travis lifted the shirt to his nose and breathed in deep. "Smells like you. You must have been wearing it all day."

"I can imagine that's a bit of an improvement over how it usually smells," she said, without really confirming that she had, indeed, been wearing it all day.

"I'd love some sweet-smelling pillow cases," Tucker said. "Wanna come over and help me out with that?"

She gave him a smile and started to reply, but Travis elbowed him, forcing Tucker back a step. "Glad to see that my invitation for tonight was intriguing, Dr. D," Travis said.

She looked around. "Yeah. I decided to get in touch with the locals."

"I'm local," Tucker said, with a cocky grin that did make her tingle a little.

She had a love-hate relationship with cocky.

But then she looked at Travis again. The cocky was about equal between the two brothers. So why did the tingles increase when it came to Travis?

The corner of Travis's mouth curled up. "He won't get you as dirty as I do."

Whatever the hell *it* was, it was there.

And the more of Travis's good-ol'-boy stuff she could get tonight, the better. She needed to O.D. on all of it…and then find that one fingernail that would turn her off and send her home.

"I'm dressed for dirty tonight." When Phoebe had described their typical river parties to her, Lauren had realized the need to be prepared for water, mud, camp-fire smoke, grass, beer and who knew what else.

Travis's gaze tracked over her again, causing zings of heat to zip along her nerve endings and she realized what she'd said.

"Well, girl, I can help with that."

Yep, those tingles didn't happen with Tucker. Or anyone else in Sapphire Falls. Or Chicago. Or DC, Haiti, London, Ontario, San Diego, Dallas, New York, or Frankfurt in the past two years.

Dammit.

"I figure we can go with mustard or hard lemonade," he said thoughtfully.

"Excuse me?"

"If I'm gonna get ya' dirty. That's how you and I do things, right?"

So far, yes. And having Travis get her dirty with mustard should *not* sound sexy.

"No beer tonight?"

"Well, I'd rather have the beer ending up in my mouth."

His mouth. Her gaze settled there. Said mouth curled up. "Though I guess there are ways to get it all over you *and* in my mouth, aren't there?"

"I, um…" She licked *her* lips and thought about licking his.

She shook her head and straightened. "I'll be staying away from the beer."

He must have noticed that she grimaced at the word beer.

His grin grew. "You not a beer fan?"

She shrugged. "In a pinch."

"Well, no worries. We don't get into pinches when it comes to liquor in Sapphire Falls."

She raised an eyebrow. "Did you say liquor?"

"I did."

"You mean the hard lemonade?"

"Better."

Now that was worth investigating.

"Travis Bennett, we might just be able to be friends after all."

CHAPTER THREE

An hour later, Lauren was standing sandal to boot with Steve Elder in spite of Steve being six inches taller and a hundred pounds heavier.

Travis found it all quite entertaining. His money was on the city girl.

"If I was interested in her," Lauren told Steve. "I'd already be rounding second base and heading to third by now instead of standing by a campfire telling my friends how much I want to ask her out."

"I'm taking it slow. That's how you *court* a lady," Steve said. "And it doesn't help for sexy women to be hitting on them."

"What are you so worried about?" Lauren asked. "If she's into *you*, she sure isn't going to be into *me*."

The way Lauren took in Steve's seed cap, T-shirt and blue jeans, made it clear that she didn't exactly mean that as a compliment.

But Steve didn't understand that.

"It just gives her more options. Even *more* people for her to compare me to," Steve said.

Travis saw something soften in Lauren's expression and he felt a kick behind his ribs.

Oh, crap.

If Lauren had a soft side, he might be in trouble. She looked like the very definition of tempting in that red bikini top and the shorts that showed off a whole lot of skin he'd like to know more intimately. He'd almost swallowed his tongue when he'd seen her stroll up with Phoebe.

She looked like a country girl.

Except for the stupid high heels. Who wore high heels to the river? But she'd quickly kicked them off and had been walking on the sand in her bare feet.

Which made his blue jeans a lot tighter in front.

Sure, her hair was still streaked with highlights that had not come from the sun, but with it pulled up into a ponytail, he suddenly had the urge to see a few pieces of straw in it from a quickie in the barn. Sure, the bikini she wore likely cost more than his jeans, shirt and hat put together, but paired with the denim shorts and those bare feet with their dark red nails, she looked like she could maybe be convinced to go for a ride on his tractor.

Of course, she wore her usual makeup, along with a gold necklace and earrings—girls in Sapphire Falls didn't wear earrings to river parties—but Lauren looked country enough to get his blood stirring in ways and places he didn't like. He also didn't like that it was obvious she was stirring up most of the single men at the party.

He didn't want any of them getting involved with her. They were all small-town guys. They all lived and worked here and intended to keep doing both of those things. They were also nice guys. Not that they didn't ever screw around or hook up with someone for just a night, but for the most part, they were looking for girls to settle down with. And they loved their hometown. If one of them got involved with Lauren, he would think he could win her over and settle her down. And he'd be nursing a broken heart as of the first of July.

If she was going to mess around with a Sapphire Falls boy, then it needed to be Travis.

He wouldn't be falling in love with her.

He knew who she was and had no illusions about her feelings and attitudes about the things he loved. He could keep his distance. Partly because she wasn't a very nice person.

Unless she was.

It would have to be deep down, behind quite a bit of arrogance, of course. Still, he was a sucker for a nice girl. Especially one who could do what Lauren was doing to those shorts. Even one from the city.

"Don't be silly." Lauren smiled at Steve. "If she wants *you*, options don't matter. Trust me."

The last two words were more or less muttered, and Travis found himself leaning closer, trying to get a better look at her face. He almost tipped off the edge of the tailgate of his truck.

"Still, you can have any *guy* in town. Can't you leave the girls alone?" Steve almost sounded like he was pleading with her.

Travis shook his head. Steve was probably right to be worried. Straight or not, even women noticed Lauren, and if anyone could tempt someone to try something new, it would be her.

He found her incredibly exasperating and yet he couldn't help but think that even he could be convinced to try caviar or something if it meant seeing her *without* the bikini top on.

"I don't want any guys or girls in this town, Steve," Lauren assured him. "She and I were talking about shoes."

"Still...I saw you put your hand on her arm."

Lauren laughed and Travis felt his gut tighten. Damn, he might eat fish eggs just to hear *that* again. The woman was dangerous.

"Honey, if she's horny enough that a hand on her arm is enough to get her going, then you should *really* get over there and take advantage," Lauren told him.

Had Lauren just drawled a little?

Travis eyed the bottle of alcohol sitting beside him on the tailgate of his truck. How much had she had? Lauren was calling someone *honey*?

Steve looked across the campfire to Kelli Dillon, his crush. "You don't think she's into you?" he asked Lauren.

Lauren shook her head. "*She* doesn't think she is anyway, so you're okay."

Steve's eyes went wide. "But *you* think she is?"

"Give me fifteen minutes with her and she will be,"

Lauren said. Her voice held a sultry note now.

Steve didn't respond at first. His eyes widened and he swallowed hard.

Travis grinned.

Sapphire Falls had never seen a woman quite like Lauren Davis. She was smarter than any of the other women in town and she strutted around like she owned the place even though she was an outsider. They all thought of her as a kind of Good Samaritan, bringing more business and attention to their little town. But many were too intimidated to actually talk to her. When she was around town, she seemed in a hurry, preoccupied and, frankly, uninterested in conversation with the common folk.

And then there was the sex thing. Everyone knew Lauren liked men *and* women. *That* news had gotten out quickly. Travis was pretty sure it was Phoebe Sherwood who had first mentioned it, in fact. But if the simple idea of Lauren being bisexual wasn't enough to get the town whispering, she wore her sexuality like an expensive designer coat—on display for everyone to see, admire, judge and talk about. Most of the people in town watched her with a kind of awe, like she was fascinating but scary.

Travis didn't find her scary. Exactly. And fascinating seemed like a bit of a stretch, but…watching her give Steve a pep talk on how to hit on Kelli, and then watching her turn the man and nudge him in Kelli's direction, made Travis admit that maybe she was a little fascinating. Sometimes.

Then she started dancing. And singing. To Brad Paisley.

And she knew every word.

Well, fuck.

That song was new enough that it told Travis that Dr. Davis listened to country music. At least some of the time.

Damn.

He didn't want to have things in common with her. He

especially didn't want to have country music in common with her. That was big stuff. Important stuff. Like religion.

Music said a lot about a person, and he had a hard time not liking someone who loved country.

If she could sing along to Kip Moore, he was going to have to be nice to her. If she could sing Johnny Cash he might have to call her ma'am instead of darlin'. A woman who knew Johnny deserved more respect than he'd been showing Lauren so far.

On top of all of that, she looked damned good moving that long, tight body to fiddle music next to a campfire.

He wasn't sure she was exactly moving to the beat, but his body didn't care. She was moving. Apparently, that was all it took to make every inch of him want every inch of her. Sure, singing to Brad didn't hurt. Well, that and the denim cut off nice and short. But the way she moved made him think about a little secluded spot just up the river.

He knew he should sit back and let someone else approach her, dance with her, share the secret mosquito repellent. But as she swatted at another bite on her shoulder, he found himself across the sand and practically on top of her, a T-shirt in one hand and a palmful of bug repellent in the other.

"You're going to get eaten alive."

She stopped moving and looked at him. And licked her lips.

God, he hadn't meant by *him*, but suddenly that seemed like a hell of an idea.

"Here. You need to cover some of that skin up." He pulled the T-shirt she'd returned to him over her head. Maybe that would help the mosquitos *and* him leave her alone.

She looked down and recognized it. "You really want me to have this shirt." She put her arms through the sleeves and tied the bottom again so it hugged her flat stomach just above the curve of her hips.

"As much as I like the bikini top look, it's gettin' dark and you're gonna be one big bug bite tomorrow if you're not careful."

All of the other women who partied with them at the river knew this and had not only brought clothes to pull on after the sun went down, but each had a jar of the magic mosquito repellent—the recipe for which was a Sapphire Falls secret, passed down in the Bennett family from generation to generation—in with their stuff.

"Well, thanks for your concern," she said. She hesitated just a second before trying to turn away.

It was that hesitation that made him react. That hesitation that said she couldn't dismiss him quite as quickly and easily as she'd like him to believe.

Travis reached out and took her arm. "There's more."

Head-to-toe itching the next day might keep her away from their parties in the future, which could be a good thing. He honestly didn't give her much thought when she wasn't around. She wasn't his type. She wasn't a friend or a relative. They had nothing in common. There was no reason to think about her.

But when she was around, he seemed unable to think about anything else. He'd been distracted all night. Not that he needed to pay close attention to keep up with most of the conversation around the fire. It was the same stuff—baseball, the town festival, a few new calves, some new truck tires. But Lauren had occupied most of his attention since she'd shown up with Phoebe. She'd taken two long draws on his bottle of Booze before she'd let Phoebe drag her around the party site and introduce her to the gang.

He'd been watching, cataloguing the ways she didn't fit in, taking note of the things she did and said differently from the country girls he was used to—the girls like the one he expected to end up with one of these days. She didn't know anything about NASCAR, she admitted she didn't watch cooking shows and she didn't read romance novels. It was like she was blaspheming right to their faces.

But the women didn't cast her out. They didn't laugh at her or give her any attitude.

Instead, they were fascinated to hear about the tree-nut oil she'd discovered on a trip to the Middle East that worked wonders on hair, skin *and* nails. She'd promised to send some bottles from Chicago when she went home next. And they were a rapt audience when she told them about a lunch she'd had in LA with the head of Outreach America—the group she worked with on her trips to Haiti—and Angelina Jolie.

Lauren was still staring up at him and he kept the eye contact as he held up the hand where he'd poured some of the bug repellent.

Okay, so lunch with Angelina Jolie was kind of cool.

"This will save all that sweet skin." He rubbed his hands together, spreading the oil out and warming it. The scent of vanilla, the key ingredient, floated up.

Lauren didn't move back as he reached out and slid a hand under each of the shirt sleeves. He dragged his hands from her shoulders to her hands and then up again.

"It smells sweet. How will this help?" she asked.

Was her voice a little husky?

"Mosquitos don't like vanilla," he said with a shrug. "You should put some on your legs too." And he'd happily help. But that was a bad idea, and he somehow kept from saying that out loud.

"Okay."

Yes, her voice was definitely a little husky.

He tamped down the surge of pleasure at that realization and turned back for his truck.

Lauren followed. She hoisted herself up onto the tailgate and reached for the bottle of alcohol he'd let her sample before. She took two long drinks of the strawberry-flavored liquid.

He should probably warn her about the kick the stuff

had. It was a carefully guarded—though surely not complicated—recipe of alcohol and local fruits. They simply called it Booze and you couldn't find it anywhere outside of Sapphire Falls.

It was good. And it was strong.

Really strong.

So he should warn her.

In a minute.

Seeing Lauren Davis tipsy was already interesting—and that was the only explanation for her singing and dancing and being nice to everyone. Seeing her flat out drunk would be…very interesting.

"This is so good," she said after swallowing.

It really was. It also cleared the sinuses and could burn the lining right out of your stomach.

"You like it?"

"I do. It makes me feel…warm," she told him. "And it makes the conversation about truck tires more tolerable."

At that her eyes went wide and she thrust the bottle at him.

"Here, I can't drink anymore."

Travis took the bottle. "Why's that?"

"This is not about things being *more* tolerable. I need to be irritated by all of this."

Travis chuckled and tipped the bottle back for a drink of his own. He swallowed, letting the booze burn its familiar trail down his throat. "Girl, you seem perpetually irritated."

"Well, yeah, when you're around. Because you irritate me."

"No kidding," he muttered. She irritated the hell out of him too. At least usually. When she wasn't giving advice to one of his friends on women or sharing her miraculous skin-care secrets with the girls in Sapphire Falls like they were BFFs.

She'd rolled her eyes twice that evening—that he'd

noticed—and *that* was a little annoying. She'd snorted in derision at least once. But she'd also laughed. And danced and sang—to country music.

Maybe she was human after all.

Maybe the Booze was the key.

He needed to pour more into her if that was the case, because it looked like she was staying for the duration of the party.

If the talk about the dead rats Marcus had found in his barn and the conversation about the guy they all knew from Pierce, a town just up the road, chopping off three fingers on his left hand hadn't done her in, she was probably staying.

Travis handed her the vanilla oil for her legs and then got busy studying the fire instead of watching her apply it. At least, he was mostly studying the fire. Problem was, his peripheral vision worked just fine.

She pulled her foot up and rubbed oil into the long expanse of skin between the hem of her shorts and her crimson-red-tipped toes. "Do you know what's going on in Ukraine right now?"

He resisted looking over at her. Her leg pulled up like that demonstrated that she was pretty flexible. And she was now going to smell like vanilla. Neither were real turn-offs. "Huh?"

"Ukraine. The country. It's in Eastern Europe."

Okay, now he had to be careful. That was also irritating about having her at the party tonight. He had to keep up the dumb-farmer thing he had going. He'd gotten some strange looks from his friends over the course of the evening.

"What about it?" he asked.

"Do you know what's going on over there? Between them and Russia?"

Travis shifted on the tailgate. He did know. At least the basics. But was world politics common campfire conversation? No. Definitely not.

"We can Google it on my phone if you want," he offered, digging his phone out of his pocket.

Lauren seemed to sigh in relief. She switched legs, rubbing the oil along the second long, silky expanse of skin that Travis refused to notice.

Just like he refused to notice the tiny pink butterfly tattoo on her ankle.

"No, that's okay," Lauren said. "I was just wondering what you knew off the top of your head."

"Is it important that I know about what's going on in Ukraine?" he asked, finally letting himself glance at her fully.

What was going through her pretty, brilliant head?

She looked at him with a big smile. "As a matter of fact, it's important that you *not* know."

"Well, then I'd say we're just fine." It was definitely safe to say that the things he *didn't* know about Ukraine outnumbered the things he did know.

She sighed again. Undeniably, a happy sound. "That's what I thought."

She finished applying the oil, lifted her hands to her nose and breathed in. "Wow, wonder if my boutique in Chicago would have something like this."

Travis didn't say anything, but the word boutique made him tense for some reason. People here didn't talk about— or go to—boutiques. They went to stores.

Lauren sat facing the fire, her legs swinging off the end of his tailgate, smelling like vanilla, and Travis really wished she'd go...somewhere else. Back to Chicago would be great. But even to the other side of the campfire would be helpful.

Why'd he have to save her from the mosquitos?

"I can't believe you all do this every weekend," she said after a few blissfully quiet seconds.

He glanced at her. "People in Chicago don't have a good time with their friends on the weekends?"

She smiled. "I mean *this*. The same spot, the same beer, the same people. The same conversations, I'll bet."

Travis didn't say anything.

"Seriously." She turned partially toward him. "How many times have you heard that story about the time Drew rescued the three-legged dog from the drainage ditch?"

Travis shrugged. "I was there when it happened."

She rolled her eyes. Again. "And how tall has that tale gotten over the years?"

Well, the dog had had four legs as far as Travis could remember. "What's your point, Doc? You don't like it? I'll take you home right now."

"My *point*," Lauren said, "is that there is a great big wide world out there. It's full of new people to meet, new things to eat and drink, new stories and traditions to hear, new things to learn."

Travis reigned in the urge to snap at her. "I guess I'm just lucky that I found the corner of the world I like best at an early age."

She didn't reply right away, and when he glanced at her, she was staring at him with wide eyes. "You really believe that *this* is the best place on earth?"

He really, really did. But he didn't expect her to understand. "I really hate when you talk," he told her bluntly.

She looked intrigued by that. "About what?"

"Pretty much everything you talk about, honestly."

His mom had raised him to be nice to women. To be respectful. To be polite. But she'd also raised him to love this land and these people and this way of life. He knew that if she was here right now talking to Lauren, she'd be defending all of it too.

Rather than look offended, Lauren nodded. "I feel the same way about you."

Yeah, he wasn't shocked to hear that. "We have something in common then."

"Yep. That and wanting to sleep together."

He arched an eyebrow. The doctor was full of herself. And right.

She grinned. "Come on. You do too."

He took a casual swig of beer from the can he held. "You're so sure?"

"You sure didn't like your brother hitting on me earlier."

He hadn't. But he hated that it bugged him. And that she knew it.

"Just because I don't want to watch him drool over you, doesn't mean anything about how *I* feel about you."

She just looked at him as she tipped the Booze bottle again.

"What?" he finally asked.

"Just wondering if you have any dumb dog stories."

"Stories about dumb dogs? Or dumb stories about dogs?" he asked.

"Either really."

Probably. "Why do you ask?"

"'Cause," she said, emphasizing the word with a fake drawl. "When yer talkin', I don't wanna kiss ya'."

Her country twang was sad. And he had to work not to smile.

"And when I'm just sittin' here, mindin' my own business?" he asked, putting extra emphasis on his drawl as well.

"I have the urge to risk some bug bites in some very uncomfortable places."

His mind went to each and every one of those places instantly.

"But you don't want to want to kiss me?" he asked.

"Exactly."

"I feel the same way," he told her honestly.

"Really? You want to kiss me, but that pisses you off?" She looked almost excited about the fact.

City girls were strange.

He shook his head. "Girl, you are the *last* woman I would ever want to get involved with."

She turned to face him fully, her eyes lighting up. "Really? Why?"

"You want me to make a list of your flaws?" he asked.

She actually smiled at that. "My flaws, *in your opinion*," she said, "could be very important to our new dating relationship."

"I'm not sure I remember agreeing to that."

"But you don't want me to stay here in Sapphire Falls. And you're about to tell me the reasons why I would never fit in here for good."

Okay, hell, he could humor her. There were several reasons why she was never going to sit at his mother's dinner table.

"Do you eat fried chicken, mashed potatoes and apple pie?" he asked.

"Absolutely not." She even wrinkled her nose.

"So my grandma wouldn't like you a bit."

"And you base your decisions about women on your grandmother's opinion?"

"She and my grandpa were married for forty-eight years. I think she might know a thing or two about good matches."

Lauren nodded as if she accepted that. "So, based strictly on what your grandmother would think—"

"Oh, my dad wouldn't like you either."

She looked surprised. "Really?"

He chuckled. It probably *was* uncommon for a man to not like Lauren Davis. "Do you like basset hounds, Tim McGraw and the Bachelor?" he asked. "And by the way, that's an *and* in there. No two out of three here. You have to have the trifecta."

"The Bachelor? As in the TV show?" Lauren asked.

Travis couldn't help but grin at that. "Yep."

"I've never seen an episode."

"Well, those are the things my dad loves and looks for in people with good character. That and things like honesty and hard work."

Lauren frowned. "I have those things."

He shrugged. She did. "But you don't love basset hounds."

"They're...cute."

He grinned again, picturing Lauren with one of his dad's hounds lovingly slobbering all over her. It was pretty hard to imagine.

"Okay, what about your mom?"

"Can you shoot a gun, make a skirt from scratch and sing "How Great Thou Art" straight through, every verse?"

She gave a little laugh. "What are the chances?"

Yeah, things would never work out for them.

Lauren tucked a foot under her other leg on the tailgate. "You want to hear the reasons *I* don't think it will work out?"

"Oh, I'm thinkin' I can come up with one or two all on my own."

"Tell me where you want to be in ten years."

Easy. "Here," he said simply.

"Here. In Sapphire Falls," she clarified.

"Yep."

"And farming. You want to keep farming," she said.

He nodded. "It's what I know."

She nodded, smiling widely. "It is, isn't it? You know farming."

He smiled. "I do."

"What else do you know?" she asked, leaning in, bracing her weight on one arm.

"What do you mean?" There was no way she was hitting on him—this was the opposite, in fact—but for a moment, his mind went to a bunch of things he knew and had, as a matter of fact, practiced on the banks of this very river in this very truck.

"Do you play the piano? Are you a gourmet chef? A Civil War buff? An aspiring novelist?" she asked, her eyes on his.

He shook his head slowly. "None of the above."

"So what are you good at? Besides farming?"

He couldn't help but study her mouth for a moment. He loved women's mouths and he'd been getting up close and personal with them since he was fourteen.

Lauren Davis had an amazing mouth.

He had a few skills to brag about in that area.

"I bet you fish."

He blinked and looked her in the eye again. "Fish?"

"Yeah. You fish, right?"

"Well...yeah." Every male within a few hundred miles of here fished.

"Do you hunt?"

"I do." Deer, ducks, whatever was in season.

"And you probably play poker."

"Yep."

"You're good at it?"

He was better at the *other* stuff he'd been on the verge of telling her about, but he didn't suck at poker. "I'm okay."

"And demo derbies. Phoebe said you drive."

"I do."

She sighed that happy little sigh again. "You ever plan to go to Paris?"

He lifted an eyebrow. "Paris? Uh...probably not." He wouldn't mind seeing the Grand Canyon, but he wasn't so sure about going overseas.

"That's...perfect," she said, leaning even closer.

Now *her* attention was on *his* mouth.

"It's perfect for what?"

"You don't have any amazing skills and you don't want to leave your hometown. So I will never want to be involved with you long term."

"Gee, Doc, I'll try not to cry myself to sleep at night." She would never fit into his world. He would never fit into hers. It was good.

So why did this whole thing irritate the shit out of him?

"But you're saying you don't go for guys who are charming, funny, good-looking, intelligent, hardworking—"

"Stuck."

He blinked at her. "Stuck?"

"I don't go for guys—or girls—who are stuck. And you, Travis Bennett, are stuck."

He opened his mouth to tell her where she could *stick* her ideas but then realized the opportunity that had just presented itself.

He'd been on the verge of liking her a little. If all it took to soften him up was a little Brad Paisley and short shorts, he was clearly weak. He needed to hear the rest of this as a defense against thinking that eating his grandma's fried chicken wasn't all that important.

"What do you mean by stuck?" he asked.

She swept her arm to indicate the party and some of the people he cared about most in the world.

"Stuck here. Stuck in your routine. Stuck in your work, your life. You're never going to leave. You'll spend your whole life right here, doing...*this*."

She was right. If he was lucky, he'd spend his life in this town with these people.

"So you don't want to be involved with me," he said, thinking *thank God*, "because I have a life here that you think is boring?"

She shook her head. "Boring isn't the right word. It's...unremarkable. You're an average Joe. A regular guy. A hick farmer."

His eyes widened. "A hick farmer?"

She nodded. "You love blue jeans and country music

and you hang out with the same guys you've hung out with since fifth grade and you don't know anything about Ukraine."

He'd hung out with these guys since kindergarten, actually, and while he couldn't write a term paper on Ukraine or anything, he did watch the news.

But she was right on with the blue jeans and country music.

And the more she *disliked* the things that made him happy, the better. Because he didn't want to be involved with her either. And because then she'd stay away from him. Because if she thought she was interested and danced her short shorts over to him and looked up at him with those big brown eyes, and—heaven help him—sang a little Hank Williams Junior, he'd have to haul her up into the cab of his truck and show her how they passed the long *boring* weekends in Sapphire Falls.

For his own sake, he needed to give her a whole list of things for her to dislike about him.

"I play in a pool league every Tuesday night."

Her smile was bright. "That's awesome."

He knew she didn't mean that the pool league was awesome. What was awesome was that Ms. I'm Better Than You would find pool league a turn-off. While he loved it because it was one of the few times he got to spend time and have some fun with his older brother T.J.

"I know every word to every one of Willie Nelson's songs," he said.

She frowned a little at that and shook her head. "I need more than that."

Oh, really? Miss City might be a Willie Nelson fan? Well, *that* wouldn't help him not like her. She was right. They needed more that they didn't have in common.

"I…" He tried to think of something.

"Do you rearrange other activities around Nebraska football games?" she asked.

He nodded. "Yeah. Everything stops on football Saturday." As it did in small towns all across the state.

Of course, fancy scientists in Chicago probably didn't care about football.

"How about hunting? Have you ever asked someone to reschedule something because it conflicted with a hunting trip?"

His buddy Drew's birthday bash had been moved back a day so they could hunt. But Drew had gone with them. And how did Dr. D know about hunting trips? She hunted for shoe sales—not really the same thing. Still, he said, "Yes."

"Do you think Larry the Cable Guy is funny?"

Everyone thought Larry the Cable Guy was funny. "Definitely."

"Do you watch the Simpsons?"

"Of course."

She was grinning at him like he was the most fascinating person she'd met. When, in fact, it was the opposite.

She was a pain in the ass. He did *not* want to be involved with this woman. At all.

Even the bare feet weren't as sexy now. Well, they were still a little sexy...

"I happen to be the Sapphire Falls horseshoe champion," he added for good measure.

"Oh, good," she said enthusiastically. "We will *never* work out."

He sat looking at her.

He still wanted to sleep with her.

That was the stupid part. Everything she said and assumed about him was insulting. But he wanted to sleep with her.

"I don't like you much," he told her honestly.

"I'll try to get over it," she said.

And she was sassy.

69

But he liked sassy.

"You're full of yourself," he added.

"Look who's talking."

Okay, she had a point. Travis didn't have any self-esteem issues. "You're too hoity-toity for me, Dr. D." And she was.

But he still kind of hoped she could convince him it didn't matter.

"I like beer that's cold," he told her. "That's my only stipulation. It doesn't have to have a fancy label or be from some special microbrewery. I like music that's about something. Music that's just instruments and no words doesn't do it for me. I like clothes that feel good and help me do what I have to do. I don't care about who made them or if they match or if they're the latest trend. And I like women who swear on Saturday and pray on Sunday and who visit their grandmas and who can drive a four-wheeler and wear boots because they're practical rather than because they make the boys hot."

She blinked at him for a moment.

"You used the word stipulation."

He sighed. "I don't want to sleep with you either." It was a lie, but wanting her didn't make any sense. No way could she drive a four-wheeler.

"I didn't say I didn't want to *sleep* with you. I just don't want to park my rocking chair next to yours on your front porch for the next eighty years."

He laughed at that. "Glad to hear it." He took another drink of Booze and eyed the girls around the fire. He should take one of them home. Tonight. Right now.

Instead, he drank again.

Because he'd never do that. He was riled up because of Lauren, but he'd never make another girl a substitute. He needed to get over this urge to show the city girl just how great rockin' a truck bed could be. Or he needed to do it and get over it that way.

"You want to do this too," she finally said.

"I don't sleep with girls I don't like." Which was true. And had seemed like a no-brainer right up until Lauren Davis knew the words to a Brad Paisley song.

There was a second of silence and then Lauren laughed.

He looked over, one eyebrow up. "That's funny?"

"Well, who's hoity-toity now?"

"Having morals is hoity-toity?"

She was still grinning. "Maybe it was the I'm-better-than-you tone of voice you used."

"You should recognize that tone pretty well."

She tipped her head. "I definitely do."

They sat looking at each other.

He had a few standards and Lauren didn't fit any of them. He slept with nice girls that he sincerely liked and it was never a one-night thing—he dated them for at least a little while. They were girls his mother would like, girls whose mothers liked him. It had never worked out long term—obviously—but he had every intention of getting married to someone from the area eventually, having kids, raising them on the farm just as he'd been raised.

The woman who looked down on everything he loved was the last woman he should even be drinking Booze with. Booze and bare feet with red toenails were a dangerous combination.

"I guess I'll need to be very careful not to tell you anything about my humanitarian efforts in Haiti and my trip to West Africa next fall and how I fly my grandmother to Chicago for a fancy, all-expenses paid shopping and spa weekend for her birthday every year," Lauren said, watching him closely. "Because I wouldn't want you to like me. That would make all of this even harder."

He knew all about Haiti. But yeah, the grandmother thing didn't make her *less* appealing. "I'd appreciate you keeping quiet about any other good things," he said lightly.

"Yeah, ditto," she said softly, looking at him with a

hard-to-read expression. "But I have an idea that might be even more effective."

"In keeping us from wanting to sleep together?"

"Yes."

"I'm listening." *Not* sleeping with her was a good idea. And he was a pretty self-disciplined guy. He could fight it. Probably. Of course, it would be better if she *never* showed up at a river party again. Or went barefoot again. Or laughed where he could hear her again.

But anything that would help him curtail the urge would be welcome. He'd already listed all the reasons she was not the woman for him. And he still wanted to get those shorts to her ankles.

"Have you ever heard of operant conditioning?" she asked.

Travis paused, one eyebrow up. "What are the chances of that, Doc?"

"Okay, go with me here. This whole thing is about me finding ways to get *over* my affection for Sapphire Falls, or at least over my desire to become a permanent citizen."

"Right."

"And part of that is for *you* to give me a taste of real life here."

"Okay."

"But some of that real life might be very appealing," she said.

"Like sex with me."

She stopped and pulled in a deep breath through her nose. She nodded. "For instance."

Travis grinned and took another big drink of Booze.

"So I need to experience negative things, the things I *don't* want about life here. But I can use operant conditioning—using punishment—to condition myself not to like the good things too."

Travis thought about that for a moment and then shook his head. "Not following."

"Every time something *good* happens, or I feel good about something, I need to follow it with something bad, a punishment, so I stop wanting it."

"Give me a for instance here, Doc."

"Let's say kissing you is a really good thing," she said.

"Totally with you so far on that."

She rolled her eyes. "So every time we kiss, I would need something negative to happen. Like..." She paused for a moment. "Okay, we kiss and then you say something like, 'Ain't that somethin'''". That positive feeling will be followed by my shuddering over your word choice and drawl. If that happened often enough, I would stop associating kissing you with good feelings and would automatically think of it as a negative thing."

She sure made it sound simple. Travis turned to face her more fully. "Thing is, Doc, there's no way kissin' me—and all the other stuff you wanna do with me—could ever be negative. I don't care what you try to follow it up with."

She didn't look worried. "It's science. It's been proven over and over. Conditioning human behavior has been successful for decades."

She was crazy. But she was hot. A hot girl could get away with a lot of crazy before a guy turned her away. That had also been proven over and over.

What the hell was he doing considering *any* of this? Protecting his friends and brothers. That's what he was going to keep telling himself.

"I really think it's worth a try," Lauren said.

Travis shrugged. He wasn't completely clear on what she was proposing here, but he did understand that she was talking about kissing him some more. He was down with that. Though he knew he shouldn't be.

"I'm here to help, City," he said. "God knows, you living here permanently seems like a bad idea on several levels."

Like the level where she was messing him all up just by

being here on his turf, looking and acting like a country girl.

"It really is a bad idea."

Until she talked to him, of course.

Maybe there was something to her theory. His fascination with her ability to chug Booze, her tattoo and the way she made his T-shirt smell was certainly reduced when she spouted off about Ukraine and not liking fried chicken.

Lauren Davis was not the kind of girl he wanted to settle down with. He'd spend his life not quite keeping up and not quite satisfying her. Mason Riley was the only man who could really impress Lauren and that guy was a literal genius. Travis didn't have a chance. He had a simple life and he needed a woman who would appreciate that.

So what the hell was he doing teasing Lauren with the fact that she wanted him? He didn't want her to like anything about Sapphire Falls, and she *would* like sex with him. A lot. In that way, he'd satisfy her and then some. And then he'd never get rid of her and they'd spend their life making each other hot...and miserable.

Lauren was about a thousand times smarter than Travis, so if she said she had an idea about how to make this chemistry thing less strong, he should probably listen to her.

"Fine. I'm in. But," he added, "I think *I* need a punishment after something feels good too."

She gave him a little smile that almost seemed accidental. She quickly sobered and nodded. "Not a bad idea. The less we *both* want to kiss—and do things—the better probably."

"Okay, let's do this."

Lauren nodded. She leaned in, bracing a hand on the truck bed between them. She wet her lips and motioned him closer with her finger.

He obliged.

Because when a barefoot girl on a tailgate asked him to get closer, he was never going to say no.

Travis jumped to the ground and faced her. Lauren spread her knees wider so he could move in between. Very close. Without conscious command, his hands went to her hips.

"We're going to kiss," she explained, her voice soft, her eyes on his. "But afterward we're both going to say something or do something that will be a turn-off to the other person."

"So I could belch or something?" Travis asked.

The corner of her mouth curled and she put her arms around his neck. "That would work."

"And you'll say something uppity."

Her eyebrows rose. "Uppity?"

"Yeah, like something you know I don't have a clue about."

"Ah, okay, got it." She took a deep breath.

His gaze dropped to her mouth. She had a great mouth. When it wasn't talking.

"You gonna kiss me or am I gonna kiss you?" he asked, his entire body feeling like it was preparing for something big. It was just going to be a kiss. And they'd already had a hell of a hot lip lock earlier. Still, he felt primed.

She lifted a shoulder. "We'll kiss each other."

He felt his smile. "On three?"

She laughed lightly. "Okay."

"One." He leaned in until their lips were millimeters apart. "Two." He felt her catch her breath. "Three."

Their mouths met.

And...*something*...broke loose. He just wasn't sure if it was hell. Or heaven.

CHAPTER FOUR

They opened their lips simultaneously. Their moans mingled. His hand went to the back of her head at the same time she threaded her fingers through his hair. They both tipped their heads to the right, fitting their mouths more fully together. Travis curled his fingers into her hip at the same time she tightened her knees around him.

He stroked his tongue deep, drawing on her mouth as he pulled her closer to the edge of the tailgate.

The heat and want built over the course of several seconds that could have been hours, until Lauren finally pulled back.

She was panting and staring at him with huge pupils.

"Do you know what *Legim* is?"

He blinked at her. The woman who he wanted more than he'd ever wanted any woman. The woman who wanted to hate his lifestyle and hometown. The woman who drove him nuts in too many ways to count.

The woman who had just asked him about something he'd never heard of.

"Another foreign country?" he asked.

She shook her head. "It's a Haitian food."

"I'm a meat-and-potatoes kind of guy."

She frowned. "They eat meat and potatoes in Haiti."

"There's no way they make fried potatoes as good as my mom's." So he wasn't an adventurous eater. So what? When you had sirloin steak and meatloaf and homemade chicken pot pie, you didn't go looking for different food—it would never be better.

And her theory was working. He loved kissing her, but this was a great reminder that unless they spent twenty-four-seven kissing—which was tempting, but not all that realistic—then they wouldn't have much else to do that wouldn't make him nuts.

"Now you say something to turn me off," she said.

He didn't have much practice with turning women *off*, but with Lauren it seemed that he pretty much just needed to be himself.

Along with the food theme… "Fried pickles are some of the best things in the world."

Sure enough, she shuddered. Then she smiled.

"That was pretty good," she said. "But—" her gaze dropped to his lips "—I think we need to keep going. I still want to kiss you."

He focused on her mouth as well. "Yeah. You need to be bitchier."

"And you need to be more of a slob."

They both leaned in simultaneously, joining their mouths in a full, hot exchange. There was a lot of tongue, some groaning and a hunger that seemed to only increase.

They pulled apart a moment later.

"I think everyone in the world should know what's going on in Ukraine," she said, panting slightly.

Okay, that was a little bitchy. But she wasn't totally wrong either.

But he was supposed to be a slob. He could do that. "I have a huge compost pile at the back edge of my yard."

Her eyes widened. "You compost?"

Was that a note of enthusiasm in her voice? "You're *interested* in that?"

She pulled back farther. "Of course. Composting is a fantastic practice. How did you get started? Does Sapphire Falls have a program? Did you build a bin or is it open? You said it's huge. How big?"

He sighed. This woman was weird. She wore high heels that cost more than his house payment, she got manicures and pedicures, she wore lip gloss to river parties, but she got excited about composting. Even the country girls he knew didn't find composting interesting. "And here I thought having a big pile of garbage on my property might be a turn-*off*."

She shook her head. "It's a very responsible environmental practice. We teach it along with almost all of our presentations. We've established village-wide composting in three villages in Haiti."

Unbelievable.

"We do have a program in Sapphire Falls," he felt compelled—for some reason—to say.

She looked pleased for a moment. Then her eyes narrowed. "Don't tell me you started it up."

And the reason he'd felt compelled was suddenly clear. He liked surprising Dr. Davis. She thought she had him pegged. This was one of those moments he'd been waiting for—to prove her wrong.

He nodded. "My composting pile is everyone's composting pile."

She shook her head. "Dammit. It's supposed to be a turn-*off* when you talk. We might be in trouble here."

Trouble. That was one word for this.

"I better not tell you about our water conserving irrigation practices then. You'll be all over me."

She groaned. "You're right. The way to really get to me is to talk about recycling and conservation and alternative energy."

He couldn't help but chuckle. "Duly noted." Then he shook his head. "You don't like to get dirty, but you get excited about composting?" he asked.

"Composting is…getting dirty for a purpose. It's worth a little dirt under your fingernails."

"Ah," he said. "And planting and harvesting crops isn't worthwhile?"

"That's not what I mean," she said. "I respect and value farming, Travis."

"Just not the farmers who do the farming."

"That's not true."

"But you want nothing to do with life here. In a town

full of farmers, who farm."

"I'm talking about...the rest of the lifestyle here. The lack of interest or knowledge about anything *but* farming."

He was still standing between her legs, her hands resting on his shoulders and his hands on her hips.

And they were talking about garbage and she was insulting his lifestyle and his friends. Again.

"Well, congrats, City. If me talking doesn't turn *you* off, *you* talking definitely turns *me* off."

He started to step back, but she tightened her knees against his hips. "Wait. That's *good*. And I'm sure we can find some way for you to turn me off."

He was torn between laughing...and telling her to fuck off. For the second time that day.

Well, she was right about one thing—he was sure he could find a way to turn her off. Or at least to piss her off.

He reached for the bottle of Booze, with the remaining third of the strawberry liquor inside. "Okay, if rotting vegetables and grass clippings don't do it, maybe this will." He tipped the bottle, sloshing red alcohol down the front of her.

She gasped, slipping her arms from around his neck and glaring up at him. "What's the matter with you?"

"It's not a grape slushy or chicken poop, but you are now dirtier than you were a minute ago. You're welcome."

Lauren plucked the wet, sticky T-shirt away from her skin. She reached for the bottom of the shirt and pulled it off over her head. "Keeping my clothes on around you is really tough, you know that?" she asked.

The liquor had soaked through and she had red streaks on her stomach and chest. And just like the sand on her feet and the smell of campfire in her hair, it made him want her even more than he did when she wore her expensive skirts and her silky blouses. And that was saying something.

He leaned in. "I'm going to need you to repeat what you said about people here not being interesting here in a minute."

"Why?"

"Because I'm going to kiss you and I'm going to enjoy it too much. So be ready with something bitchy, okay?"

"I'll do my be—"

He covered her lips with his before she even finished the sentence.

Her hands were back in his hair, his hands were gripping her butt, her legs were around him, his cock was hot and hard and rocking against her when he heard a chorus of wolf whistles from the crowd around the fire.

He pulled away, breathing hard. Dammit. This wasn't working. They clearly needed more practice with this conditioning thing.

"How long does operant conditioning take?" he asked her.

She too, was breathing hard and fast.

"Um." She pressed her lips together and then wet them. "Longer than this. We need to consistently pair punishment with the behaviors we're trying to change."

"Which means consistently engaging in those behaviors."

She nodded and cleared her throat. It was that action, the sign that she was obviously affected, that made his decision. He doubted there would be a time when he *didn't* want to kiss Lauren Davis, even if she did say bitchy, uppity things.

So they needed another way to ensure that she *wouldn't* stick around and continue messing with him long term.

If she needed to find something in Sapphire Falls unappealing and beneath her, he could help her out. "Okay, City, you've got yourself a temporary Sapphire Falls boyfriend."

Her eyes widened. "Really?"

"Really."

"Great." She seemed relieved. "And no trying to

impress me or win me over," she warned. "I want real life, how it would really be to live here and be involved with someone from here long term. We need to skip ahead like two years into a relationship. Pretend that we've been together a long time. Way past the point of romance, okay?"

He cocked an eyebrow. She thought guys in Sapphire Falls won a girl over and then reverted to their old caveman ways? Well, who was he to argue?

"Whatever you say, baby doll."

No romance? No trying to impress her? Just show her his everyday life? Yeah, he could do that.

ৡৄৎ

"So the plan to hate Sapphire Falls isn't working?" Phoebe asked. "That's too bad."

She didn't sound sorry at all.

Lauren frowned as she slid mints off the refrigerated tray with a spatula in the kitchen of Adrianne's shop.

"I don't want to *hate* Sapphire Falls." Why did people keep saying that? "I just need to not want to live here for the rest of my life."

"You know what? This is getting old," Phoebe said, pouring melted chocolate into molds. "I'm about to start telling you just to shut up every time you talk about this. And I might not do it nicely."

"Adrianne," Lauren said, turning to the woman who was *taking it easy* by running the huge mixer while sitting down. "Help me out here. You know what I mean."

Adrianne shut the mixer off and shrugged. "I love it here, Lauren. So does Mason, so does Joe, so does Nadia. Lots of people who have lived the city life have decided they like Sapphire Falls better. You're kind of the minority here."

"I'm the minority? The population of Sapphire Falls is

less than two thousand," Lauren said. "The population in Chicago is over two million. There's a reason for that."

Phoebe set the bowl she was holding down hard. "Shut up. Definitely. Seriously."

"I'm just saying—"

"I *know*," Phoebe said. "I know what you're saying. You don't want to live here. You don't want to fall for someone here. We've got nothing you want or need. Yeah, we've *got it.*"

Lauren started to respond but immediately realized that she had nothing to say.

"But just so you know, the people in Haiti aren't the only people in the world who need things."

Lauren opened her mouth again.

"And around here, we take care of each other," Phoebe went on.

Lauren closed her mouth.

"I mean, just because it's in your backyard, kind of, doesn't mean it doesn't matter. And our tragedies aren't as big as what's going on in Haiti, but we have droughts and tornados and floods. Things happen here too, and guess who comes to *our* rescue? Guys like Travis. Travis himself in fact," Phoebe said. "He spent a week in Lawson when a tornado hit them. He helped sandbag the river bank at Tompkin Grove last summer. He walked the woods and fields for ten hours straight when the little Martin girl went missing. And so did all of the other guys here. These are good men, good people. You don't have to live here, but I'm glad I do, and you can keep your opinions about it to yourself."

Lauren stared at Phoebe. The redhead was always upfront and sassy but...wow.

"I could really use your passion in DC, you know that, Red?"

Phoebe's eyes narrowed. "I don't *want* to go to DC. DC can suck it."

"And *that's* the attitude that makes it imperative that I accompany *Mason* on all of his trips to DC," she said with a sigh.

"You're missing my point."

She wasn't. She was trying to process Phoebe's point.

"I think that you're trying to prove to *Mason* that Sapphire Falls is nothing special," Phoebe said, pointing a chocolate-coated wooden spoon at Lauren. "I think that you're ticked that all these people are finding *happiness* and you're not. So instead of entertaining the idea of getting happy yourself, you're trying to undermine *their* happiness."

Lauren felt like Phoebe had slapped her. And she felt defensive…and very uncomfortable. She was *not* so easy to read, dammit.

"First of all," Lauren said, using the voice she used when White House staffers wouldn't let her talk to whoever she wanted to talk to, "Mason Riley is my best friend. I want nothing more than for him to be happy and fulfilled."

She lifted a finger in front of Phoebe's nose when she started to respond.

"Second of all, I *am* happy. I'm doing what I always dreamed of doing."

Phoebe again opened her mouth, but Lauren gave her the look she gave to the members of Congress who wouldn't do what she wanted them to do.

"And third, Joe *offered* to go to DC for that meeting tomorrow; I didn't ask him. But it *is* his job. I'm sorry if you're going to be lonely for a few days, but this is how it's going to go sometimes."

Phoebe opened her mouth and got a little squeak out, but Lauren wasn't done.

"And fourth…" She sighed. She liked Phoebe. The other woman was sincerely one of the nicest people she knew, and it was really hard to be mad at her. It was equally hard to lie to her. "You're right. A little."

Phoebe pressed her lips together, clearly wanting to say something but now hesitant.

"Now you," Lauren said, gesturing for Phoebe to speak.

Phoebe took a deep breath. "*You're* right that I'm crabby about Joe leaving. We were supposed to meet with a bunch of people about the wedding. But you're also right that it's his job and that he offered to go. So I'm sorry about that."

Lauren nodded.

"But *I'm* right?" Phoebe asked, her tone much less formal now. "You don't want to find happiness?"

That wasn't it. Exactly. She wanted it. In fact, she'd thought she had it. But then things had started to change. Things that she'd always counted on.

"I just…" She took a deep breath and looked from Phoebe to Adrianne. "Okay, here's the thing," she said. It wasn't that she didn't know this about herself, she'd just never pondered it for long. Or admitted it to anyone else. "I grew up in a town where fitting in was valued. Everyone was like everyone else. Farms and businesses were handed down from one generation to the next, no one ever moved farther away than the house on the other side of the section from their parents. People met in fourth grade and got married the summer after they graduated. Some people went away to college—like those who wanted to be teachers or doctors—but they always came home. Others might drive into the nearest bigger town to get their real estate license or train in welding or something. But they also came back home."

Lauren took a breath. "Being new or different was a negative thing. I moved in for my junior year of high school. Not only was I new, but I dressed differently, I had social experiences that went beyond bowling at the local alley and movies at the drive-in. I had been in a school where there was a diverse student population. We had exchange students and an active student government. I moved to a town where the same guy had been class president since seventh grade because he was cute and where no one had even traveled outside of the state."

It had taken her only about a week in Longview to realize that she was going to have to learn to blend or she was in for the longest two years of her life.

She'd been an independent thinker, used to the freedom to express herself however she needed to in a school where there was room for diversity, but she'd also been sixteen, and no matter how strong and sure you were at sixteen, peer pressure was often stronger. It took about twenty-four hours in her new hometown to understand that conformity was the path of least resistance.

And then she'd met Shawn. He'd made her feel accepted, loved.

"I got stuck. I got sucked into it all because I wanted to belong. I was the smartest one in my class, but people didn't value that. Or discussions in American History about the political conflicts in other countries. Or even wearing something different or out of the box. So I started to blend. In a town where everyone knew their path in life—own the hardware store, farm with dad, open a daycare, do hair— from the time they were ten, being smart and applying for scholarships and college wasn't important."

Lauren shrugged. "Eventually, fortunately, my fiancé cheated on me, so I left him at the altar and headed to Europe."

Phoebe and Adrianne were watching her with rapt fascination. Their eyes widened at the same time.

"The *day* I stepped off the plane, almost the *minute*, I felt the difference. I felt free. I knew I was never going back. A few months later, I started college. And I met Mason."

She smiled at the soft look on Adrianne's face when she heard her husband's name. In Lauren's opinion, Adrianne's best feature—and she had a few—was her love for

Lauren's best friend.

"I sat down next to him in organic chemistry. We started talking and I saw his eyes light up when I knew the Markovnikov Rule. He was the one who first made me feel like I was special and could do something important with what I was good at. Mason didn't care what I wore or how I did my hair."

Adrianne and Phoebe both snorted at that. To say that Mason didn't care about clothes and hairstyles was an understatement. Lauren had given him a makeover three days after sitting down next to him in that class. He dressed like a GQ model now. He was sexy and sophisticated and completely put together.

But he still didn't *care.*

Lauren grinned. "Mason thought my brains and ambition were awesome. And I found people who *celebrated* my intelligence; they respected it, they admired it. And I could be different. I could be myself, whatever I wanted."

"Is that when the bisexual thing came up?" Phoebe asked.

Just to mess with her, Lauren leaned in and said, "You know, you are *really* interested in this whole thing for someone who's only into guys."

Phoebe, predictably, blushed. "It's a legit question."

"Okay, yes, part of my freedom was being able to express *whatever* I felt or wanted. But that was only part of it."

"But this isn't high school anymore," Adrianne pointed out. "I think the *adults* in Sapphire Falls are more accepting."

Lauren nodded. "The acceptance isn't the issue now. Now I know what I want to do with my life, and I can't do it in Sapphire Falls."

"Joe and Mason are making it work," Adrianne pointed out. "They're making IAS work while living here."

Lauren felt the stab of irritation that had been becoming more and more familiar over the past year. "Joe and Mason are working for IAS and living here, yes."

Adrianne frowned. "There's a but there. Or something."

"Joe and Mason, Mason in particular, are not making IAS work. Not like they used to," Lauren said.

She hadn't brought this up with anyone so far. She'd hinted at it with Mason, but Mason didn't do very well with hints and subtleties. They'd almost gotten into it when she was trying to convince him to go to Haiti, but he'd given in before she'd had to get really blunt.

"What's that mean?" Phoebe asked, sounding a bit defensive. Which was understandable.

"It means that since Mason and Joe have fallen in love, something—or someone—else is taking precedence over their work," Lauren said.

Phoebe drew herself up taller—putting her at five-four. "You're upset that they've got people in their lives that mean more to them than a job?"

"I didn't say that," Lauren said calmly. "I'm stating it as a fact. I'm not judging it. But now that you mention it, for Mason in particular, IAS isn't—or at least it *wasn't*—a job."

"For Joe it is?" Phoebe asked.

Lauren shrugged. "Joe is amazing at what he does and I'm thrilled he's on our side. He's done a lot for IAS and he's very dedicated. But IAS is Mason's and my *dream*. It's what defined us both for a long time. Before he met Adrianne."

"Adrianne is great for Mason," Phoebe said.

"She is," Lauren agreed. "But that doesn't change the fact that Mason approaches our company and his work differently now. Which means if IAS is going to keep doing what it's always done and grow, someone has to step up. Me. I have to step up. I have to take up the slack, travel more, and occasionally push Mason to get on airplanes and do what only he can do."

"And he's not there to celebrate with you and brainstorm with you and go to Haiti *with you* now," Adrianne said. She gave Lauren a little smile. "I know he doesn't give you as much time and attention."

Lauren shook her head. "I know it sounds pathetic. But Mason is the only person in the world to really get me. I didn't realize how lonely I would be."

Adrianne looked sad for a moment. Then she smiled. "Well, you're the only person to *really* get Mason too. I don't always understand him or even fully appreciate what he does. But I love him anyway. And he loves me. I've shown him that there's more to life than that lab and that company."

Lauren couldn't disagree. "But I don't know how to do anything else, and I don't know who I am without the company," she said. "Mason has a role—your husband, and now he'll be a father. I don't have anything else."

"You need to get something else," Phoebe said.

"Maybe."

But the travel and the learning and the new experiences were so fun. She so missed the all-nighters with Mason when all they did was sit and talk, one subject flowing into the next, topics evolving as they practically completed each other's sentences, the feeling of sharing a passion like that with another person. It was an awesome experience that they'd both always respected and protected, knowing that it was rare to find someone to connect with like that.

Mason had loved the travel and discovery as much as she had. He was adventurous when it came to trying new foods, learning new customs and finding ways to solve problems.

They were a hell of a team.

She couldn't help but mourn the loss of even a piece of that.

And, though she knew that she needed to adjust to it,

she knew that she would never find someone to replace Mason in her life.

"Seriously, Lauren, you need to give Sapphire Falls a chance," Phoebe said.

Lauren shrugged. "It's great. It just doesn't have what I want."

"Chicago does?"

"Chicago and DC and Port-au-Prince and Rome and—"

"Yeah, I get it," Phoebe muttered.

"There's a lot of world out there," Lauren said.

"Yeah, well, nobody in DC knows my grandmother, nobody in DC cares that she has a kidney stone and nobody in DC will be making her a tuna-noodle casserole or a peach cobbler when she gets home from the hospital."

Lauren turned wide eyes on Adrianne.

Adrianne slid off of the stool she'd been sitting on and pulled Phoebe into a hug. "She's going to be okay."

Phoebe returned her hug. "I know." Then she looked at Lauren. "I just mean…we need things here too. We need other people and, dammit, we *can* be interesting."

"I know. I just—"

"And maybe I'm a little jealous," Phoebe went on. "Maybe I think you're pretty great and I wish that you spent more time here getting to know and take care of the people I care about here."

Lauren didn't know how to respond to that exactly. She cleared her throat. "Geez, Red," she finally said. "I knew I was getting to you."

Phoebe just raised an eyebrow.

Lauren looked from Phoebe to Adrianne. These women were very different from Lauren's friends in Chicago. And in no way was that a bad thing. They were funny, intelligent, sincere women with big hearts.

"The thing is," she said, trying to keep her voice light. "I'm not good for much here."

They both looked at her in surprise. "What do you

mean?" Adrianne asked.

Lauren couldn't believe she was about to admit this. "DC and Haiti are the perfect fits for me. I have what it takes to talk to politicians and policy makers. And I know all about soil and water conservation and alternative energies." She shrugged. "Sapphire Falls doesn't need anything I've got." And that stung a little, she would admit. She was a very valuable person. In some circles. In big circles. Important circles.

So why did she care that Sapphire Falls really didn't care who she was or what she could do?

Phoebe frowned. "We're a town full of farmers." She glanced at Adrianne, then back to Lauren. "And doesn't *everyone* need alternative energies?"

"I'm a scientist," Lauren said. "But my real skills are in negotiations and…selling." She turned to Adrianne. Adrianne had worked for her family's candy company— one of the top five in the country—in sales and marketing. "You know what I mean. I'm not selling a product—I'm selling ideas—but it's a big deal. I'm trying to convince very powerful people to take big risks on IAS and what we do. Sending our team to Haiti, the money, the political relationships, the PR surrounding it—it's all a lot to coordinate and get everyone on board and keep everyone happy."

Adrianne nodded. "I've seen you in action. It's impressive."

Adrianne had accompanied Lauren to meetings that involved smoothing feathers that Mason had ruffled. Lauren might be able to sell IAS and their ideas and their vision and mission, but no one could sell Mason like Adrianne could.

"Thank you." Lauren's job was stressful because it was important. It involved a lot of balls flying through the air at the same time. But it was rewarding because of that as well.

She didn't really think about all of that very often, but it was true that her talents were a much better match for a big stage like the White House and meetings of the Department of Agriculture and Outreach America. And, yes, Haiti. They needed a champion, someone people would listen to, someone who was impressive on paper and in person, someone who could think fast on her feet.

IAS succeeded because of Mason's ideas and passion *and* because of Lauren's ability to make the right people listen at the right time.

They couldn't do it without either piece. But Mason's piece could be done anywhere there was dirt and sunlight and water.

Lauren needed to be in boardrooms and offices and on airplanes.

"Why can't you share time between the traveling and Sapphire Falls?" Adrianne asked. "Joe and Mason are both making that work."

Lauren sighed. "I can't because Mason and Joe are less able to travel now."

Both women frowned at her. She was talking about their men, and *they* were the reason those men were more tied down.

"Joe believes in IAS and everything you're doing. He'll do whatever he needs to do," Phoebe said. "I resent the implication that I'm somehow holding him back."

Lauren frowned. Joe handled government relations and PR with Lauren. His job was to be where Lauren couldn't be, to handle the media requests, to do the buddy thing— golf, beer and so on—with the aides and contacts within the offices of the important people that Lauren needed to meet with.

And, yes, since he'd met Phoebe and relocated to Sapphire Falls, he'd been less available. But Mason and Lauren had agreed that it was worth keeping him on their team for when he could be in DC. No one could work a room of grumpy politicians like Joe Spencer. Plus, they really liked him.

"Whoa, Red, what the hell is going on? You know I don't feel that way."

Phoebe went from spitting mad to tears like someone had flipped a light switch. "I'm sorry," she said with a sniff. "I'm so touchy. It's making me nuts."

Adrianne handed Phoebe a tissue.

"*What* is going on?" Lauren asked, watching Phoebe dab at her eyes.

"It's the hormones."

"Hormones?" Lauren glanced at Adrianne. *She* was the only one with baby hormones coursing through her body. Wasn't she?

"Yep, I'm pregnant too," Phoebe confirmed. "Not even eight weeks. But I'm a mess."

Lauren shook her head. "Well, see, if nothing else, I need to avoid this town because of this latest contagious condition."

"It's not their fault."

They all turned toward the swinging door that led from the kitchen to the front of the shop.

Travis stood in the doorway, grinning, with one shoulder propped on the doorjamb.

Lauren hated that she loved his grin.

"Hey, Trav," Phoebe greeted.

He gave Phoebe a wink. "Seriously, City," he said, pushing away from the door. "You gotta look out for the fresh country air. Makes people horny."

Phoebe rolled her eyes, but Lauren noticed she couldn't seem to help her smile either. Travis had that effect on everyone apparently.

"Thanks for the warning," Lauren said dryly.

"What am I thinkin'?" he asked, coming into the kitchen and looking over their morning candy creations and taking over a lot of Lauren's personal space. "You know exactly what I'm talkin' about. You got a big lungful of country air last night, didn't ya'?"

He chose one of the mints she'd mixed and poured into molds and recently turned out onto trays. He popped it into his mouth, meeting her eyes, his mouth curling in that sexy and infuriating way that it so often did.

Phoebe crossed her arms. "Last night? Do tell."

"At the party," Travis said. "Dr. D was all over me."

Lauren scoffed. "*That's* what you think of as *all over*? Poor guy."

"Don't tell me she didn't tell you all about it," Travis said to Phoebe as if Lauren hadn't spoken. He tossed another mint into his mouth, the picture of pure country cocky.

"She told me she had fun at the party and that nothing she's tried so far to turn her off of Sapphire Falls was working," Phoebe said. She eyed Lauren thoughtfully. She looked hopeful.

"Did she now?" Travis also eyed her thoughtfully. He looked concerned.

Lauren fidgeted. And that was the final straw. No one made her fidget.

"Why are you here?" she demanded of Travis. "I'm sure the health department has rules about guys like you being allowed in kitchens."

"Gee, Doc, I don't know what you mean." He scratched his butt, wiped a wrist across his nose with a loud sniff, licked his fingers and reached for another mint.

"Oh my God!" She pulled the tray out of his reach.

He smirked at her. "You're so easy."

She didn't respond. Because that would have been easy. And exactly what he was going for.

"Why *are* you here?" Phoebe asked.

"I came to get my girlfriend."

"Your what?" Phoebe asked.

Lauren could feel Phoebe's gaze on her but she pretended to be very busy arranging the tray to cover the spaces where mints were missing thanks to Travis.

"My girlfriend. She didn't tell you?" Travis sounded amused.

Lauren gritted her teeth.

"You and Lauren are dating?" Adrianne asked.

"Yep," Travis said.

"No," Lauren said. "We're…working on a mutually beneficial arrangement."

Travis chuckled. "And I thought operant conditioning sounded sexy. You're just full of come-ons, baby doll."

Phoebe and Adrianne both said, "*What*?" at the same time.

"Operant conditioning is a behavior modification plan to—" Lauren started.

"Not *that*," Phoebe said. "The dating part."

"Oh, that." Lauren waved it away. "I told you that I needed to spend more time with him," she said. "Hanging out with Travis is a constant reminder of my reality if I stay in Sapphire Falls and all the things I *don't* want."

Except it wasn't working out that way at all.

"But you said that nothing is working to turn you off," Phoebe said.

Lauren risked a glance at Travis. Of course, he was smirking again. "We've got to put more time in on the conditioning."

"And that's why I'm here," Travis said.

"It is?" Lauren asked. Her stomach flipped and her nipples tingled. Conditioning herself to *not* like Travis's kisses and touch was definitely going to take some time and repeated punishment. And she was in.

"We need to get to work. You're only here for a month. Helping you get over this town is going to be tough. We need to work on it every minute we can." He held out his hand to her. "Let's go make you hate Sapphire Falls."

"I don't want to *hate* it," she protested. But then she sighed. And took his hand.

She stoically kept her gaze from meeting Phoebe's or Adrianne's. She knew they were looking at her with a combination of curiosity, shock and amusement. She didn't want to see any of that.

Travis led her out the door, across the street and up a block to Main Street, and then started across the grass toward the midway.

"What are we doing?" She scrambled to keep up with him in her heels.

"You'll see."

He gave her a big grin and her stomach flipped as she remembered those lips on hers. She hoped wherever they were headed was going to involve some nakedness.

Holy cow. She'd known there was chemistry between them. She'd figured he was pretty good at kissing and such, but damn. This idea to glom on to him for the next twenty-eight days seemed less and less brilliant all the time.

She realized they were headed for the Ferris wheel. And she grinned in spite of the fact that she was not thirteen, had already been kissed and had no intention of wearing Travis's class ring. Then she wondered briefly if kids still did that—the class-ring thing. If they didn't, it was too bad. She'd liked that tradition. She should have stuck with that tradition and never let Shawn exchange his class ring for a diamond. She frowned and then pushed Shawn out of her mind. She was going on the Ferris wheel with Travis.

Maybe it was silly, but she preferred that to some of the emotions Shawn had elicited.

But they walked right past the line for the Ferris wheel.

"We're not going for a ride?"

Travis looked from her to the big wheel and back. "No way, City. When a guy takes a girl on the Ferris wheel at festival time, it means he's really serious about her."

"That would be a great way to show everyone that we're dating, right?"

He chuckled and shook his head. "My mom heard about

our kiss at the kissing booth within ten minutes of it happening. I got the expected voice message about what was I doing and that I needed to call her immediately. Which I didn't. So I got two more messages."

He didn't seem bothered by any of it.

"Your mom is concerned about you hanging out with me?"

"Yep. She's sure I'm going to get my heart broken." He looked over at her. "See, even she knows you don't belong here."

"Maybe I should hang out with *her*." Lauren wondered why she was bothered by a woman she didn't even know thinking she wasn't Sapphire Falls material. Because she wasn't.

But what did Mrs. Bennett know about it? She should mind her own business.

And there was one more reason to not like the small town—people thought *all* the business was their business.

Of course, her son probably did qualify as her business.

"So there's no way I'm taking you on the Ferris wheel," Travis said.

"People will see us when we're out together anyway," she pointed out. "Won't they?"

What did dating in Sapphire Falls really consist of? Staying in and watching TV with takeout chicken or something? Yikes.

"People will see us," he agreed. "But we're past the romance part remember? After two years, I don't have to buy you flowers or be publicly affectionate. My mom won't know about the stuff we do." He gave her a wicked grin.

And her nipples responded again.

She cleared her throat. "Mason is still publicly affectionate with Adrianne," she pointed out. So much so it was a little annoying at times.

"Mason's mostly a city boy," Travis said. "He might be

from here, but he doesn't really know our ways."

"Your ways?" Okay, Sapphire Falls was different from Chicago, but it wasn't like it was a completely alien culture.

"Yeah, you know, you hook up with a cute girl in junior high, you kiss her behind the bleachers at a football game and you're more or less engaged from there. You're sweet and romantic to her when you're trying to get her pink polka-dot panties off. But once you're hitched, you can go out with the guys, hunt all weekend, crash in front of the couch after work and then rock her world every night."

"After she makes you dinner and does your laundry, right?" Lauren said wryly.

"If you understand that, maybe you can fit in around here after all."

"Be still my heart. And you don't think that's how Mason does things?"

It wasn't. Not at all. Mason didn't hunt, for one thing. And he loved being with Adrianne. Hell, Lauren had a hard time pulling him away for work stuff—which he also loved.

Travis shook his head. "I've seen Mason do things. He's still sweet and romantic and loving."

"The jerk."

"He makes the rest of us look bad."

"Maybe you could take some lessons from him. Maybe you wouldn't still be single at age thirty."

"I'm twenty-nine," Travis said.

Huh. A younger guy. Only by a year, but she'd never dated younger.

Not that they were really dating.

"Don't most people around here have three kids, a mortgage and an affair by age twenty-nine?" she asked. Her words and tone sounded harsher than she'd expected. This wasn't Longview. But there were similarities—she had to remember that.

It didn't matter that Sapphire Falls's Main Street businesses all had blue and white striped awnings and the business name hand painted on the big front window. It didn't matter that the place smelled good, even when there wasn't cotton candy and kettle corn in the air. It didn't matter that everyone smiled and said good morning or hi to everyone, friend or stranger, on the clean, white sidewalks that had big wooden planters full of blue flowers every fifty feet.

It was a small town. She didn't want a small town.

"You know, City, I'm almost interested in what made you so bitter about small towns," Travis said. "Almost. But I will say there's something to that conditioning stuff. 'Cause as cute as you're lookin' and as much as I'm lookin' forward to more kissin', when you talk, I don't wanna push you up against the wall quite as much."

Until Travis, Lauren had not ever been quite so aware of her nipples. But the guy didn't even have to *actually* push her up against a wall and she was all hot and tingly again at the mere mention.

"Tell me more about how you *won't* be romancing me or being sweet," she told him.

He gave her a knowing look but stopped under one of the oak trees that lined the west side of the town square. He faced her and crossed his arms.

"Okay. If I'm in charge of cooking, it'll be takeout burgers or pizza. I will be watching every baseball game on TV that I can and watching the high school boys play when they're in town. I watch all the shows on FX and the History Channel. I have a beer with my buddies every Monday night. We'll be partying at the river as much as possible. I don't mind if you do any of those things with me, but if you don't know what's going on with my TV shows, you'll have to catch up on your own 'cause there's no talking while they're on. If you cheer for any team from New York or Boston, you will be asked to leave my house.

Also, I won't be watching any talent shows of any kind on TV. No singing, no dancing, nothing. I don't want to talk about national news. I don't want to eat anything I can't pronounce and I do want to have sex at least five times a week. And I'll let you pick the position at least one out of five. Two if you can bake a decent snickerdoodle cookie."

Lauren felt her heart pounding. That was stupid. He'd just given her a laundry list of things that were pretty much completely unappealing—a chauvinistic laundry list at that. But he'd ended with the sex thing. Damn him. They hadn't specifically talked about having sex. It had been more than implied that they both *wanted* it. And, were she actually dating someone from here, they would surely be having sex on a regular basis. At least, she certainly hoped so.

So the chauvinistic, all-things-will-be-my-way stuff was good. Because sex with Travis wasn't going to make her anxious to leave. That was for sure.

But she could absolutely walk away from Sapphire Falls without a single regret if the men were Neanderthals.

As long as she didn't kill any of them first.

CHAPTER FIVE

"You seem to have given this a lot of thought," she commented.

"Nah. That's just how it is."

"And you being single and twenty-nine is also how it is. I wonder if that's a coincidence?"

He leaned in. "You make it sound like I don't want to be single and twenty-nine. The girls around here know how things go."

Lauren knew he was full of it. Or at least exaggerating it. The guys around here weren't *all* chauvinistic jerks. If nothing else, the girls like Phoebe would have put them in their place a long time ago. "Maybe that's how it goes with *you*," she said. "But there are some really nice guys here too."

"There are some guys here who are good at playing nice. Like I said, you have to keep that sweet stuff up at least until her panties hit the floor mat of your car."

She quite easily imagined her panties on the floor of Travis's truck. Though if he was used to pink polka dots, she might have a few surprises for him. She didn't own a single thong that was pink.

"What, there are no divorce attorneys in Sapphire Falls?" Lauren asked.

"The divorce rate in Sapphire Falls is like point two percent."

He was definitely making that up. "The girls around here just basically give up on anything resembling a decent, interesting life?"

"We instill a deep sense of family and the importance of being a good mother and then knock 'em up early."

Oh, man. She grimaced in spite of her near certainty that he was laying it on thick to annoy her. But he'd just described her own sister to her. Lea had fallen for Corey fast and deep. She'd been in love within three months of knowing him. They'd gotten married the day after she turned eighteen. She'd been sixteen weeks pregnant when she'd said I do.

"That is not the best way to get me into bed with you, Farmer Boy."

"Well, I've got Booze to use too."

Romantic it was not. Exactly as she'd asked.

"Oh, and we'll be hanging out with my friends a lot. They can help me help you hate Sapphire Falls."

He gave her a big grin, but Lauren felt a shiver of unease slide down her spine. She didn't need to *hate* Sapphire Falls, dammit. She just needed to not find it so damned perfect. She swore that it wouldn't surprise her if the birds and mice started doing housework around here. And singing while they did it.

"But first things first." He turned and started across the street.

Lauren had little choice but to follow. She could have, of course, gone back to Adrianne's shop and finished making mints, but *this* was actually what she wanted.

"I just need a taste of real life here," she said, hurrying to keep up with his long strides. "I don't need the dark alleys and abandoned roads or anything."

Travis chuckled. "I've got just the thing."

That didn't make her feel better. He seemed far too enthused about this whole idea suddenly.

"You know, maybe—"

"We'll start here."

She stopped beside him and looked up at the sign over the storefront. "Why *here*?"

"You need some Sapphire Falls clothes," he said. He pushed the door open and gestured for her to precede him.

"I don't need new clothes," she protested. She was dressed more causally today, for instance. She wore a white linen and silk blend skirt with an uneven hem that hit above the knee in front and at mid-calf in back. She'd paired it with a fitted, off-the-shoulder blue top. It was summery and light and cost half of what she'd worn yesterday.

Travis put a hand on her lower back and pushed. "You do. Trust me."

"Seriously, Travis. I'm fine. I'll just borrow something from Hailey if I need something special."

"I need to know you're committed here, City," Travis said, leading her deeper into the store, past the racks of plaid shirts and fleece jackets, past the wooden shelves that lined the walls and held stack after stack of denim, to the area in the back that displayed something even worse.

Boots.

Lots and lots of boots.

"Committed?" she asked. Maybe she needed to *be* committed. Like in an institution.

"I need to know that you're going to give this true consideration. You can't expect to be turned off of the town if you don't fully experience and absorb life here. If I'm going to really be into this, then you need to be too."

She blew out a breath. "So I need boots?"

"You can't go traipsing around where I'm takin' you in those heels."

"Where are you taking me?"

"Someplace where you can't wear heels."

"Right. Fine. Okay."

"And you're going to need jeans. Several pairs."

"Well, I guess that tells me something about the types of places you take the girls you date."

She picked up a pair of soft, light-brown leather boots. They were actually quite pretty. The swirling design on the sides was done in light colors that were feminine and understated.

"I guess it does," Travis agreed. He greeted the sales girl—he'd probably known her since kindergarten, Lauren thought with a mental eye roll—and she helped him pick out three shirts that she assured him would fit Lauren.

As if Lauren wasn't standing right freaking there.

But maybe the men in Sapphire Falls were all actually jerks who thought they needed to help their women out with their clothes. Maybe they ordered for them in restaurants and said things like, "That's women's work." That would all help her out a ton.

"So I'll be your old lady?" God, how many times had her stepdad referred to her mom that way? She'd always hated that.

"Somethin' like that. And you don't want to get any more animal poop on them fancy shoes anyway, do ya'?"

And if he kept talking like that and dropping letters all over the place, she was going to be good and over this place and the idea of dating a local boy in no time.

"We're going to be hanging out, socially, for fun, in places where I might get animal poop on my shoes?" she clarified.

"Well, you never know," he said, holding up the long-sleeved shirts he'd picked out. "It's good to always be prepared 'round here."

Awesome. She'd be prepared all right. Little did good old boy know, but she not only knew how to shoot a shotgun, she even owned one. Any more animals came near her shoes and they were going to be dinner.

She could give Travis a little taste of country girl that might just shock him right out of his blue jeans.

And *that* wouldn't be all bad. Not at all.

"I'm not wearing plaid," she informed him.

"You're going to want some long sleeves."

It was June. It was hot and humid. She did *not* want long sleeves. If he thought he was taking her out in the cornfield or out in the woods at night where she might get scratched up from corn stalks or branches, he was crazy.

"I'm not wearing plaid," she told him again.

He sighed and hung the shirt back up. "At least get this

one."

It was a Welcome to Sapphire Falls T-shirt. It was, of course, blue.

Clever.

"Fine. Whatever." She turned back to the boots. In the midst of all of the cowboy boots, she spotted something else. Something more familiar.

She reached for one of the boxes. "Are these—"

"No. They just look like Uggs," the salesgirl told her. "They're a knock-off. They're called Duggs. Much cheaper."

Duggs. Right.

Lauren pulled them from the shelf and held them up to Travis. "What do you think of these?"

They were pink. Which was a crazy, almost tacky color, but something about them kept catching her eye. If she was going to wear boots, she might as well wear *boots*. She was never going to wear them outside the borders of Sapphire Falls anyway.

"Uh, no," Travis said.

"Why not?"

"Those aren't cowboy boots or work boots."

"I'm *not* wearing work boots."

"Your feet will melt in those in this heat."

"I'm sure leather isn't exactly *cool*," she told him.

"They're *pink*."

"I like the pink. What's the problem?" If Travis didn't like them, that meant she was getting them for sure.

"Those are not…boots," he said.

"They are most definitely boots," she said, propping a hand on her hip. "They're not flip flops. Or pumps. Or flats."

"But they're not…practical."

Yeah, well, he should see some of the heels she owned. Practical was rarely a consideration in footwear.

"These will hick-ify me just fine."

"Hick-ify? Really?"

"Oh, don't get all offended."

"Gee, why would I get offended by that?"

She fought the urge to smile at his dry tone. She liked sarcasm in a guy.

"Do you prefer these?" she asked, holding up a pair of pink cowboy boots.

"*No.*" He looked completely offended. "They shouldn't even make cowboy boots that color."

"So it's the Duggs then."

"People will laugh. Duggs aren't farm wear, City."

"I don't care if people laugh, Farmer Boy. It's not like I'm *serious* about having farm wear, you know."

He sighed. "At least get the brown."

"Why?"

"Boots are supposed to be brown. Or black. Not pink. People who wear pink boots aren't taking it seriously."

"There's serious boot wearing and non-serious boot wearing?" Lauren asked, amused in spite of herself.

"Pink boots aren't for being outside or getting dirty. They're what city girls wear out to the bar or to a Luke Bryan concert."

"True city girls don't wear boots at all." She pulled the brown ones off the shelf and tucked them under her arm. "But you don't have to worry about me going to a Luke Bryan concert, even with pink boots."

"Not a fan?"

"He's way overrated."

Travis tipped his head, studying her. "You know Luke Bryan?"

Oops. She had to be more careful. "I've heard his stuff."

"Uh huh." He eyed the boots under her arm. "You're getting those boots no matter what I say right?"

"Right."

He sighed, sounding very put upon, which made Lauren

smile. Yes, she'd asked him to spend time with her as a favor and she was happy he'd accepted. But irritating him was simply too fun to give it up entirely just because she owed him.

"Fine. Then grab some jeans and let's go."

She frowned.

It did seem that everyone in Sapphire Falls had a true affinity for denim. If she was going to live life here, even short term, she supposed she had to do as the Romans did.

Bailey led her to the shelves and pulled a couple of pairs from the cubby that was labeled with Lauren's exact size. That was impressive.

Bailey turned to her. "Do you want skinny fit or boot cut or—"

"Skinny," Travis interjected.

Lauren looked over at him. "Oh, really?"

"Hey, if I'm doin' this, we're at least gonna make the other guys jealous. We need to show off your ass."

She couldn't believe he'd just said that. She turned to face him fully. "Did you really just make it sound like I'm a new toy you're going to brag about to your friends?"

He gave her a grin she was sure had gotten many pairs of panties on his floor mats over the years. "You know it."

"And I suppose I should be flattered?"

"I just told you that you have a brag-worthy ass. Sure you should be flattered."

"And these are the types of compliments I can expect as we go forward?"

"Unless you don't want any compliments at all."

She didn't actually *need* compliments from Travis. He was her pretend boyfriend. Her *temporary* pretend boyfriend. And she was confident in how she looked and carried herself.

But dammit, having Travis commenting on it still made her tingly. Even when he did it like a hick.

"Fine. Skinny jeans," she told Bailey. "Do you have

any in pink?"

Travis groaned.

With a huge smile, she went into the fitting rooms and came out with three new pairs of jeans.

Bailey rang up the jeans, T-shirt and boots and Lauren handed over her credit card. She shook her head. This was probably going to trigger the fraud alert. Her credit card company wouldn't believe she was buying boots and jeans in a place called Sapphire Falls in Nebraska.

"You were supposed to put the jeans *on*," Travis said, his gaze traveling over the expanse of bare leg shown by her skirt.

"Now?"

"Why not now?"

"Because...I..." She wasn't sure why not now. "Are we going somewhere now?"

With her bag of "country clothes," Lauren stepped out onto the sidewalk with Travis.

"Well, yeah. That skirt isn't real practical for moving."

"Moving?"

"To my place."

Lauren stumbled over a crack in the sidewalk. "Excuse me?"

"What?"

"You're talking about me moving in to your place? With you?"

"Well, darlin', I ain't goin' anywhere."

"Why in the world would I *move in* with you? This is all a pretend relationship anyway."

He stopped and faced her, his hands in the front pockets of his jeans. "But you want a real taste of what your life would be like if you settled down here. We need to shack up for that."

"As charming as I'm sure that would be," she said sweetly. "No."

"You said we were two years in. I wouldn't be in that

long if I wasn't gettin' it at home every night."

Lauren bit her tongue, literally, for a moment. He was such a caveman. Finally, she said, "You can't talk the girls into sex every night around here?" She sincerely doubted that.

He gave her a grin. "I was talkin' about dinner."

Of course he was. "Oh, good. More chauvinism. That will definitely help." It would. She wasn't anyone's cook or maid.

"So let's pack your stuff up."

"I don't need *that* much realism. Thank you very much."

"Okay then," he said with a shrug. "If we're not shacking up, we're datin'."

"Meaning?"

"Sweetness and romance."

Oh, no. Hell no. "My panties aren't going near your floor mats."

"That's what you think." He took the bag from her hand and headed back for the shop. He opened the door. "Hey, Bailey, can you hold on to this for us? We're gonna see some of the festival."

Bailey agreed to take care of Lauren's purchases and Travis turned back to Lauren. "You ready?"

She wasn't. She didn't know what he had planned, but the mischievous gleam in his eye made her sure she wasn't ready. "Where are we going?"

"On our first date."

He took her hand and started for the midway.

Lauren let him hold her hand. For now. But she had a bad feeling about this.

There was no way she could *live* with him. They were going to sleep together. That seemed obvious. But a hot encounter here and there, probably against the side of a barn, was something she could handle. Look forward to even. But *living* with him? That might be a little too real.

And not in a good way.

She loved her life as it was currently. A lot. But she was also honest enough to admit that there were times when she loved to sit on the couch with a pizza and binge watch Netflix. She also wouldn't mind having someone to do it with her. But she hadn't shared a living space on a long-term basis with anyone since she'd moved into Shawn's trailer with him two months before their wedding.

Sharing pots and pans and washing their underwear together had given her a huge false sense of security.

And she'd seen Travis's house from the field when she'd been out with Mason or doing various PR meetings. It was a cute country home. It had a porch. And a garden. And a big old maple in the front yard.

It was way more charming than that trailer could have ever been.

Living there wasn't going to do a thing to cool the desire to stay in Sapphire Falls.

They stopped in front of one of the typical carnival booths, where the object was to pop balloons with a dart to win a prize.

Travis was really good at it. Five minutes later, he handed her a stuffed bear.

"You've got to be kidding me."

He chuckled. "This is what we do with our girls at festival time. At least, when we're first trying to win them over."

She stared at the bear. No one had ever won her a prize at a festival before. "I'm probably a little old for a teddy bear," she said.

"That's part of the fun of the festival," he said, taking her hand again. "You get to act and feel like a kid again for a few days. Nothin' wrong with that."

Okay, she could go along with that.

He won her a rainbow-striped bowler hat by shooting targets with a fake shotgun and she surprised him by actually wearing it. He won her a gaudy necklace—that would surely turn her neck green—by tossing rings on to the tops of old-fashioned milk bottles and she wore that too.

Then he pulled her into a photo booth.

"We need a photo strip to commemorate our date," he explained, spreading his knees wide enough that there was no room for her unless she climbed onto his lap.

Which she did.

So far, their date had been fine...but forgettable. Nothing too exciting, nothing that would make her want to do it over and over again. It was just an afternoon at a small-town festival.

Perfectly average.

Nothing that would make her choose it over the Louvre for instance. Or an opera at the Royal Opera House or a tour of the Mayan ruins or even a day at the Smithsonian.

This was a very nice small-town festival. But it was nothing that would tempt her away from her life.

Until she sat on Travis Bennett's lap.

Her skirt was short in front and it pulled up on the back of her legs as she climbed in on top of Travis. Which meant there was plenty of bare skin to rub up against the warm denim that covered his hard thighs. The skirt also offered very little protection from the feel of his big hands on her hips, positioning her. His wide chest pressed into her shoulder blades, his thighs pressed against the backs of hers and his fly pressed against her butt.

His hard fly. His hard, hot, not-hiding-his-arousal-a-bit fly.

She worked on breathing.

"Now smile, darlin'," Travis said gruffly against her ear, pressing his cheek to hers.

She did as the machine flashed.

"Make a funny face," he coached.

She was sure her face looked funny without even

trying. But she pursed her lips and tipped her head as the machine flashed again.

Then Travis gathered her hair back in one hand and pressed his lips against her neck.

She gasped and pivoted on his lap, which was a move she wouldn't mind repeating a few more times, but he captured her lips with his before she could respond.

She was vaguely aware that the machine flashed for the fourth and final time, but with Travis's hand holding her hair, she couldn't move away from the hot onslaught of his mouth.

As if she would have anyway.

Travis stroked her tongue with his and she pressed more firmly against his erection. He groaned and ran a hand along the bare skin of her leg and then up underneath the hem of her skirt.

His work-roughened hand caused delicious friction on the skin on the outside of her thigh and made her squirm. He cupped her butt, realized she wore only a thong and groaned again.

Damn, that sound from him made her want to pile *all* of her panties on the floor of his truck. With him around, sounding like that and touching her as he was, she wasn't going to need any of them anyway.

She turned on his lap to press her aching nipples into his hard chest and wrap her arms around his neck.

With a muttered *fuck*, he grasped both of her hips and turned her fully, forcing her to straddle his lap. The movement separated their lips momentarily, but they immediately came back at each other, their mouths fusing, hungrily drawing on one another as he ran his hand back up to the bare cheek of her ass. He slipped his middle finger under the tiny string that crossed her hip and ran it around to the front, pulling the panty forward and tucking his thumb under the silk and right against her clit.

Lauren gasped, pulling her mouth from his so she could

breathe.

Travis looked up at her. Their gazes collided as he ran the pad of his thumb over her again.

She knew she was acting completely wanton. She could have said no. She could have pushed herself off his lap. But instead, she was spread out over him, his hand under her skirt and all she could do was widen her legs.

He ran his thumb lower along her cleft and, if there had been any question about her wanting him in his mind prior to that moment, the wet heat on his thumb would leave no doubt.

And if he stopped now, she was going to hurt him.

She slid her hands up underneath his T-shirt and swiveled her hips, circling her clit against his thumb. His chest was firm and hot. The hair rasped against her palms and made another wave of want course through her.

"If only I'd put more quarters in this machine. I wouldn't mind a picture or two of this," Travis told her.

She circled her hips again. "I'll text you a couple of pictures later if you're nice."

He gave her a lazy half smile. "A *nice* boy from this nice town would have never gotten into this particular situation with you." He turned his hand so that his thumb rubbed just right as he slipped his long middle finger into her heat.

She let her head fall forward as she struggled to keep from taking over and riding his finger. Damn. She liked sex. Loved it. Was very open about getting what she wanted and needed in the bedroom. But she never lost her mind.

She'd also never had someone finger her to orgasm in a photo booth. And she kind of wanted him to get on with it.

"Well, when a guy gets his fingers where yours are right now, it's *nice* to keep going until the girl has a *nice* hard orgasm. *That's* the kind of nice boy I want you to be right now."

Travis added a second finger, and Lauren felt her eyes
cross.

"I thought you didn't want to think *nice* things about
anything here," he said, pumping his fingers deeper.

"You're right," she said breathlessly. "This might be a
good time to use some of that conditioning. Say something
that will tick me off."

He stroked in deeper, his thumb somehow exactly
where she needed it. Lauren was unable to resist lifting and
lowering herself slightly, meeting his strokes and
increasing the heat.

"See why the girls around here *stay* around here?" he
asked.

That probably *should* have gotten her off his lap, but
Lauren felt her muscles clamp down as if ensuring no one
was leaving any time soon.

He chuckled...and stroked and circled again. "Looks to
me like you're a natural-born rider, baby doll," he said
huskily.

That too, probably should have worked. It was a little
more country anyway. But Lauren felt the beginning
ripples of an orgasm.

"Next time you're going up and down on me, I want
you in those boots. And nothing else."

That *definitely* didn't turn her off.

Travis must have felt her orgasm building, because he
pulled her forward as the lightning suddenly streaked
through her, covering her mouth when she would have
cried out.

He kissed her hard throughout the climax, stroking his
fingers slower and slower as the ripples faded. Then he
slipped his hand from under her skirt and pulled back.

"How do you feel?"

Her eyes widened. "How do I *feel*?" She pushed her
hair back and took a deep breath. "I feel like I like you a
whole lot more than I did when you spilled grape slushy on

me."

He nodded thoughtfully. "I've added a few things I like about you to my list too."

Lauren was stunned when he lifted his fingers to his mouth and sucked.

She knew she was staring. She was also aware that, in spite of the orgasm, she was ready to do it all again.

She'd seen and done a lot sexually. She was willing to bet good money that she was more experienced than Travis. Yet the sight of this country boy licking his fingers after making her come was enough to shock her and turn her on like she was *conditioned* to respond to him.

"So we need to keep working on this, clearly," he said, nudging her from his lap.

Lauren felt off balance in just about every way as she stood and straightened her clothes.

Travis, seeming fairly unaffected really, stepped from the booth and grabbed their photo strip from the side.

"Aw, how cute are we?" he asked, showing her the photos.

They did actually look good together. In the first photo her smile seemed forced, but the silly picture was admittedly cute. And the kissing photo—she had to suck in a quick breath as every nerve in her body responded to the picture—was hot.

Dammit.

"Well, hello, Travis."

Lauren stepped the rest of the way out of the booth as a trio of older women approached. Each was dressed in a different color—a different *bright* color—and humongous straw hats with flowers that matched. One wore carnation pink with silk carnations on her hat. One wore lemon yellow with a huge sunflower perched on the brim of her hat. And the third wore a green that, in spite of Lauren's efforts to distance herself from the country life, she knew would be called John Deere green. And this hat too had a big green flower that might have been a tulip. Or a petunia.

"Hi, ladies," Travis greeted with his signature huge grin.

Lauren ran a hand through her hair, smoothed the front of her skirt and pressed her lips together, wondering how disheveled she looked. It couldn't be too bad. They hadn't even undressed, and Travis had only touched part of her.

Of course, her intense blush at that thought was likely telltale.

"We're spreading Sapphire Sunshine." The woman in pink handed Travis a bright blue business card.

Travis looked at it, nodded and said, "I like it."

Lauren watched the exchange with some admitted curiosity.

"Oh, here you are, Dr. Davis." The one with the sunflower gave Lauren a card.

"Thank you." Lauren took the card and glanced at it.

Tell someone a joke.

She flipped the card over, but the back was blank.

She looked up at Travis, confused. He stepped close, wrapped his arms around her and hugged her tight.

That was weird. Not that it wasn't pleasant. There were certainly worse things to be pressed up against than the hard, hot body wrapped around hers, smelling like sunshine—for God's sake. But it was weird.

Maybe she would always feel like Alice did when she fell down the rabbit hole while she was in Sapphire Falls.

Travis had her arms trapped against her sides, making it impossible for her to hug him back, so she waited for him to let her go. Which seemed to take longer than a simple hug in the middle of the town's square with three grandmotherly figures looking on probably should.

When he finally stepped back, she blinked at him. "What's going on?"

"Sapphire Sunshine." He held up his card.

First of all, the typical color of sunshine was yellow.

Secondly...this was still weird.

"It's a new effort to spread happiness and a greater feeling of neighborliness to the town," the woman in green said.

Lauren turned her blinking gaze on the woman. "Sapphire Falls needs *more* happiness and a greater feeling of neighborliness?" The way it was, Lauren felt like she needed to brush her teeth more often when she was in town for fear of developing cavities from all the sweetness.

"You can never have too much happiness or too many neighbors," Pink told her.

Lauren wasn't entirely sure about the part about too many neighbors, but she wasn't going to argue with the Rainbow Girls. "Okay."

Travis chuckled. "You've heard of random acts of kindness?"

"Of course."

"This is similar. These lovely ladies—"

The trio giggled.

"—and a few gentlemen—make up the Blue Brigade."

"Get it?" Yellow asked. "Blue for Sapphire—"

"And because we're making people the opposite of blue," Green said.

"Because they say people are *blue* when they're sad," Pink added.

Right. It all made sense. At least, it did when she was standing in the town's square surrounded by the scent of kettle corn and the sound of Frank Sinatra singing about rainbows. Apparently, he'd visited Sapphire Falls. It wouldn't surprise Lauren a bit if people sat on rainbows here. With their unicorns.

"You hear the music, right?" she asked Travis. It also wouldn't surprise her to find it was all in her head. Maybe the whole thing was. Maybe Sapphire Falls was all one big hallucination.

Travis grinned. "I do hear the music. We have speakers

in the street lights."

"Wow."

"It adds to the ambiance, don't you think?" he asked.

Ambiance. That was one word for it.

"You need to spread your sunshine," Pink said, gesturing toward the card in Lauren's hand.

"What else does the Blue Brigade do?" Lauren asked, ignoring that.

"We deliver singing telegrams," Yellow said.

"For birthdays and stuff?" Lauren asked.

"No, just because."

"Who doesn't like to have people show up at their work for no reason and sing "You Are My Sunshine"?" Pink asked.

Lauren knew they weren't kidding. And in Sapphire Falls, they might be right. Maybe everyone loved being serenaded at work. She also realized that it was a sign that she'd been in Sapphire Falls too long. It didn't even occur to her that the goodness and goofiness wasn't real.

"We also send cards," Green said.

Lauren hesitated but still asked, "For birthdays and stuff?"

Pink smiled and Lauren said, "No, just because," along with the three ladies.

She couldn't help it. She grinned at the women. "What else?" She had to know.

"We hand out random cookies," Pink said.

"And books," Green said. "We have several we pass all around."

"What kind of books?" Lauren asked.

"Feel-good books. Funny ones. Romances," Green said.

"Lots of romances," Pink interjected.

"And flowers," Yellow said.

"Oh, and compliments," Pink added.

"And hugs," Yellow said.

"And cups of coffee," Green said.

"And kittens," Pink said. "But only if we know they'll take good care of one."

"And that they aren't allergic," Yellow said.

Lauren shook her head. She was falling in love with a town where they gave out random compliments, cookies and cats.

"And the Sapphire Sunshine," Pink said, pointing to Lauren's card again. "We give people assignments that help them make other people happy. Simple little things. But both people end up smiling."

Travis turned his card so she could read it.

Give someone a hug.

Well, at least it made the hug a little less weird.

"So let me see yours," Travis said.

"No way."

"Yeah, come on. What are you supposed to do?"

"No." She pressed the card against her chest so he couldn't look at it.

Travis stepped in close with a glint in his eyes. "Is it make out with someone?" he asked. "Because the rule is that you're supposed to do whatever it is to the closest person when you read the card."

Pink swatted Travis's arm. "That's not the rule."

"And none of the cards are about making out," Green said, sounding slightly scandalized.

He chuckled. "What's it say?"

"I'm not telling you," Lauren said.

"Is it run through the square naked?"

"Travis Bennett," Green admonished. "We would never write a card like that."

"It would make everyone around here really happy, Angie," Travis said.

"Not me," Lauren said.

"Well, sometimes you have to sacrifice your own happiness for that of others," Travis said.

"The card does not say running around naked," Lauren

said.

He grabbed it from her, his teasing having distracted her enough that he could get it out of her fingers.

"Oh, I see." He nodded. "Ladies, we need a new card."

Lauren grabbed it back from him. "No, we don't."

"You don't know any jokes."

"Of course I do."

"They can't be dirty jokes."

Lauren propped a hand on her hip. "I know some non-dirty jokes."

"I have a hard time believing that."

"Oh, brother." She turned and scanned the area. Two boys, about twelve years old or so, were passing by. "Hey guys, what did the lion say after eating the clown?"

The boys stopped. One looked confused, but the other grinned.

"What?" he called.

"I don't know about you, but I think that tasted kind of funny."

There was a slight pause and then both boys started laughing.

Lauren turned back to Travis with a smug smile. "Told you."

He was grinning. "They're boys. A pretty girl tells them a joke, they're gonna laugh whether it's funny or not."

"You think I'm pretty?" She knew he was attracted to her. He'd complimented her ass less than an hour ago. He'd given her an orgasm less than ten minutes ago. But the word *pretty* seemed...nicer. And more sincere.

"Every male on the planet thinks you're pretty, Dr. D."

She squinted up at him. "That's a really *nice* thing to say."

He squinted back at her. "I can be *nice*."

"I would have never guessed," she said lightly.

"I would have never guessed you could tell a fairly funny joke either," he said. "Guess we both have a few things to learn."

And just like that, Lauren was hit with the urge to teach him French and introduce him to *tzatziki* and show him the gorgeous Amalfi Coast.

How stupid was that? Travis Bennett didn't want to do those things.

Pink clapped her hands together. "We need to move on. More happiness to spread."

"See?" Green said to Lauren. "Everyone smiles."

Lauren nodded. "I do see what you mean."

The trio started down the sidewalk. The scent of kettle corn grew stronger, the notes of "I

Get a Kick Out of You" floated overhead and Lauren almost couldn't stand the cuteness of it all.

Then it got worse.

Two little boys and a little girl—looking anywhere from six to ten years old—stopped them. "We're raising money to buy our neighbor lady, Mrs. Kroeger, a new birdhouse. We drew this cartoon of you."

The taller of the two boys handed Travis a piece of paper.

The other boy elbowed him. "It's not a cartoon. It's a cari-something."

"A caricature?" Lauren asked helpfully.

The little girl beamed. "Yeah, that's what it is."

Travis looked at the picture and laughed. Lauren leaned in.

In the center of the paper were two stick figures. They were facing one another, their arms reaching out, but not touching. Neither had any hair or clothes. In fact, the only distinguishing features were the gigantic lips they each had. The lips were touching.

"And this is supposed to be me?" Travis asked, turning the picture so the kids could see it.

Lauren frowned at him. It wasn't a good picture. But these were little kids. "I think it looks nice."

Travis gave her a no-way look. "The only way I know this is me is because it says Travis underneath it." He pointed to the name under the first stick figure. "And by the way, you guys could work on your printing. That V looks like a W."

Lauren turned away from the kids and lowered her voice. "They're just kids who are trying to raise money to do something nice for someone they care about. Lighten up."

He rolled his eyes. "How much are you asking for this masterpiece that you spent ten seconds drawing?" he asked the kids.

"Ten bucks," the shorter boy told him.

Travis scoffed, dug out his wallet and handed them each a dollar. "And that's two dollars more than it's worth," he said.

Lauren stomped on his toe. "Be nice," she hissed. She started to open her purse.

"Uh, City, before you go flashing any more fifty-dollar bills around, you might be interested in knowing that Mrs. Kroeger, their neighbor, is mostly blind. She likes to attract song birds to her yard with birdfeeders, houses and bird baths. She can identify all of them by their songs."

Lauren gasped. "That's so nice. And these kids want to help her get a new house. That's amazing."

"What they didn't tell you," Travis said. "Was that she needs a new birdhouse because they broke her other one climbing her tree when they weren't supposed to, thinking she couldn't see them so they wouldn't get caught. *And*," he added, when the kids started to protest, "their dad specifically said they needed to earn the money by doing *chores* around home. Not playing pitiful and preying on the good will of the people of this town."

The kids all looked at the ground, clearly sheepish.

"I also happen to know that Carter here is a heck of an artist. He took first place in the art fair at the end of the

school year. So these stick figures are just insulting."
Travis pointed to the picture. "I'm way taller than her, for
instance. And if you want to draw a caricature and
emphasize a feature, then you *have* to draw her in crazy
high-heeled shoes."

The kids snickered at that.

"So take your three bucks and go get some snow cones
and then get home and do some actual work and get that
poor woman her bird house."

"Okay, okay." They started to turn away, but then the
older of the boys turned back. "But you like the big kissy
lips, don't you, Travis?"

Travis started toward them like he was going to run
after them. They all shrieked and took off across the street,
laughing.

"Oh, my God," Lauren groaned.

Travis frowned at her. "What?"

"I can't take it. This is all adorable. I give up. Yes, I'll
move in with you. Just get me out of here. No dating and
no more sweetness."

"Honey, living with me can be sweet too," he said with
that sexy drawl that made her want to climb all over him.

She held up a hand. "No," she said firmly. "That's what
I mean. It can't be. You have to make it…"

"Miserable?" he supplied, a little too eagerly.

"Well…no."

"Awful?"

"Not exactly."

"Horrible?" he said brightly.

She frowned. "No. Just *not sweet*. Or overboard
charming. Just…meh."

"Meh?"

"Routine. Boring. Typical. Nothing delightful or unique
or worthy of giving up Prada or Gucci."

"Ah, got it," he said with a nod. "Nothing to make you
want to give up travel to those exotic locations."

She opened her mouth to correct him and then snapped it shut. It didn't matter one bit if Travis knew what Prada was. Not one bit.

"You think you can handle it?" she asked him.

"Making you *not* want to live with me? Yep, can do."

"No Frank Sinatra?"

"Promise."

"No random acts of kindness."

"You have my word."

"And no more hugging," she said. "But that doesn't mean no touching at all."

He snorted and then nodded. "Got it."

She nodded. She just needed to make it twenty-eight more days. "Awesome. Let's go."

ço~e

While Lauren was in Hailey Conner's guest bedroom packing up her stuff, Travis made a quick phone call.

"Tucker, it's me."

"Bailey Baker said you and Lauren were in the shop buying new clothes."

The speed with which gossip spread in Sapphire Falls sometimes amazed even the lifelong residents.

Travis chuckled. "Yep. The girl needed some jeans."

"Making out with you in front of the whole town and buying jeans. What's going on with her?"

"She's…trying to get over us."

"She's trying to get over you? When was she…under you?"

Travis felt hot want flash through him. He hadn't had her under him, but he'd been under her. In a fricking photo booth of all places. He had intended to have her on his lap and maybe get a feel of those silky thighs, but he hadn't intended things to go as far as they had. It wasn't his fault though. It really was like throwing gasoline on a fire. One touch, one taste and he couldn't stop. And now that he'd heard, seen and felt her come, he was going to be her fake boyfriend, but he was also going to be her very real best-she'd-ever-had.

Travis shook his head though his brother couldn't see him. "She wants to get over her infatuation with Sapphire Falls."

There was a pause on Tucker's end of the phone. Then a, "Huh?"

"She loves it here, but she doesn't want to. She doesn't want to pull a Mason and move her life here. So I'm going to help her *not* like it here."

It sounded crazy when he tried to explain it out loud.

Of course, it *was* a little crazy. He understood where she was coming from. Lauren wasn't a small-town girl, not for good anyway. But if anyone could get how easy it was to love Sapphire Falls, it was him. He wouldn't pick anywhere else on earth to be.

Then again, it wasn't like he'd really spent a lot of time anywhere else on earth.

Still, this was home. There might be prettier places, more exciting places, more stimulating places. But none of them would have the memories or the comfort or the peace of home.

As far as he knew, anyway.

Which was fine. Really. He'd meant it when he said that all he needed was hard work, cold beer and good friends.

"You're going to make her not like it here?" Tucker repeated.

"Right."

"How?"

Travis grinned. "With a little help from my friends."

He heard Tucker laugh.

"Okay," his brother asked. "What are we doing?"

"I need you to head to my house. Like right now. And

mess it up."

"Mess it up?"

"Like a serious bachelor pad. Not fit for a lady. Some place she'll be miserable staying."

"She's *staying* at your house?"

Damn right, she was. And that was even before she'd straddled his lap in the photo booth. "I know how that sounds, but it's the easiest way to control her misery."

"So you're taking this woman to your house with the sole purpose of making her miserable."

And that sounded even worse.

"I'm helping her by showing her the real Sapphire Falls. Behind all the cuteness."

"But your house isn't usually a mess."

"She wants to know what it would be like to live with a local boy."

"But your house isn't usually a mess," Tucker repeated.

Travis sighed. "But most of the houses of the local boys are. I'm just the…representative for you all."

"But *your* house isn't usually a mess," Tucker said again, with a little chuckle this time. "That'll drive *you* nuts before it makes her miserable."

"Just do it," Travis said without actually admitting that his brother was right. "If I make her comfortable and am a good host, she won't ever want to leave."

Tucker chuckled. "Okay, okay, whatever. I'll go make your house…look more like mine."

Exactly. It wasn't that Lauren had to not love living with Travis specifically. She had to hate living in the country on a farm with anyone. A messy house was only part of that, but it was a start. This was going to be the easiest part of the whole plan. Classy, sophisticated, snooty Lauren Davis would *not* like living in the country on a farm.

He heard Lauren's footsteps overhead. "Gotta go. Hurry up. And clean out the good food too."

"What does—"

"Oh, and bring Tank and Luna over. They're staying with me for a while."

"You need my *dogs*? No way."

"And let the chickens out," Travis added.

"But what—"

Travis hung up on him.

CHAPTER SIX

"Ready to go?" he asked as Lauren appeared at the top of the stairs.

"Guess so."

He reached for her suitcase when she got to the bottom of the steps. She pulled it out of his reach and gave him a frown.

"This is going to suck, right? I've seen your house from the field. It's kind of cute."

He felt his eyebrows rise. "Is it?"

"Front porch, porch swing, hanging flower baskets."

"My mom puts those baskets up."

"They're still cute."

"I can take them down."

"That might be good."

"Done."

They stood looking at one another. And he wanted to kiss her.

It hit him out of the blue.

Well, not exactly. He'd wanted to kiss her even *before* he'd kissed her at the kissing booth. Now that he knew how she felt and tasted, he wanted more.

But she was nuts.

She thought his hometown was cute. Which it was. She was at risk of falling in love with his home. Her loving something he loved so much felt stupidly intimate.

But she was nuts. And in that moment, wanting to kiss her and realizing that they could have something so important in common, Travis realized he was in trouble.

He really needed to help her *not* like Sapphire Falls. He needed her to *not* like the things he loved. He needed her to look down on his life and his friends and family. Because if she loved any of it, even half as much as he did, he'd actually like her.

And liking her and wanting to kiss her was not a good idea.

She'd never be happy here long term, and if he liked her too much, he'd want her to stay and when she didn't, it would tear him up.

"Time to go, City. Let's turn you into a country girl."

"God forbid," she muttered, but she handed her suitcase over.

He took the long way to his house. With all of the back gravel roads, there were several ways to get to his house from town, and he knew he could drag it out for the time Tucker would need to make his house Lauren-ready. He kept the radio on—to country music, of course—and pointed out who lived where with a brief history on each family all the way to his place.

She didn't say anything, and Travis bit back a smile. There was no way she was interested in any of this.

Let the boredom begin.

They finally pulled into his yard. Three barking dogs—a black lab, a pit bull and a mutt—came bounding toward the truck, scattering the group of chickens everywhere.

"Dogs."

Lauren sounded completely un-thrilled.

Travis grinned. "You like dogs?"

"No." She opened her door anyway.

"You're not afraid of them, I hope," he said. They were big farm dogs. They stayed outside most of the time and would leave her alone if he told them to. But he hadn't really thought about the possibility of her truly being afraid.

She got out of the truck and Nellie, his lab, approached her first.

"Nellie, come," he said.

The dog looked up at Lauren and then turned and trotted to where Travis stood at the bumper.

The other two were Tucker's dogs. They were good dogs, but they weren't as used to listening to Travis.

"That's Tank and Luna."

Lauren put her hands on her hips and looked down at the dogs. Luna, the pit bull, stood watching Lauren with her sweet soft eyes. She clearly wanted to jump up and greet Lauren, but she kept her feet on the ground, wiggling her butt with excitement.

"Don't even think about it," Lauren told her.

Luna's butt dropped to the dirt. She continued to watch Lauren closely, but it seemed the risk of jumping was over for the moment.

Lauren touched the dog's head. "Good girl," she told her.

Travis knew his eyes were wide. She might not like dogs, but she knew them.

That was interesting. At best, he would have guessed she was the fuzzy, yippy-dog type. He could picture her with a tiny white ball of fluff with a sparkly pink collar around its neck. Big dogs, especially dogs used to running outside and jumping into the back of pickups and splashing through puddles as they duck hunted, took some getting used to.

Lauren turned her attention on Tank. Tank was the smallest of the three dogs and the sweetest. He wasn't a good hunter; he barely played a decent game of fetch, but if a dog could be joyful, Tank was. He ran and jumped and barked and chased and wagged with everything in him one hundred percent of the time.

It wasn't just Tank's butt that was wiggling for Lauren, it was his entire body. He was almost vibrating with the desire to shower his doggie love all over her.

Travis kind of knew how he felt.

"Tank, huh?" Lauren asked him.

He barked in reply.

"Do you know how to roll over?"

He didn't. Tank continued to shake, his tongue hanging out.

"How about sitting?" she asked.

Nope. Tank didn't know how to do anything on command. Except maybe come in for dinner. He could hear that dog food bag rustling from miles away.

"Tank," Lauren said, in a very serious voice, looking directly into the mutt's eyes. "This is Donna Karan," she said, indicating her skirt. "You will not be putting your paws on it."

Tank woofed again.

"I'm not kidding, dog."

He barked.

"Okay."

She walked right past him, up the steps to the porch and into the house.

Travis watched her let herself in through his front door like she owned the place. Then he turned and looked at Tank.

"Seriously?"

The dog barked and immediately jumped up on Travis's leg.

He patted the dog's head, laughing. It looked like they recognized the alpha of the pack when they met her.

But this was good. Very good. He could never be involved for real with a woman who didn't like dogs.

Travis grabbed her suitcase and headed into the house.

He almost ran into Lauren who was standing just inside the front door.

"Whoa, what's up, City?"

Then he got a look at his living room.

"Have you been robbed?" she asked.

No, he hadn't. But Tucker had definitely been there.

He recovered quickly. Or at least he hoped he did. Frankly, he was a bit in shock himself. There were beer cans and a couple of frozen dinner trays on his coffee table. There were jackets and shoes and shirts all over. There was a pizza box on his desk and on the seat of his recliner.

There were what appeared to be potato chip crumbs on the floor between the couch and the flat screen TV.

There were more shirts on the banister leading upstairs...along with two bras and a pair of panties that he really hoped Lauren didn't think belonged to him.

He didn't even want to go into the kitchen.

In fact, he might just have to move. He wasn't exactly a clean freak but he was...okay, he was kind of a clean freak. He liked things picked up and neat and, yeah, clean.

He worked on not shuddering. "Come on in, make yourself at home," he said, nudging Lauren forward with his hand against her lower back.

"Uh, thanks."

"I've got some chores to do," he said. "I'll take your bags up to the guest room and then I'm gonna head outside."

"The guest room?" she asked. "All the women who stay here get the guest room? You country boys really are nice."

He moved in closer until she had to tip her head up to meet his eyes. "Girls here don't stay over. Their mamas know where they sleep at night."

One corner of her mouth curled. "And a lot of time they have grass stains on their butts when they get home to their mama's house, right?"

He felt the urge to laugh but he shrugged. "I've never had a complaint."

"Well, I prefer silk sheets to grass."

"I get my sheets at Walmart."

She grimaced, and he did laugh.

"Probably still better than grass," she finally said.

"There are sheets on the bed in the guestroom."

"You really don't want me in your bed?" she asked.

"I thought you *didn't* want to like it here," he said.

"Ah." Her smile seemed grudging. "So no hot sex in comfortable sheets with breakfast in bed the next morning," she summarized. "Got it."

"That's not to say there won't be any sex at all," Travis said. There would be. Definitely. No question. Possibly right now. He lifted a hand and brushed a strand of hair away from her cheek. "And I like waffles. In case you're keeping track."

"I'll tell the cook if I see her. And I'll put in an order for scones and blintzes."

"Yeah, you do that, baby doll. And then be sure to explain what scones and blintzes are."

They stood smiling at each other. And Travis thought about kissing her. Again. And wondered if she was thinking about kissing him.

She took a small step forward…and the sound of something crunching under her shoe made him wince.

It also, apparently, pulled her out of the moment.

"You said you had chores?" she asked, leaning back.

"Uh, yeah." He did, of course. But it was nothing that couldn't wait thirty some minutes.

"I'll…make some lunch," she said, though the way she looked toward the kitchen made it clear she was also hesitant to go in.

Travis wondered what Tucker had left in the kitchen. Travis didn't make a habit of having tofu and diet soda on hand, but he ate normal—if simple—food that he prepared for the most part.

But if he was to give Lauren a true taste of life with any other single local boy, then the kitchen would be pretty bare. With the exception of chips, a few frozen dinners and some cereal.

Most of the guys around here didn't do a lot of cooking. It was a bit of a stereotype for sure, but stereotypes came from somewhere after all. The unmarried guys Travis knew made sandwiches and eggs, could grill just about any meat, and always had casseroles from their moms in the fridge. But they gave Dottie a lot of business downtown at her diner too.

The married ones, on the other hand, ate well at home.
That was just how it went. It wasn't necessarily
chauvinistic. It was just that boys around here spent their
youth hunting, fishing and farming. They were outside
from dawn to dusk. There wasn't a lot of time or, okay,
incentive to learn things like laundry and cooking. Steak
could be eaten for almost any meal and boxed cereal was a
great invention. As for laundry, it was hard to ruin clothes
that they were wearing out in the fields and barns while
they sweated and got into all kinds of things from mud to
manure. Clothes got dumped together with soap on the
regular cycle and then hung out on the line in the yard
when the weather allowed or on the line that ran across the
laundry room when the weather did not.

Travis was an exception to some of those rules. He ate
vegetables and his mom only brought him food once a
month versus once a week like his brother. He could make
chicken soup—not from a can—and French toast. And he
went to Dottie's for coffee and local gossip more than for
food. If he was in the mood for pancakes or a turkey club,
Dottie was his girl, but her pie, good as it was, didn't come
close to his mom's, and he could make a better
cheeseburger.

"Sure, help yourself to anything you can find," he said.
"I'll hurry outside. We need to get back to town around
four."

"Back to town for what?" she asked.

"The volleyball game."

Lauren blinked at him.

"It's Thursday."

"I don't know what that means."

"We play sand volleyball on Thursday nights."

"Sand volleyball."

"Do you know what volleyball is?" Maybe they needed
to start with the basics.

"Yes, I do."

Okay, good. "This is volleyball, but the court is made of sand."

"Yes, I get the general idea of sand volleyball," she said. "Why do you play it on Thursday nights? Or at all?"

"Because it's fun."

She looked dubious.

Travis laughed. "This is what you wanted, City. Real life in Sapphire Falls."

She sighed. "You're right. Bring it on."

Travis gave her a grin and a salute and headed out the door.

Feeling like she could breathe again, Lauren grabbed her bags and started up the stairs.

The difference between his first and second floors was remarkable. The first floor looked like a frat house. The first room on the left up the stairs was...lovely.

But it had to be the guest room.

The bedspread and curtains were both white with blue and yellow flowers. There were windows on the south and west sides that let in a lot of sunlight. There was a white wooden dresser, an old-fashioned, oval looking glass and in the corner was a white wooden table that held a lamp and a Bible.

No way was this Travis Bennett's bedroom.

But what did a guy like Travis need with a guest room anyway? Everyone he knew lived within a thirty-mile radius.

This room, strangely enough, made more sense to her than the living room had, though. Travis's truck was clean—inside and out. Sure, some guys took better care of their vehicles than of their other possessions, but she had a feeling about Travis. For some reason, she didn't think this was how his house usually looked. He took good care of his lawn, and even if his mom hung the pots of flowers on his porch, Lauren was sure he was the one taking care of the shrubs and flower beds that wrapped around the entire west side of the house. Including the rose bushes. The guy had rose bushes. And now that she was thinking of it…she crossed to the window and looked down at the porch below her. There were no hanging baskets of flowers.

Uh huh. They'd been there just a few days ago. And now were gone. He was up to something. Someone had come and trashed his house.

But they'd missed the guest bedroom.

It was very possible his mother had decorated the room as well, but it didn't matter. It was sweet.

So she appreciated the pizza boxes and muddy boots by the front door.

He was trying to make this unappealing, as promised.

This bedroom with its country charm décor was *not* unappealing.

With a sigh, Lauren picked up her bags and headed down the hall. She wasn't staying in the guest room. She was staying in Travis's room. Surely it was at least more lived in and no way would Travis's room be *cute.*

She opened another door to a guest bath. Also neat, tidy and cute.

The next door was a linen closet—neatly organized and smelling fresh and clean and…yes, like Travis. Her nipples tingled a little and she slammed the door quickly.

Dammit.

The next room was another bedroom, but it was used for storage as evidenced by the boxes and general accumulation of things like wooden chairs, a trunk, a few picture frames and a mattress propped against the wall. There was also a fake evergreen tree in the corner and several plastic bins labeled *Christmas*. The guy decorated his house for Christmas? Or his mother did and he stored the stuff here. Either way, she could easily picture the big country home decked out for the holidays and her heart ached a little. She'd been in Haiti last Christmas and London the year before that. London was lovely at that time of year, but…

Lauren shut all of that down as she shut the door.

Holy crap. If she wanted Christmas decorations and a roaring fire and hot chocolate with a cute guy cuddled up under a big fleece blanket, she could get that anywhere. Sapphire Falls did not hold a monopoly on any of that.

She took a deep breath and started for the last door at the end of the hall. As she got closer, she knew it was Travis's room and prayed for some dirt. Or at least clutter.

She wasn't a clean freak. Okay…she was kind of a clean freak. She liked things picked up and *clean*. She would definitely be less attracted to Travis if he had socks all over the room or dried toothpaste in his bathroom sink.

Her ex-girlfriend, Alexia, had been gorgeous, stylish, always put together and attractive. And her bathroom had been disgusting. She'd never rinsed her sink, always left wet towels on the floor and there had been long blond hair everywhere.

It had made their break-up easier to get over.

But Travis's room was neat. And clean. Very neat and clean.

Because that's how her luck was going.

The bed—the huge bed with the massive wooden frame—was made, the top of the dresser was orderly, the floor clean and recently vacuumed. The only thing out of place was a pair of jeans draped over the arm of the chair in the corner and the two books on the floor beside the chair. The chair that sat in front of a floor-to-ceiling bookcase.

And he read.

Well, wasn't that just great?

Not that she thought he was illiterate. But reading for pleasure said a lot about a person. As did *what* they read. Yes, it was cliché and judgmental and some other not-nice things, but she'd been picturing Travis as the *Sports Illustrated* or a *Field & Stream* kind of reader.

She dropped her bags and crossed to the books on the

floor, unable to help herself. The first book she saw was *Life, the Universe and Everything.*

The guy who said ain't and gonna and darlin' read Douglas Adams? Uh huh.

The book under it was *A Connecticut Yankee in King Arthur's Court.*

Dammit. She had to stop looking. If she found any more of her favorites she'd have to *really* like him, and that went against their entire plan.

But she couldn't help letting her gaze drift over a couple of other book spines.

She felt a surge of relief when she saw *Investing for Dummies* and thought she should be relieved, but also felt a bit fascinated at the biographies in Travis's collection including Hank Williams, Brad Paisley, Carrie Underwood and Faith Hill. And, on the other side of his chair near the window was, thank God, a stack of *Hunting* magazines and...yes, she knew it... *Sports Illustrated.* Along with several issues of the magazine called *Nebraska Life*— which, yes, Lauren had read a time or two—and *Huskers Illustrated.*

Okay, so he wasn't a complete enigma. Good thing.

She ignored the rest of the books and headed for the master bathroom.

Just because he read and maybe knew the word ain't made him sound ignorant, didn't mean that he wasn't just a good old boy deep down. He wore blue jeans every day and had chickens running around his front yard and played sand volleyball every Thursday night.

But it wasn't what was in his bathroom—which was done in soft browns and tans with gorgeous ceramic tile and a huge Jacuzzi tub—that surprised her. It was what *wasn't* there.

There was no clutter, no dirt, no soap scum, no laundry.

There was also no cologne, no moisturizer, no hair gel. There wasn't even men's body wash. There was a bottle of shampoo, a bar of soap, a can of shaving cream and a razor. Period.

Lauren picked up the shampoo bottle and lifted it to her nose. Just a nice clean smell. Nothing frilly, nothing flowery, but also nothing musky or even manly—whatever that meant exactly. It was just a clean smell.

That made her want to run her fingers through his hair.

Her nipples hardened—from his fricking *shampoo*— and she quickly set it back on the shelf and took a deep, un-Travis scented breath.

Damn.

On a whim, she opened the cupboard next to the door.

His towels were also basic blue and cream-colored terry cloth. But they were folded and stacked on the shelves neatly.

She returned to the bedroom and contemplated what she'd gotten herself into.

She was here, in Travis's house, to get a taste of the humdrum everyday simple country life in Sapphire Falls. She didn't really know the guy she felt safe enough to live with temporarily.

It wasn't that she was concerned for her physical safety. She was, however, concerned for her sanity. She liked Sapphire Falls. To the point that she'd picked the guy she liked *least* to help her like it less.

But Travis was surprising her.

That wasn't good.

If the Travis she didn't like was not exactly the Travis she thought he was, then there was a real risk that she could maybe actually, well, *like* him.

Which wouldn't help her un-like the town. In fact, it might make her like it even more.

Of course, there was always the sand volleyball game. If anything could turn her off it would be a sporting event, outside, in the sand.

The last time she'd played volleyball—or any kind of

organized sport—was sixth grade P.E. class. She was a much better individual competitor—on teams you had to put up with other people's shortcomings. Lauren preferred to run. It worked off a lot of stress, kept her in shape and could be done anywhere she traveled. All she needed to pack were her shoes. So the volleyball thing wasn't really up her alley. Plus, it was going to be played in *sand*. Sand was only a slight step up from dirt. She didn't mind dirt when she was working in Haiti or even helping Mason in the greenhouses. But that dirt had purpose. It was necessary.

There was nothing necessary about playing volleyball in the sand.

But fine. As Travis had said—if she wanted to be turned off of the town, she had to fully experience and absorb life here. She had to be into it.

She picked up a pair of her new jeans and looked down at her shirt. She wasn't sure what the proper attire for sand volleyball was, but her Donna Karan skirt and top were *not* it. And that left her with cotton and denim.

At least the denim would help her blend in. They would all be wearing denim.

But denim was hot. It was June. And, as far as she knew, sand meant they were going to be outside. Not that she intended to play volleyball, but if she was going to watch, she wasn't going to sweat while she did it.

Just like she sometimes got dirty, she also sweated. It wasn't that she was allergic or too good to sweat. But when she did it, she was running to stay healthy or in Haiti digging in the fields and putting up walls and making the world a better place.

That sweat was worth it. Sand volleyball...not so much.

She rummaged in her stuff and pulled out a pair of scissors from her travel sewing kit. She'd used it exactly twice—once to sew a button back on a suit jacket in DC and once to sew the arm back onto a doll for a little girl in

Haiti.

Lauren breathed deep. This was good. DC and Haiti. Those were the places she needed to be. Two places so different from Sapphire Falls in many ways. That's what she needed to focus on.

She worked for almost five minutes before she admitted that the tiny scissors were not going to get this job done. Dammit. She eyed her bag. She supposed she could wear the jeans Phoebe had cut off for her last night, but she shuddered even thinking about it. Not just because they hadn't been washed yet, but wearing the same thing two days in a row—even cheap denim—rubbed her the wrong way. Finally, she sighed and headed for Travis' kitchen, jeans in hand. She dug in drawers until she found a sturdy pair of scissors that sliced through the denim easily. Strangely, she didn't have one qualm about cutting up a perfectly good pair of new jeans. Or maybe it wasn't strange at all. These were not exactly going to become a wardrobe staple for her after her time in Sapphire Falls was over.

Finally satisfied with her second pair of shorts, she went back upstairs to complete her ensemble. She wasn't going to win any fashion shows, but she was, by God, going to fit in in Sapphire Falls. For now.

She pulled on her Welcome to Sapphire Falls T-shirt, brushed out her hair, pulled it back into a ponytail, applied lip gloss, wiped it off—that was probably overkill for volleyball—then put it back on. Nothing wrong with looking nice. In Sapphire Falls, the women's makeup tended to be one of two extremes—nothing at all, even when out on a Friday night, or way too much, even when just stopping at the post office. Not that any of that was her business or her problem, Lauren reminded herself. Makeup tips would likely not be welcomed.

She reapplied her body spray and the scented lotion that went with it.

Feeling feminine in spite of the T-shirt and denim, she slid her feet into her new boots and smiled. Not that she'd admit it to anyone, but she liked those boots.

She made her way downstairs to the kitchen and hunted for only three minutes before she realized that she was faced with a problem. There was no good food in Travis's house. Either he'd cleaned it out in a further effort to turn her off, or he really did exist on fruit-flavored cereal, frozen pizza and burritos and Twinkies.

Sighing, she looked around. There had to be something she could use for sustenance. There were chickens right outside which, presumably, meant eggs. But there was no way she was going to try to get eggs from real live chickens. She'd have to Google how to do it. For *one* thing.

The kitchen window looked out on Travis's backyard and her gaze landed on the garden.

It was huge. A guy who had a big vegetable garden like that did *not* survive on burritos and Twinkies.

It was only June, so there might not be a lot out there, but there had to be *something*.

Thirty minutes later, when Travis came into the kitchen, she had a salad made up.

The look on Travis's face was worth the dirt under her fingernails, the scuff on her new boots and having to sit outside to watch a volleyball game later.

He looked…flummoxed.

She liked that. A lot.

She wasn't sure if it was her outfit or the salad, but she liked it.

His eyes were wide, his mouth hung open and he seemed frozen in place.

"I told you these boots were good."

He came forward slowly. "Holy shit, City. What are you wearing?"

"My country clothes."

"You cut the jeans off."

"Yep." She turned to face him fully, loving the feel of his gaze tracking up and down her body.

"Really short."

"The less denim, the less heat, Farmer Boy."

"Really? Doesn't seem to be working that way for me."

She grinned as his meaning set in. "Do I look country enough?"

He shook his head and cleared his throat. "You're wearin' those crazy boots. I told you about that."

She lifted a foot and smiled. "I like them."

"Though the guys on the other side of the net aren't gonna be able to see any balls coming, so there's that."

He had a streak of dirt on the side of his face and his shirt was dirty and rumpled, but she still felt her body heating as he came closer. Maybe the less-denim less-heat thing wasn't working for her either.

She should *not* be turned on by dirt and sweat. And his stupid cap and his scuffed up work boots and his faded blue jeans.

Good grief. She had seven course dinners with men who wore three-piece suits and shoes that cost more than Travis's car payment.

She tried not to show that her breathing increased the closer he got. "What is that? Cow or pig that I smell?"

He continued forward with a grin. "Take a deep breath, City. That's the smell of hard work."

And sunshine. For God's sake.

He crowded close, making her left butt cheek press into the round knob on the drawer that held silverware.

"You mean that's the smell of sweat." Though she certainly didn't mind it. If all men in Sapphire Falls smelled like Travis after working outside—a stupid combination of sunshine, fresh air, fresh grass and man— all the women who set foot in this town were screwed.

As she well knew.

He leaned in and reached around her and Lauren felt

her breath catch in her chest as his cheek brushed her temple.

"Yep. Good old-fashioned sweat." He leaned back with a cherry tomato in his hand. He popped it into his mouth and chewed while his gaze tracked over her face.

She worked on meeting his gaze and not his lips.

Then he put a hand on her hip.

She sucked in a quick breath, but he simply moved her to the side so he could get to the sink. "I'm gonna shower before we head to the Come Again."

A big strong drink sounded like a great idea. "That's where you play volleyball?"

"Yep." He lathered his hands with soap and rinsed.

How had she missed that? People playing volleyball outside the Come Again? Of course, she generally avoided social events in Sapphire Falls. It was easier to tell herself there was nothing fun going on in the small town if she avoided any hint of a good time. Though she was plenty familiar with the Come Again and their vodka stock.

Travis grabbed three more tomatoes from the bowl and continued to study her. She frowned. She'd sampled as she'd cut everything up and the vegetables were one hundred times better than anything she could get in Chicago. But come to think of it, that was just another plus in the stay-in-Sapphire-Falls column that was getting far too long as it was. He could eat it all.

And she should eat frozen burritos and pizza, have a stomach ache every day and gain twenty pounds. Maybe *that* would get her butt back to her regular life.

Because the idea of a naked Travis showering upstairs sure wouldn't work.

"You know, I should probably warn you," he said after nearly a minute of silent chewing.

A minute during which she refused to speak for fear of saying something akin to, "Take me now."

"Us guys who like to work with our hands tend to get

pretty riled up outside in the fresh air. The testosterone is flowing, we're feeling all manly, and if there's a cute girl around she might just find herself thrown up on the nearest firm surface."

He glanced to her left where the sturdy looking kitchen table sat.

Lauren felt her heart rate increase. "Is that right?" she asked, trying for cool but pretty sure it came out as breathless. "Sometimes you just have to work it all off, huh?"

"You got it."

Finding sweat and dirt attractive worried her. Finding that Travis was not who she'd expected worried her.

But the idea of making out with him on his kitchen table really worried her.

Because she really wanted to do it. After all, if the country guys and gals went at it on various random surfaces, who was she to argue? And his explanation about getting worked up outside made a little sense.

And maybe, just maybe, it would suck.

That was actually what she was clinging to at this point.

That all the attraction and heat and flirting and teasing would add up to a big fat unimpressive sucky nothing.

Because there was the fresh-air thing to consider. She'd been out in it too. Maybe that was what made the guys around here so attractive. Maybe that was what made her feel like she was going to die if she didn't get a chance to run her tongue over the ridges of Travis's stomach.

There was also the possible genetic component to her attraction. Lord knew, her mom and sister had fallen fast and hard for country boys like Travis. Lauren couldn't fully fight her genetics, could she? But that didn't mean that she and Travis specifically had a connection. It was her DNA making her crazy, not *him*.

Then there was the boredom factor. In a small town like Sapphire Falls, there wasn't as much going on to distract or interest her. Or Travis for that matter. If the guy had a few more hobbies, maybe he wouldn't spend so much time grinning and swaggering and drawling around her.

So if they did actually act on all of this supposed chemistry, maybe there would be nothing to it. Because really, how many women could Travis have possibly been with? Lauren knew that he was considered something of a playboy around here. She knew that there were lots of women who *wanted* to know what his master bedroom and bathroom looked like. But this was a small town and she, unfortunately, knew more about relationships in small towns than she wanted to.

It wasn't so easy to sleep around.

First, there weren't as many options. He'd likely graduated from high school with forty kids, give or take. Statistically, half of those would have been boys. Even if he dated both older and younger than him, that still left fewer than a hundred eligible women. Then relatives, friends' girlfriends and simply the ones he wasn't attracted to had to be subtracted from that total. Not to mention the BFFs of the girls he *had* dated and dumped.

Seriously, there were maybe ten girls in the entire town that Travis could have dated.

"So you just go at it anywhere the mood strikes?" she asked, looking around the kitchen thoughtfully. The table really was the best option. Or the counter right behind her.

"There's no fighting Mother Nature," Travis said with a shrug.

Or a genetic predisposition to go for tight butts in blue denim. "You just have to give in to those base urges sometimes, I suppose."

"It's survival instinct, baby doll." He leaned in and braced a hand on the counter beside her hip.

And in this kitchen, at this moment, with this man leaning in, Lauren found herself making a mental list of all the things from her apartment that she'd want to bring

when she moved here and doing a quick mental tour of
Travis's living room to decide where she could put her
floor lamp and roll-top desk.

Holy crap.

This was really bad.

But it was also something worse…inevitable.

She couldn't possibly spend a month with him and *not*
end up in his bed—or on his kitchen table as the case may
be. And the option of not spending the month with him
was, frankly, damned unappealing.

Which left her with her only hope—that Travis Bennett
would suck in bed.

"Hey, Trav?" she asked. He wasn't going to like this.
Or maybe…

"Yeah?"

His voice was husky and she felt a shiver of
anticipation dance over her spine.

"I think our conditioning has moved to a new level."

"Does this level involve nakedness?"

She nodded. God, he had gorgeous eyes. "It does."

"I'm in."

"But the thing is…you can't make this good."

One eyebrow arched over one of the gorgeous eyes.
"Pardon me?"

"No fancy tricks. Nothing that you know for sure is a
homerun. In fact…" She tipped her head. "You know all
the things that guys want to do but girls aren't always into?
Or things you're afraid will be a turn-off?"

Travis was looking at her with amused skepticism.
"Yeah, okay, I'll bite. What are you talking about?"

"Sex. Basic. No bells and whistles. Do what you want
with no worries about me or if I'm having a good time or if
I'm going to have an orgasm or if I think you're a god. Just
do what you want and get it over with."

He leaned back slightly, looking a little more irritated
than amused now. "Are you kidding me right now?"

"What?"

"You want me to be a selfish dick during sex?"

"Definitely."

"Because you want it to be bad?"

"Yes. Very much. But don't worry," she said quickly. "I'll be bad too."

His mouth curled even while it was clear he was wondering why he put up with her. "You'll be bad too? Give me an example of how that's gonna go."

"I'll just lie there," she said. "You can do all the work."

"Awesome," Travis said dryly. "Can't wait."

"Oh, come on," she said with a little laugh. "You do *not* want me to turn on everything I've got."

"Is that right?"

"You'll never be able to be with another woman again," she told him with a shrug. "And you already told me your mom won't like me, so…" She decided to let him finish that thought.

"So we're going to have sex, but we're going to make it bad. Like every cliché about how sex can suck?"

"Right."

"You're just going to lie there. Maybe even yawn or something—"

She laughed. "Yes, perfect. Maybe I'll comment on how I need to get my nails done."

"Uh huh. And I won't need to waste any time on foreplay. Or kissing. I'll just go for the good stuff."

"Right." Though in her opinion, their kissing so far had been very good stuff.

"I could just bend you over the table and thrust," he said, looking at the table, his tone thoughtful.

Her heart kicked and her thighs squeezed together. "Uh, no. Not that."

He looked at her with a sly grin. "Oh, you'd like that, huh?"

She cleared her throat. "Yeah, behind isn't going to be

bad for me."

There was a wicked glint in his eye now. "Maybe we need to run down the list of positions that are *good* for you. You know, so I can avoid them."

She licked her lips. This felt like foreplay. But damned if she could keep from saying, "Me on top—forward or backward, you behind—in any position, or up against the wall—or fridge or whatever."

The heat radiating off his body was enough to make her want to start stripping her clothes off in the heavy silence that followed her recitation.

"Duly noted," he finally said, his voice rough. "So missionary it is."

"The table will also make it less bad," she said. "But I'm okay with that," she was quick to add.

Suddenly she *needed* to have sex on Travis's kitchen table.

"I probably need to leave the whipped cream in the fridge too," he said. His gaze was tracking slowly over her face.

Lauren felt her skin begin to tingle and everything in her body tightened.

"Yes. No whipped cream. Or any other food."

"Food during sex is on your good list, huh?"

"Right."

"Got it."

"And no dirty talk," she said.

"You like dirty talk."

"A lot."

"Will do."

"No," she said, shaking her head. "*No* dirty talk."

"Right," he agreed. "I will do the no dirty talk." He lifted a hand to her hair and ran it from her temple back and down her pony tail. "What if I grab on here at some point?" he asked, taking her hair in his hand and tugging slightly, tipping her head back. "That's probably a turn-off, right?"

Not one fricking bit. She shook her head as much as he would allow. "Probably no hands on my hair."

That sexy mouth curled up at the corner again. "Well now, we can't go completely hands free, you know? Even sucky sex involves hands."

But hopefully not big, rough, knowing hands that could turn her to needy mush with a single stroke.

The photo booth had been enough of a warning that Travis knew how to use his hands.

"You can use them," she agreed. "But not...well."

He gave a soft laugh. "I'm not sure I know how to not be good with my hands, darlin'."

She closed her eyes and gave a soft groan. "No nicknames. No darlin', no baby doll, no honey, no City."

"You like it when I call you City?"

She could feel that he'd leaned in closer and she opened her eyes to his intense gaze. Damn. She was giving way too much away here. "Maybe instead of talking about the things you *shouldn't* do, we could list some things that you can do that would be a turn-off."

"I could get the handcuffs out. Or have you dress up in only a kitchen apron. Or insist you go down on your knees and suck me for a while."

Her entire body flooded with heat. The jerk. None of that would turn her off. How did he know that?

He must have seen something in her eyes, because he gave her a knowing grin. "Well, *some* girls would be turned off by that stuff."

She puffed out a breath and tried to gather her thoughts. At least, the thoughts that weren't *why are my clothes still on?*

"Maybe you could eat some garlic and breathe on me a lot."

He nodded, as if that was a serious suggestion. "Or I could give Molly a call."

That shut her up quick. "Molly?" she asked, her eyes

narrowing.

"Two girls at once is something guys like but girls don't generally want to do."

Lauren frowned. Dammit. It wasn't like this was the first time *this* subject had come up with a guy. But just because she was attracted to both men and women didn't mean that she was any more inclined to want to be with both at once than anyone else.

"I was wondering when the oh-boy-she's-a-lesbian thing would come up."

He caught her wrist when she tried to push him back. "I thought you were bisexual."

She looked up at him. "And that means I'm into everything? There's nothing I won't do?"

He shrugged, still standing way in her space and holding her wrist firmly. "I figure people who are bisexual are pretty much like everyone else. Some are into threesomes, some are into handcuffs, some aren't."

She stared up at him. That was surprisingly enlightened of him. "I'm not into threesomes."

"Good. Me either." He gave her that infuriating almost-there grin. "I don't like to share."

She sighed. "Then what's with the Molly suggestion?"

"I thought I was supposed to be turning you *off*. I was hoping you *weren't* into threesomes." He frowned. "What's with the jumping to conclusions about the girl-on-girl action?"

"It's maybe come up before," she muttered.

He tugged on her wrist, bringing her up against his body in full chest-to-pelvis contact. "And you assumed that I was like the other guys who've been assholes?"

Well, when he put it like that...She nodded. "Yeah."

"Not cool, baby doll. I don't assume that liking girls *and* guys makes you a slut, and you don't assume that me driving a truck makes me a dick, okay?"

She was aware that she really liked being pressed up

against him. And she felt a little bad about making the exact assumption he'd just accused her of. "Okay."

He ran a hand down her back to her butt, pressing her closer to him. "Now what else can I do or not do to make sure that the hot, sweaty, sweet sex we're about to have will *not* rock your world?"

Hot, sweaty and sweet.

Those seemed like some really good words.

And her entire tactic changed in the blink of an eye. There was no way sex with Travis was going to suck. There was also no way she was going to be able to not have it anyway.

"I was just thinking that maybe you should put everything into this," she said.

"Everything? Meaning?"

"Give me all you've got," she said, wrapping her arms around his neck. "Otherwise, I'm always going to wonder how it could have been. That might be worse than reality— I mean, I could really build it up in my imagination. I probably need to have your best, so when I'm over it, I'm *definitely* over it."

"You think you're going to get over it?"

She nodded, trying to seem sincere. "I do."

"We'll see about that," he muttered.

CHAPTER SEVEN

In this case anyway, Travis acted exactly as she'd predicted. He met her challenge, cupping her chin with one hand and covering her mouth with his.

The kiss, thankfully, saved her from admitting that not inviting Molly whoever-she-was over had less to do with Lauren's disinterest in threesomes and everything to do with her not wanting to share Travis.

Flags didn't get much redder than that.

Still, she kissed him like having sex with a farmer on his kitchen table was the last thing on her bucket list and she had one day to live.

Because they *were* going to have sex on that kitchen table. It was suddenly an unfulfilled fantasy she hadn't even realized she had.

Travis lifted his head, his breathing ragged. "So let's talk about a few things I *do* like during sex. Then I'd love to hear more from your list." He reached between them and unbuttoned the top button on her shorts. "I also like dirty talk." He lowered the zipper and pushed her shorts to the floor.

Lauren had to kick out of her boots to get the shorts completely off.

"Those are goin' back on," he said, jerking her shirt up and over her head.

Boots only? Sure that would be a good look.

She got him unbuttoned and unzipped as well as he stripped his shirt off.

"I like oral," he said.

Lauren's fingers fumbled getting the denim over his tight butt.

"Getting or giving?" she asked, her voice wobbly.

He grinned. "Both." He stripped her panties off and kicked them across the floor. But—" He put both hands on her ass and lifted her up against him. She wrapped arms and legs around him and he walked to the table.

Thank God.

"You'll be happy to know," he went on, depositing her on the edge of the table. "That giving is one of my favorite things in the world."

"As far as conditioning me *not* to like you, that is *not* going to work," she said. She *loved* oral sex as well.

He went down on one knee and Lauren held her breath. But instead of putting his mouth where she wanted him, he reached for her boots. He slid one onto her foot, kissed her knee, then held the other boot out for her to put her foot in. Just like Cinderella.

But the fairy tale had left out how Prince Charming looked at Cinderella when she was wearing nothing but the glass slippers.

The heat in Travis' eyes made Lauren's breath catch in her throat. Maybe this was a good look after all. She reached behind her, unhooked her bra and sent it flying over his shoulder a moment later.

"See, now here's where your whole let's-make-the-sex-suck plan would have fallen apart anyway," he told her.

"What do you mean?" she asked, her nipples beading and straining toward the guy who made them tingle almost constantly.

"Well, I don't care what kind of deal or strategy or conditioning thing we have going." He cupped one breast and brushed his thumb over one of the nipples that *loved* him.

As he touched her, the look in his eyes was hot and sweet at the same time and Lauren tried to close her eyes. Except that she didn't want to close her eyes. Already, she was torn between wanting this to be nothing at all…and wanting it to be everything.

"I would have never been able to resist doing this to you," he went on. He put his hands on her knees and slowly spread them apart.

Lauren caught her breath.

"And I just don't know that I would have been able to keep from being awesome at it."

He grinned up at her in the way that usually made her grit her teeth. But when it came from between her knees, Lauren admitted she loved that damned grin. At the moment, it was making her want to grab the back of his head and pull him forward to where she ached for him.

"You like naughty words, right?" she asked.

"I really, really do," he said sincerely.

"Then you'd better fucking get on with this or I'm going to kick your ass," she told him.

His eyes widened, his grin widened, and then he put his hands on her knees and widened the space between her thighs.

Travis Bennett was a tease. A flirt. A laidback, drawling, sauntering country boy.

But when he had his face—and tongue and lips and fingers—between a girl's legs, he didn't mess around.

He licked long and firm and then sucked, swirled his tongue around her clit and made zings of sensation and heat zip through her body. He slid one finger deep and then another. Lauren tipped her head back, put her hand on the back of his head and needy moans were coming from her throat within minutes.

But he didn't take her all the way to the summit. It was close—the muttered, "Fuck, you taste so good," and the, "Damn, I could eat you all day," and, "That's right, baby doll, move just like that," got her *so* close. But he lifted his head before she went over the edge.

"Trav—"

"Hang tight, City."

She wanted to protest, but she couldn't lie, when he got to his feet, bare chested and wearing blue jeans unbuttoned over the hard ridge of his cock, and gave her his grin, she almost went the rest of the way into her orgasm.

His eyes on hers, he stripped out of his jeans and underwear. He, unlike her, had lost his boots at some point. He also had a condom handy.

She did appreciate a guy who was prepared for anything.

Her gaze was pulled from his by the delicious sight of him rolling the condom onto his long, thick cock. She went hot and wet all over again watching his hand stroke down the impressive length. He was gorgeous. Gorgeous. Big, solid, tanned from the sun, defined by his hard work.

Of course he was huge. Why not? If he'd been small or didn't know what he was doing with a clitoris, or didn't say City in exactly the tone that he used, she might not be in hopeless lust with him. But he was big, talented and sexy as hell. And she was in deep.

ॐ∞ॐ

"Come here," she said.

That husky voice, the look in her eyes, the fact that Lauren Davis was buck naked on his kitchen table…there was no way in hell he was going anywhere but *here.*

He stepped between her knees and moved to put his hands on that very sweet ass to get her closer. But her hand on his chest stopped him.

"Hang on, Farmer Boy. I've got some stuff to do."

He lifted an eyebrow but didn't protest a bit when she leaned in and put her mouth against his chest. She kissed her way across his left pec and then traced the B tattooed on his shoulder.

The tip of her tongue outlining the symbol he and his brothers all had inked onto their bodies was probably the hottest thing he'd ever experienced.

"Lauren," he said roughly, balling his hands into fists to keep from grabbing her. "That's making me nuts. I want to throw you back on this table and make it really hard for you to walk later. Just so you know."

He heard the quick intake of air and then felt the puff of her breath on his skin. "Just a little more."

She pushed him back, slid to the floor and bent her knees while cupping his ass with both hands. She ran her tongue over the ridges of his abs on the left, up the middle of his torso and then down the right side.

He was panting by the time she hovered over his cock.

"Almost done." She looked up at him through thick lashes. "You got another one of these?" she asked, indicating the condom.

"Two boxes. I stocked up after the grape-slushy incident."

She smiled. "See, you're such a *nice* guy."

Then she pulled the condom off and took him in her mouth.

He groaned and grabbed her ponytail, mostly to ground himself, though keeping her right where she was made a lot of sense too.

The feel of her hot, sweet mouth around his cock was sheer heaven. Travis stared down at her, absorbing everything about it—the feel of her hair in his hand, the perfect suction of her mouth, the sight of her taking him in and the glistening wetness she left behind when she lifted her head. And those damned boots.

"We're to the this-is-the-fucking-greatest-sex-ever part, right?" he asked, leaning over and scooping her up and putting her down on the edge of the table again. "Because, darlin', if that was you tryin' to make this *bad*, you failed miserably."

He pulled another condom from his jeans, rolled it on, stepped forward and took one of her knees in each hand.

"This is gonna be longer than eight seconds...barely...but it's gonna be a helluva ride." He didn't bother wondering if she'd get the bull-riding reference. He just thrust deep and hard.

Lauren gasped and her hands flew to his shoulders to hang on.

She was gorgeous. Spread wide on his table, her breasts bouncing, lots of smooth tan skin and pink glistening heat. He thrust harder, unable to control his speed or intensity, spurred on by the pure instinct to possess her and be the best she'd ever had.

But she didn't seem to mind. She was watching where they were joined, her breathing ragged, her chest, throat and cheeks flushed. She made the hottest sounds he'd ever heard and she gripped him with her inner muscles as if she would never let go.

That was just fine with him.

"City girl, you look good on my country table." He reached with one hand to tug on one of the nipples taunting him. He hadn't even had a good taste of those yet.

Her pussy clamped down on him as soon as he touched her breast, and she moaned.

"Oh, you like that." He did it again, a little harder this time, and got a hissed, "*Yes,*" from her.

He was still holding one thigh, but she wrapped the other leg around his hip and pressed close, the heel of the boot digging into his ass.

"Travis. Damn. Yes."

"What else do you like?" he asked. He wanted her screaming. His name. Definitely. "You want me to tell you that your pussy is making me fucking crazy? That I feel like I can't get deep enough or move fast enough? That I would gladly stay right here, making you come again and again, every day for as long as it takes to make you get wet even hearing the word *table.*"

She gasped and then moaned. Her heel dug in harder and her muscles rippled around him.

"Lie back," he said roughly, pulling her hand from his shoulder.

She lowered herself back on the table. The angle change pressed him against a new spot that made her cry out, and Travis tightened his butt and pumped harder and deeper.

Having sassy, sophisticated Dr. Lauren Davis spread out on his table, her head moving side to side, her thighs wide open to him, was more than he could take. He was going over the edge.

He pressed his thumb to her clit, circling and rubbing, bringing her along with him. "Come for me, City," he muttered. "I want to see and hear that."

She arched her back and gasped and then tightened around him like a hot fist. He thrust twice more and felt her orgasm grab her and suck him in hard.

"Yes!"

Seeing this woman undone because of him made him feel like a fucking king. *Damn right.* And a second later, he came on the heels of her orgasm.

Several seconds passed with only their heavy breathing filling the air. Lauren flung her forearm over her eyes, her legs hanging loose over the edge of the table.

He braced his hands on either side of her hips, breathing in and out and wondering how long he had to wait to have her again.

It had never been like that before for him.

"I was wrong about the boots," he finally said.

She moved her arm and peered at him. "Oh?"

"They're awesome. You gotta keep 'em."

"If I'd known boots would lead to *that*, I would have bought a dozen pairs long ago."

He chuckled and pushed himself back from the table and then held out a hand to help her up. Her cheeks were still flushed and Travis felt like crowing.

She looked up at him and sighed. "Well, damn."

He grinned. He knew she was talking about how complicated this made things, especially considering she didn't want to like him. But he still grinned. Because he'd just had the best sex of his life and he felt fairly confident about being in her top three. And he was good with that. He had time to move up to number one. "Sorry." But he wasn't. Not at all.

"You're not sorry." She pushed him back, slid off the table and bent to retrieve her clothes.

"You're not sorry either." Pathetically, he wanted to hear her say it.

She straightened, pushed a stray strand of hair behind her ear and sighed. "Not exactly *sorry*, no."

Not exactly the glowing review he'd been hoping for, but he should have known better.

"Well, if you like my kitchen table, you should see my shower." He grabbed her hand and started for the steps upstairs.

"Trav—"

He turned and sighed too. "I know, City. I know." Wanting *and* liking her wasn't exactly going to make his life any easier either.

"But—"

"Look," he said, cutting her off again. "I can't make the sex suck. For us, that just isn't possible. But I can feed you fried food, mediocre beer and make you play a sport you're clearly unimpressed with in sand. That's your only hope right now of not having one of the best days ever in Sapphire Falls."

She looked like she was considering arguments and denials. But finally, she shook her head and said, "Okay. Amazing shower sex followed by boring, dirty volleyball. Let's go."

Travis ended up following *her* up the stairs.

ค∞จ

"Well, this isn't helping a bit," Lauren muttered as she

lifted her glass for another sip.

She was in a small-town bar watching sand volleyball, but the Come Again definitely knew how to make a Cosmo.

"What?" Phoebe asked, reaching for a nacho from Adrianne's plate.

"Half-naked guys jumping and diving and hitting and sweating," Lauren said.

The volleyball court was full of good looking guys— none of whom should be allowed to wear a shirt ever— playing volleyball, yelling insults, laughing and having a great time.

But her eyes were on Travis.

Tucker was there too. He looked a lot like his brother. He had the same ornate B tattooed on his shoulder and he was actually a better player as far as she could tell.

But her eyes were on Travis.

Even Joe Spencer looked good without a shirt and had some surprising athletic ability for a guy who'd been raised in casinos and had spent his time prior to Sapphire Falls at poker tables and in dance clubs around the world.

But her eyes were on Travis.

Lauren was actually supposed to be in the back row of the north volleyball court at the moment, but she'd told them all she wasn't playing, and after standing with her arms crossed and letting eight serves from the other team hit the floor, they'd believed her.

"So how goes the anti-Sapphire Falls efforts?" Adrianne asked, sipping from her bottle of water. Mason wasn't here and wouldn't have been playing volleyball anyway, but Adrianne had a thing for the Come Again nachos and her boss was here tonight. Hailey was back from her trip to Denver and some of the mayor's and her assistant's best ideas came about over margaritas and nachos, no matter the location or time of day. The good thing for Adrianne was that when it was a *work* meeting, the nachos were on Hailey.

"It's not an anti-Sapph—" But it was. Lauren shrugged. "Horrible."

"I told you that would happen," Phoebe said smugly. "Sapphire Falls rocks."

"What's going on?" Hailey asked with a frown. "*Anti-*Sapphire Falls efforts?"

Lauren let Phoebe fill her in, interjecting only when Phoebe said things like, "Lauren wants to hate Sapphire Falls," and, "Lauren thinks she's too good to live here."

"So you're trying to like living here *less* by hanging out with Travis Bennett?"

Lauren didn't confirm it. She did drink again.

"There are very few people in this town who love it *more* than Travis," Hailey said.

"No kidding," Lauren commented dryly.

"And there are very few people in this town who are more fun to hang out with than Travis," Hailey said.

"Sure, if you like bonfires and blue jeans and sand volleyball," Lauren said.

"So explain to me how having sex with Travis is going to help you *not* like it here," Hailey said.

Adrianne and Phoebe both turned to Lauren for her reaction. Neither looked surprised.

Lauren narrowed her eyes. "How did you know that?" Travis was spreading the news?

"You're glowing," Hailey said, lifting a shoulder.

"I am not." People didn't really glow after sex.

"You are."

"Bullshit."

"And you have whisker burns on your collarbone." Hailey lifted her own martini glass for a sip.

Lauren's hand flew to her collarbone and she could feel her cheeks heat. Holy crap. When was the last time she'd *blushed*?

"Well, it was…unexpected," Lauren answered.

Phoebe, Hailey and Adrianne all snorted in unison. "What? It was."

"Then you were the only one who didn't think you would sleep together," Phoebe said.

Lauren rolled her eyes. That was probably true. And *she* was hardly shocked.

"Fine. We had some kitchen-table sex. No big deal." She wouldn't mention the shower. Which had been absolutely as good. Travis had a nice...shower.

"The plan is still solid. I'm getting a taste of what it's really like to live here so I can compare it to my amazing and wonderful life in Chicago and traveling the world to make it a better place."

Phoebe rolled her eyes, Adrianne shook her head and Hailey laughed.

Lauren sighed.

Even to her that sounded a little...stupid.

"You sure you don't want to play front row, City?"

Lauren looked up—past Travis's loose shorts, his flat belly, the chest she constantly wanted to lick, the tattoo that made her belly quivery, the mouth that had done lots of things she was very, very fond of, to the eyes that made her quivery down lower.

He tipped his head, letting her check him out.

"I'm really good right here, Farmer Boy," she finally said, lifting her glass.

He tossed back a drink of water from one of the bottles on the edge of their table. He swallowed and set the bottle down. "You know, you do look good right there." He gave her a wink and then jogged back to the court.

As did the other guys. Who she hadn't even noticed coming over for water in between matches.

As soon as Travis turned away, she groaned and put her head down on the table. "I'm in trouble."

The other women just laughed.

೪೯

Travis tried to keep his mind on the game. He really did. He loved the sand volleyball games and had a great time with his friends. Usually.

Tonight, he was distracted. To say the least.

Lauren was sitting at one of the wrought-iron tables on the Come Again patio with her Dugg boots propped on a chair, her short shorts on and a drink in hand. She should have looked ridiculous. But instead, she looked…right. Good. Really good. She was talking and laughing with local girls who loved Sapphire Falls as much as he did. And she fit right in. Something in his gut clenched at that realization.

He felt a strange sense of…something. Contentment maybe. Optimism—though that didn't make a lot of sense. Anticipation. Yes. That worked. There was a definite feeling that something good was coming. And fun. That seemed to fit best.

He liked having her here. He loved having her eyes on him and he'd felt them all evening.

It was fun to have her mingling with his friends and he could imagine it happening week after week for…

Travis almost got hit in the face by a ball.

Happening week after week for what? Forever? Yeah, right.

It was his turn to serve and he used his frustration to send the ball flying past the out-of-bounds line at the back of the court. Fuck. What was he doing? What was he thinking?

He'd given her three orgasms—four including the photo booth—and now he thought she was going to stay and get together with his friends? What were they going to do, have a weekly game night? Potlucks? Sure. Instead of dining by the Eiffel Tower or picnicking along the Nile, she'd barbecue in his backyard and watch the Sapphire

Falls football team compete for their second conference championship.

No problem.

The second match seemed to drag on and on. Everyone playing was getting hot and drunk. It wasn't just water in the bottles they kept at the tables to sip during their time sitting out of the rotation or during timeouts. Timeouts that were usually taken so that everyone could grab another drink or two.

But as the drinking continued, the play got sloppy and the laughter got more frequent and louder.

Except for Travis. He wasn't laughing at all. Every time he stopped by the table, there were more people sitting there and he heard words like soil erosion and political ideals and understanding how public perception plays a role in pushing for policies that can mold everything from growing programs to imports to the introduction of new plant and animal species that can work together for the overall agronomy of the area.

She was talking about work. And all of the reasons that she could never be satisfied in Sapphire Falls.

"Jesus, let's go!" Travis yelled across the net. "Serve the fucking ball."

"Relax, Bennett," his buddy Matt yelled back. "This ain't the Olympics."

Travis growled, and when Matt finally served it, Travis jumped and hit it right back into the sand on the other side of the net.

The game finally ended and he headed for the table.

Drew and Steve, two local guys and friends of his, had joined the girls nearly thirty minutes ago, and they were listening intently to whatever Lauren was saying. Travis frowned as he drew closer and realized they were passing Lauren's phone around.

"The girl on the left is the one who's helping get the kids to school. She's only fifteen, but she understands that the future of their village depends on the kids. She goes around to each home and gets the kids and walks with them to the schoolhouse."

Lauren leaned in, giving Drew a nice shot of her cleavage and making Travis's blood pressure rise. She pointed at the phone. "The boy in the middle has been Mason's shadow. He's only twelve, but he loves everything about the growing program. He goes everywhere with Mason when he's there and Mason's great. He's very patient and takes the time to work with the kids because again, getting them involved is key for the continued success long term."

There was mighty Mason. He wasn't even here and Travis felt a stab of jealousy. It was clear, even in the short and infrequent interactions Travis had witnessed, that Lauren and Mason could practically read each other's minds. They were a team, best friends, they shared a true passion for what they did and, frankly, no other man would likely ever be able to be what Mason was for Lauren.

That pissed him off, and then he was even more pissed about being pissed off.

Good God. Two days ago, he'd thought Lauren was stuck up and too cool for his taste. Now he was feeling jealous of other men and irritated about the fact that she would never think bonfires at the river were a good time.

He was losing his mind.

"So Mason was saying that your biggest job is the relationships with the politicians," Drew said, handing Lauren's phone back. "He says you're amazing."

Lauren smiled a smile that jabbed Travis again. Clearly, Mason's praise meant a lot.

He grabbed a water bottle that required him to lean into Lauren's space. Juvenile maybe, but he didn't care. "What're we talkin' about?" He tipped the water back but kept his eye on her.

"Haiti," she said with a big smile. Her face lit up with

that one word.

Dammit. Why did he care? It wasn't like this was a big revelation. Why did it piss him off? So the sex had been good. Big deal. It wasn't a first or last for either of them.

"She's telling us about the kids over there," Drew said.

"And the water conservation program," Steve added.

They both grinned like she'd told them the secret to understanding women.

And maybe she had.

When she talked about her work, she was softer and brighter and clearly thrilled. Wasn't that the key in any relationship, to getting close to the other person—to be interested in what was interesting and meaningful to them?

And Drew and Steve had figured it out.

Awesome.

Well, she was going home with him, so they could just suck it.

"So what does Mason mean by government relations really?" Drew asked.

"I talk with policy makers, representatives on various committees, that kind of thing. Joe and I are basically the lobbyists for IAS, and that turns into lobbying for agricultural policy and programs in general—here and overseas."

"I don't know how anyone could ever say no to you, girl," Tucker said, coming up beside Travis.

Lauren gave him a smile. "Too bad you can't get elected."

"I'd give it a good shot if girls like you were coming into my office every day," Tucker told her, tipping back his beer.

"I'd never want to leave DC if all the guys I met with were like you," Lauren said, flirting right back.

Travis was going to slug someone. And that was so unlike him, he had to stop for a minute and just breathe.

"So you were saying something earlier about Ukraine,"

Drew said.

Lauren wiggled in her chair. "Oh, okay, so the coast in Crimea is gorgeous and I really love the Carpathian Mountains, but there is this little town in Ukraine that is almost perfect. I haven't been there in forever and well, now…" She paused and looked at Drew thoughtfully. "Do you know about what's going on in Ukraine?"

That was the final straw. She was *not* going to tease his friends with the same stuff she used on him, and she was *not* going to rub it in that they were less knowledgeable or worldly than the other men she was used to spending time with. And, most of all, she was not going to flirt her way across Sapphire Falls.

Travis grasped her upper arm and pulled her from her chair. "Time to go."

"Hey," Lauren protested as she tipped over a water bottle on the edge of the table, sending water down the front of her T-shirt and barely-there shorts.

"Whoa, Trav, take it easy," Tucker said, stepping close.

Travis leveled his brother with a serious stare. "I've got this."

Tucker held up both hands. "Settle down. Just don't be an ass."

Travis didn't look at Lauren, but he said through gritted teeth, "City, tell him we're good."

Lauren sighed and pulled her arm from Travis's hold. "We're fine, Tucker."

"You sure? 'Cause he's bigger than me, but I'm guessing I'll have backup if I need it."

Drew got out of his seat and Joe moved in closer.

"Jesus," Travis muttered. He held up his hands this time. "Lauren, I have some thoughts about Ukraine and was hoping we could discuss them. Privately."

She looked up at him with wide eyes but nodded. "I would really love to hear your thoughts about Ukraine."

Drew looked from Travis to Lauren and back. "Wait a

second. Ukraine is code for sex? *I* want to talk more about Ukraine, Dr. D. You asked me first."

Lauren didn't take her eyes from Travis. "Actually, Drew, I started this conversation with Travis the other night at the river."

Drew slumped in his chair. "Damn, Bennett, you noticed that she knew Brad Paisley the other night, didn't you?"

"That was one thing," Travis agreed, still staring at Lauren.

She lifted an eyebrow. He mimicked the action.

"So we'd better go," she said. "We can probably cover all of my thoughts about the way they can use their natural resources to make a political impact by midnight."

Yeah, that's what they were gonna do.

He gestured for her to step in front of him toward the door. As she did, he caught a whiff of her scent. Maybe it was sitting on the Come Again patio, maybe it was hanging at the festival and his place earlier, but damn if she didn't smell like sunshine.

Travis rolled the windows down, turned the radio in his truck up loud, blasting Kip Moore and heading for a spot on his land that was perfect for what he was going to say to her. But he didn't have anything else to say until they got there.

Lauren didn't seem inclined to start a conversation either. She didn't reach for the volume knob. In fact, she was singing along.

Which at any other time would have thrilled him.

When they got to the spot, he threw the truck into park and shut everything off.

The complete silence and the near-complete darkness after the music was almost deafening.

And now that he had her here, he wasn't exactly sure how to start.

"God, it's beautiful here."

He turned to her. She was staring out the truck's windshield.

And the view in that direction was beautiful. The land rolling away from the front of the truck was his. The trees on the south edge of the land were his. The creek running along the east side of the land was his. But that wasn't *the* view.

"Come on." He got out of the truck, trusting she would follow him.

He went to the back of the truck and stood, hands on his hips, looking out over the view that never failed to soothe him.

Tonight was no different. Lauren stirred him up, there was no question. Physically, of course. More than any other woman ever had. But emotionally too. He hadn't been expecting that, and *that* stirred him up as well.

But looking out over his fields, his house sitting in the distance, the trees he'd climbed as a child, the creek he'd fished in, the far hill where he and his brothers had sledded winter after winter, he felt the usual peace wash over him. This was who he was, where he belonged. This was where he knew himself best. Regardless of the thoughts and emotions the city girl in his truck stirred up.

Lauren joined him, and before she could say a word, he turned to face her and spoke. "*This* is beautiful, Lauren. And those people you were teasing are honest, hardworking, do-anything-for-me people, and I won't have you looking down at them. You might have seen some amazing things in your travels, I know you rub elbows with some important people, but for you to think—and *say*—that this is any less amazing or that these people are any less interesting is insulting. And I won't have it." He moved in closer to look down at her from the seven inches he had on her. "If that's how this is going to go, you've just been to your last Sapphire Falls social event. I'm not going to subject them to your judgments."

She didn't look offended or angry. She looked almost intrigued when she stepped closer. "Are you done?"

Even now, he was having a hard time keeping his hands to himself. "Yeah. For now," he added.

"Well, even though you don't deserve it, I'm going to explain to you that I was talking to your friends about my travels because they asked. And they asked because I made a comment that I'd never seen anything quite like the beauty here. I was talking about the effing sunset *here*, Travis, and talking about how the land is so flat and how all I can think is that it seems to go on and on forever and yet it feels...intimate." She gestured toward the field lying to her left without even glancing at it. "Like this field. I know that the crop there is new this season, but that field has been planted over and over for generations. It's constant and predictable, and somehow that makes me ache inside."

He stared at her, emotions hitting him in waves of surprise and pleasure and disbelief and wonder.

"You did not tell Drew that it makes you ache," he said, somehow knowing that she didn't share stuff like that easily and, at the same time, humbled by the fact that she'd shared it with him.

"No. I'm telling *you* that," she said. "But I did tell him—and everyone—that I think it's beautiful here. Yes, I've seen a lot of beautiful places, but this is one of the few places that has actually gotten to me beyond the *wow*." She took a deep breath. "No matter how beautiful the places in Italy and Greece and Africa are, I just like to look at them. Here I feel like I can...*be*."

And that made *him* ache inside.

"Jesus, Lauren." He reached for her and pulled her up against him, his mouth hungry on hers. There had never been another woman like her in his life, and there was definitely a part of him thankful for that. Being turned inside out had its pros and cons, for sure.

But he was sad too. Because he would never find another woman like her…and he couldn't keep her.

He started stripping off her clothes. He couldn't keep her, but maybe he could convince her that there was something more here than the obligatory visits she'd been making so far because of her best friend. And if not that, then he sure as hell could enjoy the time he did have her.

"There is one view here I haven't seen, but I've imagined it."

She helped him pull his own T-shirt off and slid the athletic shorts over his hips. "What's that?"

"Looking up from your face out over my field and home while I plunge into you over and over." He undid her bra and dropped it, then skimmed the panties down her legs. "I want your cries in this air and I want this air all over your body as I—"

"God, Travis."

She pulled his head down for her kiss this time, sliding her tongue against his as he ran his hands all over her body—up and down her back, over her ass, up her sides to cup her breasts. He needed to possess her, brand her as his somehow, make sure that this place—that *he*—was imprinted on her.

She ran her hands over his back and then down to his butt, pulling him close. His cock nudged her belly and they both groaned.

"Hang on. Dammit." Travis pulled back and went around to pull out the sleeping bag and foam mattress that he kept rolled up behind the seat. He unrolled them in the truck bed a moment later, climbed up and turned to offer her a hand. She let him pull her up into the back of the truck.

"You just happen to have a makeshift bed with you at all times?" she asked. "Convenient."

"I do," he said honestly. "Sometimes I'm struck by the urge to do some night fishing or just sleep out."

She laughed, glanced up at him and realized he was serious. "Sometimes you just want to sleep outside?"

"Yes."

"*Why?*"

"This." He grasped her shoulders and turned her to face the view behind the truck.

There was a pause as she took it in. Then she said softly, "Yeah."

The word was soft and there was awe in her tone that made Travis's chest tighten.

He pulled her back against him so they both faced out over the fields.

The dark fields twinkled with fireflies. The moon was bright overhead and the stars shone like sequins scattered across black silk. The only manmade light was the tall yard light near his barn nearly a mile away. All the combined muted illumination made the winding gravel road look like a white ribbon twisted over and around the dark grays and midnight blues and nearly black purples of the landscape.

His cock pressed against her lower back and he reached around to cup her breasts. He played with her nipples and her head fell back against his chest.

"This is all yours?" she asked breathlessly.

At her question, Travis felt a surge of possessiveness that included the warm, soft woman in his arms. Only a few days ago, he would have never believed that he would have Lauren Davis in the back of his truck surrounded by fireflies. But here she was. And it felt damned good.

"We're right in the middle of my land here," he said. He slid one hand down over her belly and pointed with the other. "That house over there is my brother T.J.'s. That's where my land ends and his starts."

"That's what I mean," she said.

She sucked in a quick breath as Travis's fingers

brushed over her mound. He grasped her hip in his other hand, holding her still as he touched her.

"This land has been here, in your family forever, and you share it, you all live on it, you take care of it together."

He was amazed and in love with the fact that she seemed to get his connection to this land and his family and, more than that, that she seemed to be impressed or touched, or something, by it all. He slid his hand lower, his middle finger contacting the hot nub of her clit and making her gasp.

"T.J. and I flipped a coin for the house," he told her, sliding his finger up and down over the sweet spot, feeling the heat and wetness building.

She pressed back against him.

"Grandma and Grandpa lived out here as long as I can remember. I played on this land, grew up here. Some of my best childhood memories happened here. But my brothers felt the same way."

He circled over her clit and she grasped his wrist, holding his hand against her as she arched her back and pressed into him.

"Ty left to go to Colorado," he went on. "And Tucker wanted to build his own house. So that left me and T.J."

Travis slid his finger lower and her gasped *"Travis"* washed over him.

"One Sunday dinner, Grandma pulled out a coin and told T.J. to call it. I won the house and then helped T.J. build his across the field."

Lauren moved against his finger and he slid into her heat.

After her heartfelt *"Yes,"* she asked, "Oh, my God, you guys can build houses? Literally? With your own two hands?"

He pumped his finger in deep. "I'm good with my hands."

"You country boys really take that manual labor thing

seriously."

He added a finger and stretched her as he thrust three times. "Damn right," he muttered in her ear.

There was something so crazy hot about touching her like this while talking about his roots and his home. He would never be able to explain it to anyone, but it felt right to have his hands all over her while letting her into his life.

He added his thumb, circling it over her clit as he pressed in and out of her and cupped her breast, plucking and tugging at her nipple.

The air had cooled since sunset and the breeze that washed over them made the contrast with the heat between them even more pronounced.

"Lauren, I—"

"*Travis.*"

At that moment, he felt her clamp down around his fingers, the waves of her orgasm pulling him deeper. His cock responded, hardening and pulsing, and he needed her. Now.

"On your back, baby doll," he told her, pulling his hand from her body and turning her.

He didn't let the ripples of her climax fade. He knelt with her on the makeshift bed and rolled on a condom as he drank in the sight of her bathed in the moonlight and took a deep lungful of his country air.

She readily opened her legs for him as he moved between her knees. Damn, he liked her compliant in sex. But he liked her feisty otherwise, because it made her submission here all the sweeter.

He hooked his wrists under the backs of her knees, grasped her thighs and pulled her close. He looked out over his land to his house where the porch and kitchen lights glowed, and he took another deep breath. Then he looked down at her and was hit upside the head by a revelation that felt new and awesome and yet at the same time not surprising at all. It wouldn't matter where he was—as long as it was Lauren he was looking at, he was in the right place.

Home.

That word, that one four-letter word had never felt so true. And considering that he was in the bed of his truck, parked on his land and looking at his house…that was damned staggering.

He lifted her, looked into her eyes and slid deep with one hard, possessive thrust.

Everything else faded. They could have been floating on the Mediterranean Sea, lying in the Egyptian sand, rolling in the grass in Ireland…and he would have been home.

Lauren arched her neck and clamped her legs around him, digging her heels into his ass.

Maybe she felt something different now too. Maybe this vibe, this revelation, this feeling of rightness was connecting them.

"Travis. Yes, oh, yes."

Or maybe it was the truck.

Trucks seemed to have that effect on some women.

A second sweet orgasm swept through her, and Travis's climax climbed fast and erupted hard in response.

CHAPTER EIGHT

They lay together long after the ripples had faded and their breathing had returned to normal. They were on their backs, looking up at the stars.

The same stars that shone over the entire fricking planet. So why did *these* seem better and brighter?

Lauren was afraid of the answer to that question frankly.

"There's something I've been thinking about," Travis said as he pulled the sleeping bag from underneath them, unzipped it and flipped it over their naked, cooling bodies.

There were about a thousand directions they could go from that introductory comment. However, probably not the potential political impact of the natural resources in Ukraine. She braced herself. "Okay."

"I've seen the photos and read what Joe writes up about Haiti. It isn't a big city you're in love with over there. Even Port-au-Prince is not Paris or Rome. Yes, you travel to those other places, but you don't spend a month at a time there. You haven't given your heart to any of those places like you have in the small village you work with in Haiti."

Lauren shifted to her side to look at Travis. He sounded very sincere about all of this, as if he'd given it a lot of thought. "What big revelation do you think you've had, Farmer Boy?"

"I don't think it's about the excitement or exotic locations or food in other places."

"You don't think *what* isn't about that?" she asked, unease niggling at the back of her neck.

"The aversion to small towns."

She started to protest. It *was* about those places having things the small towns didn't. But she couldn't make the words form. Partly because she kind of wanted to hear what Travis thought he had discovered about her. And partly because…he might be right.

Initially, when she'd first left home for Europe, it had been about the adventure, about seeing and experiencing new things. She'd loved the new sights, the foods, the languages, the cultural differences, the architecture and music and art. The things that made it different from the life she'd left behind. But most of all, she'd loved the traditions and the history. She'd loved the stories and the customs. The things that made a place unique.

"What do you think it *is* about?" she asked.

"Well, see that's the thing." Travis shifted to put a hand behind his head and slid the other under her to pull her up against him.

His big warm body felt…good. Not hot, not arousing, but good. Comforting. Secure. Solid.

And she knew she needed to put some distance between them. Secure and solid were dangerous words. They were words that had nearly sucked her into a small town life with a sixth-generation farmer who had no desire to learn anything new—and no desire to stop fucking other women just because he was engaged to her.

But she didn't want to get away from Travis.

She almost whimpered as the realization hit her.

She was already sucked in. She was already considering giving some things up to have more of *this*. More of him.

And while the rational part of her brain acknowledged it, her heart was chanting *Travis, Travis, Travis.*

"Where you work is a small village," he went on. "And you go there because you care about the people. And I'll bet there are some cute and charming things going on there. Maybe even a festival of some kind. Like the Rara Festival or Carnival."

She stared at him. "Someone's been using his Google."

He grinned at her and then went back to studying the sky. "Admit it, City, you get dirty there sometimes."

She swallowed hard. Travis Bennett had been

researching Haiti because of her. He'd blown off her comment about it, but she knew somehow that he'd looked up festivals in Haiti or some such search term because of her.

"No grape slushies…or kitchen tables," she said, liking the sexy curl of his lip at her words. "But yeah, there's dirt."

"I think that there is a sense of community and history there that you're really drawn to," he went on. "And I think Sapphire Falls makes you feel the same way."

The crickets and other night noises seemed to be amplified in the sudden silence after his statement.

Lauren felt a strange warmth swirling in her belly. She was surprised and flattered and pleased. He'd been really thinking about her. Not just the sex or how to best turn her off of Sapphire Falls, but what made her tick.

He didn't know why she was how she was. But he wanted to.

It had been a long time since someone had tried to figure her out. She didn't need to share intimate details of her thoughts and feelings with anyone else, even her boyfriends and girlfriends, because she had Mason. Mason knew her, understood her and accepted her, so she didn't need that from anyone else.

"So you think that Sapphire Falls is filling a gap for me right now while I can't be in Haiti?" she asked, hoping that wasn't really what he thought. And hoping that wasn't really true.

"I think that there's a sense of community and roots here that you're really drawn to," Travis said. "I think there is a definite lack of those things in your life. I think you're looking for a home, a place to belong, and I think *Haiti* is filling that gap."

She blinked several times.

When she didn't respond, he rolled his head to the side to look at her.

"I can even *spell* the word insightful," he said gently.
With just a touch of smugness.

"Can you spell speechless?" she asked, all kidding
aside.

"I can spell 'I'm as surprised as you are,'" he told her
sincerely.

"That you're insightful?"

"That I'm insightful about *you*."

She nodded and took a deep breath. His arm was still
around her, his hand resting on her hip. He spread his
fingers, spanning his hand over more of her hip, and she
felt the possessiveness coming off of him.

And she liked it.

Which had to be something like the thirty-seventh red
flag in her relationship—or whatever it was—with Travis.

That also made it the thirty-seventh red flag that she
was ignoring in her relationship—or whatever it was—with
Travis.

"Small-town life isn't so bad, baby doll," he said
quietly.

She sighed. "Small town life is...small."

"Why do you need things to be big all the time?"

"Because small is easy to do and hard to get out of."

"But clearly your big-city life isn't giving you what you
need either, or you'd quit leaving it."

"I leave it for *work*."

"And to travel. And to come here," he pointed out
calmly.

"I come here because of Mason," she argued. Travis
was so, so close to all kinds of truths. And if he figured
them all out and then started talking her out of her fears, it
wouldn't take much for her to put on some blue jeans and
start raising some chickens.

"There are phones and Skype and airplanes that go *to*
Chicago that Mason could use too," Travis said, his tone
even and steady. "The first year Mason was here, you came

every three to four months. This past year, it's been every other month, and the past four months it's been every month."

"You've been paying attention."

"You're hard not to notice, Lauren."

His words alone made her want to kiss him—as did his husky drawl, his eyes, his lips—but the use of her name instead of the variety of nicknames made her want to do a lot more than kiss.

"What is it about life in Sapphire Falls that has you so spooked and yet keeps you from staying away? You haven't really experienced—"

"I lived in a small town for two years, Travis. I was *this close* to settling down there as a farm wife."

Travis gaped at her and she almost laughed.

"Hard to believe?"

"A little. You don't seem like a small-town girl."

"You'd be surprised." He'd likely be *very* surprised. "I even know about party barges. I've skinny dipped. I know how to country line dance. I can tell a Chevy from a Dodge, a John Deere from an International—"

"You grew up in a small town?" he interrupted. "Where?"

"I moved to Longview for my junior year of high school. I graduated in a class of thirty four."

Travis sat up and pivoted to face her. "Longview, *Nebraska?*" he demanded.

"Yep." Longview was about four hours southeast of Sapphire Falls.

"Holy—"

"But I grew up in Lincoln until my junior year. So I'm pretty citified under the country dust."

He was frowning now. "And Longview was so horrible that you now can't stand *any* small towns?"

She sighed and sat up too, pulling her knees up and wrapping her arms around her legs. "Not exactly."

"Come on, City. You have to tell me this."

"Well, I—"

"Hang on." He pushed to his feet and climbed out of the truck—completely, gloriously naked in the moonlight—and dug behind his seat again. "Beer, hard lemonade or Booze?" he asked, holding up a beer can and a mason jar.

"These are my choices?"

"It's a cooler in my truck, not the bar in the Ritz Carlton, baby doll."

"Yeah. You have a cooler in your truck." Apparently, the Boy Scouts in Sapphire Falls learned how to always be prepared for different things than most—like spontaneous parties popping up in places without things like refrigerators, or glasses or good liquor.

"I also have a tackle box," Travis said when she still didn't answer. "Want me to get that out instead?"

"Uh, no, I'm good." She motioned him forward. "Booze, I guess." The stuff really was pretty tasty. And potent. That might be a good thing tonight.

He handed the jar over and she unscrewed the top and took a big swig. Travis climbed back up beside her with a beer and got under the sleeping bag with her. It covered up the nice view he'd been giving her, but the feel of his warm, hard body against hers made it tough to be too upset.

"Okay, now it's story time." He took a drink of beer. "How'd you go from Lincoln to Longview?"

She took another swig of Booze, shivered a little as the liquid burned its way down her throat to her stomach, took a deep breath and started the story.

"My mom had a friend who had grown up in Longview. Teri talked Mom into checking out the Longview Annual Festival with her one year. There was a street dance and a beer garden with a local band and stuff, so Mom went along."

"Your dad didn't care?"

"My mom and dad divorced when I was ten and my

sister was eleven. He stuck around for a couple of years but then got a job in Tennessee and moved."

"Ah."

Lauren gave a soft snort at that. Travis sounded understanding, but Travis Bennett had no idea about divorce. She doubted there was a divorce anywhere in his family tree.

"So Mom went to the dance in Longview and met Jim, a small-town local farmer."

"Ah."

She snorted louder this time. Jim was only the top of the small-town-local-farmer iceberg.

"They fell in love and we moved three months later."

"Whoa."

"Yeah. Mom gave up her job, the big money from that job, her friends, her life—*our* lives—for Jim. My sister and I had huge plans. We were going to travel around Europe for a year and then go to college and study international business and see the world. My sister is even smarter than I am. And she has a huge heart. We were dreaming big and we were going to change the world."

"And your mom didn't like that idea?" Travis asked, with a frown.

"It wasn't that really. But after we moved, we had less money, we had fewer opportunities. The only foreign language offered at Longview High School was Spanish. I had been two years into French and Lea was three years in. We were both going to spend our summer with a humanitarian group. There was no such program—and no money left for it anyway after they remodeled Jim's farmhouse—in Longview."

Lauren took a long drink of Booze. "Then Lea met Corey. Corey was also a local farm boy. She fell head over heels. They were inseparable by October, pregnant by February and married by June."

"*Whoa.*"

"So all of my plans were screwed up."

"By small-town farm boys," Travis added.

She nodded. "And then it got worse."

Travis took the jar of Booze from her and drank. "I'm guessing there's a small-town farm boy involved," he said after he'd swallowed. "And I'm guessing this one has to do with you."

"You're pretty sharp."

He sighed. "Yeah." He didn't sound enthusiastic at all.

"I can stop talking and we can kiss some more."

He gave her a small smile. "While that is very tempting, I do want to hear this story." His tone said otherwise.

"You don't sound like it."

"I don't really want to hear about how you fell in love with some guy who obviously didn't deserve it."

Lauren arched an eyebrow. "How do you know I fell in love?"

Travis shrugged. "Seems to be the pattern with the women in your family."

She laughed. "Yeah, we seem to have a weakness for a particular type of guy."

He nodded. "Guys like me."

Her smile died. He wasn't wrong. "Yeah."

"And they mess up your plans."

Again, accurate overall. But she felt a strange jumble of emotions when he said it. "Yeah," she finally agreed. "Those guys did."

He took another swig of Booze and handed it back to her. "Okay, let's hear it." He sounded unhappy but resigned.

"I said no to every guy who asked me out when we first moved to town. I liked them. I was attracted to a lot of them. I thought their river parties and bonfires sounded like fun."

Travis gave a strange grunt at that but said nothing.

"But I did not want to fall for anyone. I had all these big

plans that did not involve staying in Longview, and I knew any relationship would end in heartbreak. However, once Lea was in love and pregnant, I gave up all of those big dreams of world domination and started saying yes. I started going to the parties and hanging out and, just before my senior year started, I started dating Shawn."

Travis gave another grunt. Lauren ignored him.

"I fell hard and fast once I let myself. It was a lot like Corey and Lea. We became inseparable. My niece was born in November, my family was happy and together all the time and they all loved Shawn. He and my brother-in-law were buddies. He and Jim had known each other forever. Shawn's family came over for barbecues and for Christmas. I just got sucked in and surrounded by all this family time and all these connections and feeling a part of everything."

Travis took the jar of Booze back again.

"It was all great. I had given up the idea of traveling and was imagining my future very differently. Shawn's dad started talking about where to build our house on the family land. My mom started talking about how we could get married on the same day my sister had. And then one night Shawn and I were making out and—"

"I don't want to hear about your sex life, City," Travis cut in sharply.

"It's an important part of the story."

"I seriously don't need to hear that Shawn was the best you've ever had."

She snorted. "That's *not* what I was going to say. I was going to say that he didn't want to use a condom. He insisted it didn't matter if I got pregnant since we were getting married anyway, and he said, 'You don't want your sister's kids to be too much older than ours, do you? They should grow up together.'"

"Jesus," Travis muttered.

"I got instantly claustrophobic," she confessed. "I

hadn't even turned eighteen yet, and my wedding and my future were entirely laid out."

"So you punched him in the face and got the hell out?" Travis asked sullenly.

That would have saved a lot of future heartache.

"No." She sighed. "I went along with it. It seemed fast and crazy, of course, but my mom was so happy with Jim and Lea was so happy with Corey. I loved being with them and the sense of community and the idea that I had this huge family unit. I told myself it was good and I was lucky. Which," she said quickly, "I was. I had a ton of people I could count on. They all loved me and they were wonderful people. There was definitely comfort in the whole thing and we had a great time."

"But?" Travis asked. "I mean, obviously you didn't marry the guy and have his babies and become a farmer. So there has to be a but."

"There's a big but," she said with a nod. "I was called into the school counselor's office one day and she told me that I'd been chosen for an exchange program to France for the summer after my senior year. I had applied for it the year before but had been late turning in my paperwork because my mom had balked at the idea. But they'd been impressed with my application and had kept it. It was an all-expenses-paid trip that would go for three months and would get me six college credits. I was thrilled."

"And that was when you realized you loved crepes more than you loved Shawn," Travis interjected.

She shook her head. "When I told him, he proposed."

Travis frowned. "What?"

"Yep. I told him I wanted to go to France for three months and he dropped to one knee and pulled out a ring."

"What's that got to do with going to France?"

"He told me he wanted to get married that summer. So obviously I couldn't go."

"And you told him to shove his ring up his ass and that

185

you *might* marry him, *someday* down the road, after you did all the things you wanted to do," Travis said, his frown deepening. "Right?"

"Uh, no."

"You turned France down." He said it with clear disgust.

"Yep. He told me he couldn't handle me being gone. So I turned it down and started planning our wedding."

For some reason, Travis's sigh of disbelief made her feel better about telling the story. She felt like a fool when she thought back to that time and her decisions. But something about telling Travis made her feel lighter.

"This guy must have been something," Travis said grimly, "to make you give something like that up."

She shook her head. "It wasn't just him." It had felt like it was mostly him at the time, of course. She'd believed that she was madly, deeply in love with her soul mate. "It was *everything*. I was inundated. My family, his family, our friends. Everything in my life involved Shawn. It's hard to walk away from *everything*."

"But you did," Travis pointed out. He seemed to really like focusing on the fact that she and Shawn had clearly not worked out. "You did walk away."

She nodded. "It took me a while. I was then chosen by my teachers for a leadership camp over Spring Break. I was so flattered and it was only a week, so I agreed. But when Shawn found out, he didn't want me to go."

"Fucker," Travis muttered.

Lauren felt a surge of pleasure at his obvious displeasure. He was upset *for* her. That was…nice. It made her feel warm and protected and…like kissing him again. Of course, his *breathing* made her want to kiss him.

"I went anyway," she told Travis. It had been hard, especially when Shawn had yelled and then not spoken to her for the week prior to and during the camp.

"Good."

"And he cheated on me while I was gone."

Travis's eyebrows slammed together and she could feel the anger coming off of him. "Are you fucking kidding me?"

"Nope."

"So you kicked him in the nuts and got on a plane to Europe," he said.

She wished. "No. I did break up with him though." Or at least she'd tried.

"Good."

"And then I took him back."

Travis sighed.

"And then I decided that I needed some space and talked my sister into going to visit our dad for a few days." She paused. "And Shawn cheated again."

Travis was obviously gritting his teeth.

"But I took him back again," she said, still mad at herself and feeling particularly pathetic saying it out loud to Travis.

"Can we skip to the part where you finally dumped him for real? Or where he got hit by a bus? Or whatever finally happened to break you up for good?"

Lauren smiled. She was in the midst of telling her most embarrassing story, the thing that had shaped her life the most, the story she didn't even like to think about in the privacy of her own mind, and yet she was smiling.

Travis was so…outraged. She loved that.

"Well, he finally cheated again…when I was there, in town, two blocks away, planning our wedding," she said. "And I knew I couldn't do it. I had given everything up—my plans, things that made me feel good about myself, chances to do big, wonderful things—and he couldn't even give up fucking other girls."

"So you kicked him in the nuts and got on a plane?" Travis said, almost hopefully.

"Nope. I planned our wedding, sent my mother and

187

bridesmaids to the church, changed *out* of my wedding dress and got on a plane. For France. With the money I'd gotten from selling my engagement ring."

Travis looked at her for a few seconds. "You left him at the altar. In front of the whole town and all the people who thought he was so amazing."

"Yep."

Travis's grin grew slowly and finally he said, "That's my girl."

My girl. She liked that far more than she should.

Lauren cleared her throat. "I traveled around Europe that summer working in hostels, then I came back and started college. Suddenly, I was surrounded by people who really cared about my talents and brains."

"Your family *didn't?*"

"My talents and brains didn't matter much for the life that was mapped out for me in Longview," she said honestly. "But in college, I realized I could do anything. I studied in Paris for a semester, met Mason, did a trip to Haiti with one of my professors. Started changing the world."

"You've never gone back home?"

"Rarely. I fly them all out to visit me sometimes. We spent Christmas in Colorado one year and in Hawaii one year. I took them all to Disney World for my niece's birthday."

"And you fly your grandmother in for a spa treatment for her birthday each year," he added.

He'd remembered. She nodded.

"And you were right," he said. "That does make me like you even more."

She pulled in a deep breath. She hadn't realized it until that moment, but having Travis Bennett like her mattered.

"My mom and sister now live vicariously through me. They love the photos and stories of my travels. They are very proud of IAS and me and Mason. They've said several times how glad they are that I didn't end up stuck in Longview with Shawn."

"What's Shawn doing now?"

"The same stuff. He's married. Farming. They never go anywhere. He hangs out with the same guys he's always hung out with. He's...the same."

Travis was quiet for a moment. Then he muttered, "Like me."

Lauren pulled in a long breath. That was...true. Or it seemed true. But it also didn't seem fair at all to say that Travis was like Shawn in any way. He was so much...more.

But it didn't really make sense. Travis *was* like Shawn in many ways. He still lived in the same town he always had, he hung out with the same people he always had, he was living in the house he'd live in until he died and he was making a living doing something he would do until the day he died.

But here with Travis, at this moment, it felt wonderful. Right. Good. Admirable. Tempting.

Very tempting.

Just as it had with Shawn. In spite of his possessiveness and narrow thinking and cheating.

Dammit.

"Travis—"

"Let's not talk about that," he interrupted. "So you keep doing all of this because you want to prove to all of them that you're happy and made the right choice?"

"I am happy."

"Obviously. But if all of those people didn't have these expectations and weren't watching, would you still do it? The travel and stuff?"

"I feel like—" She swallowed and then laughed lightly. "I don't think I've ever been this open and honest with anyone other than Mason."

"Well, Mason isn't here," he snapped. "So talk."

She raised an eyebrow. "My mom and sister have things I don't. They have neighbors who bring them food when they're sick, people who notice when they're not in church on Sunday, who are almost as excited as they are when one of the kids gets a ribbon at the fair or when they get the lead in the school play. My sister has four kids and my mom never misses a ballgame or a recital or a program. They have pizza together every Friday and my mom and sister go for pedicures and margaritas once a month, and Corey helped Jim remodel their bathroom and…" She trailed off and sighed. "They have each other. No one is ever lonely. No one is ever stranded or stuck. Because they have each other."

"You could go back."

"It's not my home. It wouldn't be the same for me as it is for them. They have their roots and their history there. I feel like I gave up my chance at security and comfort and…family…and now I have to make it count."

"You can change, Lauren." Travis reached for her hand.

And even that mattered.

"People change," he went on. "You didn't want to be married to a guy who couldn't keep his pants zipped. That doesn't mean you can't ever want those things. That you can't have your adventures *and* the comfort. Everyone needs someone."

"And I have Mason and our work and the village and…"

"You can want more."

"I do want more."

And she couldn't believe she had just admitted that out loud. But now that she had, she wanted to go on. "I do want more. I want the community and the family. But I'm also afraid of what I will do to have it, what I'll compromise, what I'm willing to give up and change to have it. And then I'm afraid I'll regret it. I gave up things that really mattered to me before. And I took Shawn back after he cheated…just to have that comfort and sense of family."

"You don't have to give up and change everything."

"But I can't have it all."

"Why not?"

"Because no one can have it all. We all have to make sacrifices. And I'm willing. I'm *too* willing."

"You just need someone who understands you. Who understands what you do and that it's important to you and to the world."

Her heart thudded in her chest. That was what she needed. But even if Travis thought he understood…did he really? Would a guy who could trace his roots back five generations on one plot of land understand her need to make her mark on the *world*?

She didn't even always understand it. Why did she need to make sure that the people in Haiti were cared for or make sure that not just the US policy makers, but those in France and Germany and Russia and Egypt understood how to use their power to make things better worldwide? Why did she think she could make a difference anyway, and why couldn't she be content on a farm in Sapphire Falls?

Farming was noble work. What Travis and his family did mattered. Maybe on a smaller scale, but she knew better than anyone that those small pieces could combine into a big, beautiful picture. She couldn't do what she did without Travis and these people doing what they did. But even if she couldn't explain it, even if she couldn't go back and point at one moment that made her so passionate about the work she and Mason were doing, the passion was there and real and strong.

"I have someone like that," she finally said. "Mason."

"But Mason doesn't give you two orgasms in a row or make you scream on the edge of a kitchen table."

Her body heated and she nodded. "That's true."

"Has Mason *ever* done that?" Travis demanded. "With that genius brain of his, he's probably better in bed than most men too."

Lauren liked the jealous note in Travis's voice. Red flag.

"Maybe," she said. "But the first time we got naked together—"

"You *have* been naked with Mason?" Travis asked.

"Yes."

Travis looked to the sky. "Why did I ask?"

Lauren hid her smile. "We were—"

"I don't need details about how hung Mason Riley is or how seductive you find his ability to recite the periodic table backwards in Japanese."

"Mason doesn't speak Japanese and—"

"Tell me more about *not* sleeping with Mason," Travis said.

She smiled. She definitely liked him a little jealous.

"We were naked and kissing and I suddenly remembered I wanted to ask him something about a trip to Haiti. He was really interested and we started talking about it and just like that all the arousal and physical attraction was gone and we talked for an hour, naked, about Haiti."

"I hate Mason," Travis muttered.

"Why?"

"Mason matters to you. More than anyone. He gets you."

That sounded more than a little jealous. But she liked it too. Because Travis wasn't just jealous of the near-sex with Mason. He was jealous of the connection she had with her best friend. Did that mean Travis wanted a connection like that?

And if so…that would be terrible. It didn't *feel* terrible at the moment. It might not feel terrible for the next several moments. But it was. She knew that. On some level.

"Mason gets me," she agreed. "He's the only one to really understand what I do and fully support it."

Travis was quiet for a long time, and Lauren somehow

avoided looking at him. It was stupid to want him to want to know more, to get more involved in what she did and to believe in it. How did it matter at all that a farmer in Sapphire Falls, Nebraska, understood IAS and its impact? Or *her* impact on IAS? The farmers in Sapphire Falls were an important part of their growing program, but all that mattered was that they agreed to participate and understood that *they* were important. They didn't even really need to know Lauren's name.

But she wanted Travis to know. To understand.

"I can't decide if I should hug you or shake you," he finally admitted.

"What do you mean?"

"I mean, you're in love with my hometown whether you think you *should be* or not."

She couldn't respond right away. He wasn't wrong. "I gave all of this up," she finally said. "I had my chance."

"Well, you don't have to like the random acts of kindness, the strawberry festival and the nursing-home residents teaching the kindergartners ballroom dancing but—"

"The nursing-home residents teach the kindergartners ballroom dancing?" she repeated.

He nodded.

"Oh, my God," she groaned.

He shook his head and sighed. "I know, it's cute and silly."

"No," she was quick to respond. "I never said any of this is silly. It is, however, cute." So cute. And comforting. And just damned nice. What was wrong with having as much nice in her life as she could?

Travis went on. "No matter how cute or silly or crazy you think Sapphire Falls is, and no matter how many great foods and museums and dinner parties you experience, I bet you think about us when you're gone. I'll bet some night you'll be drinking wine in some fancy restaurant and you'll think about the taste of Booze. I'll bet you'll be sitting around a conference table in a meeting and you'll have the urge to tell some grumpy politician a stupid joke. I'll bet you'll be walking along a gorgeous beach and you'll think about sand volleyball. And I want you to remember something. Home isn't a place you never leave, it's just the place you always go back to."

Lauren couldn't swallow or speak for a moment. Emotions—and the distinct urge to cry like she did at the commercials that came out at Mother's Day—kept her from replying right away.

After Lauren could swallow past the lump of emotions in her throat, she asked, "So you're saying whenever I'm back, I can come have sex with you?"

"Yes. Absolutely. And hang out at the Come Again and watch volleyball and listen to country music at the river."

That all sounded very appealing. Too appealing.

"Are you asking me to stay?" she asked softly. She didn't know what she was going to say if he said yes. She couldn't stay. But she wasn't sure she could say no. She hadn't been able to when she was eighteen, but surely now—she was a grown woman. A strong, independent grown woman who knew what she wanted.

"No. But I am asking you to come back."

Air whooshed out of her as if someone had squeezed her lungs like a sponge. He *wasn't* asking her to stay but...coming back to him between trips sounded too tempting to say no to.

"What about Chicago?"

"Sapphire Falls has some things that Chicago doesn't. Things you need."

"Oh?"

Travis took the jar of Booze away from her and set it out of the way. "Let me show you." He moved to his back and pulled her down next to him. "Sleep out here with me tonight."

He wrapped his big arm around her and her breasts pressed into his rib cage, her nipples tingling and sending sparks through her body.

"Sleep outside? With the dirt and bugs and weather, huh?" she asked, snuggling in next to him anyway.

"If you think the sunsets are pretty here, you should see the sunrise."

"If you say so, Farmer Boy."

She shouldn't stay out here with him. She should leave and go back to Hailey's house right now before she found anything else to love around here.

Or *anyone*.

But she yawned and when Travis sandwiched her feet between his, she knew she wasn't going anywhere.

"If I end up with bug bites, *you're* putting the calamine lotion on me."

"I know a few places I hope get bit in that case." He pulled her up on top of his body and kissed her hot and hard on the mouth.

Then he proceeded to kiss her all of the places where a bug bite and calamine lotion would be *very* uncomfortable.

And then Lauren Davis spent the night in a truck bed with a farmer who called her darlin'—without the G.

That was the trifecta of red flags.

But she ignored every one of them and slept better than she had in years.

৩০৫৫

Damn, but the girl looked good in his sleeping bag in the back of his truck.

He might have made a mistake keeping her out here.

As they'd been talking last night, a crazy thought had occurred to him. Then, waking that morning next to her with the birds singing—literally—and the sun shining— also literally—the thought was as clear as the blue sky above.

He was falling for Lauren Davis.

Dammit. How had this happened? She was amazing, of course. That wasn't the surprise revelation. What *was* startling was how fast he'd gone from attracted to smitten.

Wanting her was one thing. And not new. Liking her, wanting to spend time with her, *understanding* her was definitely new, however.

And doomed for failure.

But when he'd asked her to come back to Sapphire Falls, to him, she hadn't said no. She hadn't said yes. But there had not been a hell no either. He was clinging to that at the moment.

"Hey, baby doll," he said softly, nudging the firm ass that was pressed against his hip.

No response.

She was lying on her side, facing away from him, her hands tucked up under her cheek. Her hair fanned out on his chest, her butt against his hip, his arm underneath her. Asleep.

He rolled toward her. "City." He leaned in to put his nose in her hair and breathed deep.

Her scent was familiar, her usual perfume faint, but she also smelled like fresh air and definitely sunshine.

He ran his other hand over her shoulder, down her arm, to her hip. He sensed a change in her breathing and realized she was waking. But she didn't make a sound. He grinned and pressed his hardening cock against her butt.

"I'll fuck you awake if that's what you're holding out for."

She moaned and pressed back hard on his erection.

"That's what I was hoping you'd say," he told her gruffly, rolling her to her back. "There is a lot of fresh air out here after all."

"And here I was thinking it must be the truck making me so horny."

Oh yeah, he was falling. For sure.

He covered her mouth with his, immediately stroking in deep and firm against her tongue, possessing her. And she let him, opening and accepting him, pressing back, making him even hotter and harder.

He'd thought ahead enough the night before to have several condoms lying under the edge of the foam mattress. He pulled one out and on within seconds and then skimmed his hand over her stomach and slid his middle finger into her heat while taking a nipple into his mouth and sucking hard.

He already knew that firm suction on her nipple made her hot and that she liked hard, deep, fast strokes—fingers or cock.

She was already wet and immediately began writhing against him. "Travis."

"You want me to get you off first or just take you now?" he asked against her breast.

"Now."

He lifted his head and kept moving his hand. She looked wild and free, bare naked in his truck, her hair spilling around her, the sun shining on every gorgeous inch and she arched and squirmed. "You sure?"

She nodded. "Inside me. Now," she gasped.

He moved into position and thrust before she could even take another breath.

It was as if he'd been without her for years. His body craved hers even as he was buried as deep as he could go.

"Damn, Lauren," he muttered, thrusting deep and hard and fast, unable to go slow. "I need you so damned much."

She tipped her pelvis and wrapped her legs and arms around him. He slid deeper and they both shuddered.

He pumped hard, wanting to touch her everywhere at once, wanting to imprint himself on every inch of her. He wanted this to go with her when she left. He wanted this to bring her back. He couldn't keep her. He couldn't make her stay. He wouldn't even try. But he would be here when she returned, and he would do his damnedest to be whatever she needed in the time she was here.

And how that had happened so fast, he had no idea.

CHAPTER NINE

After they'd recovered, he sat up. "We have a little time before we have to be in town. I'll make you breakfast."

She pushed her hair back from her face. "And I need a shower."

"Showering before the mud run doesn't make a lot of sense, does it?" He pushed to his feet and waited for her to get up so he could reroll their bedding.

"Before the what run?" she asked.

"Mud run."

"Mud."

He grinned. "Run."

She looked really, really good naked. Even with one hand on her hip. "What the hell is a mud run?"

"It's a five K charity run. It's part of the festival."

"Of course it is."

She stepped off the mattress and sleeping bag so he could bundle them up.

"Don't any of you people work during the day?"

He pulled on his shorts and shirt from the night before and stored everything back behind the seat of his truck. "That's the thing about corn, baby doll. It kind of grows whether you're there or not."

"Right."

He laughed. "We take extra time off around festival time. Yes, we typically work during the day."

"I'm going to take a wild guess and say that this five K run happens in the mud," she said as she pulled on her clothes as well.

"That it does. There's mud, water, more mud, a few obstacles and more mud," Travis confirmed.

"More mud," she repeated. "More getting dirty."

He laughed. "And then everyone heads to the river to clean up."

She arched a brow. "Skinny dipping?"

He shook his head. "Not quite that much fun, but a lot of splashing around."

"In the river."

"Yes."

"River water is dirty."

"Well, river water is cleaner than mud."

"Right."

He climbed up into the truck. She did the same.

"Tell you what, City," he said, starting the truck and heading down the narrow path that led back to the main road. "You run in the mud run with me and I'll do something you want to do tonight."

She looked over at him. "You want to do those things too."

He laughed. "Darlin', I'm not gonna complain if you want to spend the whole time naked. But I wasn't talking about sex, actually."

"What did you have in mind?"

"Whatever you want. Something you like to do that would be unusual for me…like the mud run is for you."

He glanced over to find her watching him thoughtfully. "Really? Anything?"

"Sure, why not? You've been doing all this Sapphire Falls stuff."

"That was part of the plan to make me like it here *less*."

Travis shifted on his seat. That had been the plan all right. And he'd been doing his part. He'd been showing her real life in Sapphire Falls. Just because she didn't seem all that turned off yet didn't mean he'd been shirking his responsibility. Even if he had been more recently thinking about the things he could do to make her like it here *more*.

"But this might work," she went on.

"It might?"

"Well, maybe I should give you a taste of *my* life. Show us both that we're not a good fit since this Sapphire Falls thing isn't working."

So she was thinking about them fitting. Interesting. "Um, what does that entail exactly?"

"You'll see," she said, seeming very pleased with whatever was going through her head.

They pulled into Travis's drive. Three dogs came running, thrilled to see humans again.

"Let me get them quieted down before you get out," he said, opening the door.

"I'm fine." Lauren pushed her door open and got out.

Luna was the first in line to greet her.

"Good girl," Lauren told her.

Luna panted lovingly, looking up at Lauren with clear adoration, but her paws didn't leave the ground. Lauren rubbed the dog's head, then behind her ears, then on the spot just above her nose. Luna's bliss was clear.

Tank stood to the side, his tongue hanging out. He woofed at Lauren happily and wiggled all over, but he also stayed down.

"Good boy," Lauren praised.

Then she surprised them all by dropping to her knees. "*This*," she said to them. "Is *not* Donna Karan. So come here." She patted her thighs.

They both came forward eagerly. Luna bumped Lauren's arm with her head while Tank climbed right up into her lap. She rubbed their heads and accepted their kisses and laughed and talked sweetly to them.

She looked over to where Nellie stood next to Travis, his hand on her head.

"So Nellie's yours, huh?" Lauren asked.

"Is it that obvious?"

"Luna and Tank like you, but Nellie loves you," Lauren said. "She'd rather be with you than get the new girl's attention."

"She wants to lick you badly," he said. And so did he. He would have never believed that watching a woman play with dogs would be an aphrodisiac, but he was raring to strip her naked and do her up against his truck.

"And Luna and Tank are Tucker's?"

"How did you know?"

"You're trying to drive me away and Tucker would do anything for you. Come here, Nellie." Lauren reached her hand out toward his dog.

Travis lifted his hand from Nellie's head and she trotted forward. She nudged Lauren's hand and then licked it. She moved in closer and Lauren rubbed behind her ears and let Nellie lick her cheek.

"You like dogs."

"Of course. But I also like my Donna Karan skirts."

Seeing a softer side of Lauren with any dog made him want her. Seeing her with *his* dog made her unable to resist.

"Nellie, go inside," he ordered.

Lauren let her go and got to her feet, signaling to the dogs that the snuggling was over.

Nellie turned and trotted toward the garage door that he kept partially raised for her.

"Luna, Tank, come," he said.

The dogs really liked Lauren. But they listened to him. They came to his side and he patted them both for their obedience and then pointed to the garage. "Inside."

They headed for the garage as well.

"You sure can be bossy," Lauren said breathlessly.

He strode toward her. "Yep."

"I kind of like it."

"I know." He pushed her up against the side of his truck.

"Right here?"

"Right now."

He stripped her T-shirt off, tossed her bra away, slipped her shorts off, lost her panties in the rose bushes and repeated the same actions with his clothes.

They'd done this. Repeatedly. On his table, in his

shower, in his truck—twice. And he'd never get enough.

A minute later, he donned a condom, lifted her against the side of his Chevy and thrust deep.

It was short and sweet and hot and they both came hard.

She was still sweaty and breathing hard when she said, "It's gotta be the truck."

He let her legs drop to the ground and pushed himself away from her.

"Let's go in the house. I have several surfaces that will prove that theory wrong."

"You have a mud run."

"*We* have a mud run."

"I'm not running in the mud, Travis."

"It'll be fun."

"You know what?" She tipped her head and looked up at him. "You're probably right. Everything else I've expected to hate has turned out fun. Which means I *shouldn't* do it."

Oh yeah. Dammit.

"Well—"

"But while you're off getting dirty again, I'm going to make a few calls."

She looked excited and sly at the same time. He worked on not looking worried. "About plans for tonight?"

She nodded. "Plans for your introduction into my world."

Yeah, that's what he'd been afraid of. "You need to *plan* it?"

She nodded again.

"Great, well then…" He looked down at his clothes. He was actually dressed fine for the run. "Go make your calls. I'm gonna check on a couple of things in the barn."

Travis headed for the barn, his gut knotted for reasons he didn't want to analyze. But he couldn't keep from analyzing every single one.

He was falling for Lauren Davis. In the span of two

days. And she was still the last woman he'd ever take to dinner at his grandmother's house.

Maybe that was the answer. He'd take her for a family dinner. That would convince him, and Lauren for that matter, that this could never go anywhere.

He climbed on his four-wheeler and headed out into the pasture. Travis had more corn than livestock, while his brother T.J. had more animals than crops, but Travis still had a few cows he kept. One was pregnant, and he'd been waiting for her to calve for a couple of days.

He found the cow in the north corner of the pasture, still pregnant. Which meant another trip out here tonight. "You just have to be difficult, don't ya?" he asked her.

She just blinked at him lazily from where she was lying in the grass.

He sighed. He should bring Lauren out here to check out the baby calf when he or she finally showed up. That was definitely not a typical occurrence in a day in the life of Lauren Davis. Of course, just when he thought he knew how she'd respond to something, she surprised him. She'd probably find the whole messy process fascinating. As long as she wasn't wearing designer clothes.

He gripped the handles hard as he rode back to the barn. She might surprise him at times, but he knew her. Which also surprised him. She was looking for a place that could be a home. She'd left hers and felt compelled to keep going, to not go back, to not admit that she still wanted some of that.

Not the unsupportive, cheating bastard boyfriend of course. Travis tightened his hold on the handle grips. He wanted to punch that guy. Because of him, Lauren felt like wanting a home, wanting a place to belong, was settling.

He avoided going back into the house after checking the cows. Instead, he got into his truck—not without lots of hot, sweet memories from the night before bombarding him all the way to town—and headed for the mud run.

"Where have you been?" Tucker asked the moment Travis stepped to the starting line.

"Out."

"All night?"

"Yep."

"Alone?"

"No."

Tucker chuckled. "You're in trouble."

"No shit."

The starting gun fired and they took off. Travis worked out his pent-up frustrations—or whatever they were—on the huge mud puddles, climbing wall, fallen logs and more mud puddles. Beating his brother felt good.

He was tired when they were done. And covered in mud from head to toe.

And still twisted up over Lauren.

As he floated down the river in an inner tube tied to the back of Tucker's party barge, he looked around. This was home. The guys and girls on the barge and in the other inner tubes were his friends and family. The beer in his hand was ice cold, the sun overhead hot, the scenery familiar and comforting and beautiful. This was what he loved, what he wanted.

And he missed Lauren.

It had been two hours since he'd last seen her, and he missed her.

He sighed.

"You really are in trouble, huh?" Tucker asked from the inner tube floating alongside Travis's.

Travis nodded and drank. "I really think I am."

"Because you had great sex with a woman who hates everything you love?"

Travis looked over at his brother. That sounded like a good reason he might be in trouble. At least that reason made sense. But the problem was it wasn't that easy. "She doesn't hate it here," he said. "In fact, in spite of my best efforts, she likes it here."

Tucker nodded and took a long drink from his bottle. "So problem solved. She likes it here, she stays and you live happily ever after."

Travis chuckled. That also sounded reasonable. If only it could be that easy. "She can't stay."

"You mean she *won't* stay."

"No, she *can't*," Travis said. "Well, okay, maybe she *won't* either." It wasn't like he'd asked her. "She's tempted though." That he knew for sure. And that idea made warmth spread through him that was surprising in its intensity. "But even if she wanted to stay, I wouldn't let her."

Tucker laughed at that. "I don't think anybody *lets* Dr. D do anything."

Of course not. "Well, she can't stay. The world needs her. She's got big stuff going on."

"And you're just fine right here."

He was. He was just fine.

And suddenly that didn't feel quite as good as it used to.

"You don't think I could make it in Chicago? Or Paris? Or Haiti?"

Tucker snorted.

"What's that mean?" Travis asked with a frown.

"Of course you *could*," Tucker said. "But why would you want to? You've got it all right here."

He'd thought so too. Right up until he'd spilled grape slushy on Lauren Davis. "I could travel."

"Hey, I'm not sayin' anything bad here," Tucker told him. "You're content. You're like the most *satisfied* guy I know. You know exactly what you want and what you don't."

He did. He really did. Dammit. "I've just been thinking…" He trailed off because he didn't really know exactly what he'd been thinking.

"I know," Tucker said sincerely, as if he felt sorry for Travis. "She's hot and she's been all these cool places. But you know where you belong and you know where she belongs. And it might not be together. Even if the sex is amazing."

Of course he was right. But his words made Travis's stomach cramp.

"The thing is, she's made me think about things *here* differently. I mean, things I've always taken for granted are even better now."

"So you definitely don't want to leave. Showing her all about life here has made you love being here even more." Tucker nodded. "That's cool."

"But she's gonna leave."

"Well, yeah." Then Tucker's eyes went wide. "You've been hanging out with her for like two days, man. No way has she changed your mind *that* much."

"Well, it wouldn't *hurt* me to experience some new things, would it?"

"I don't know. Maybe not. But there's nothing wrong with being happy with what you've got. You don't always have to want more."

"She wants me to have a taste of her life. Since I've shown her mine, she wants to show me hers."

Tucker, predictably, grinned at Travis's choice of words. "I s'pose there's nothin' wrong with that."

"Tonight."

"I thought you saw hers last night?"

"She has a whole night in her life planned tonight." He wasn't nervous about it. Exactly.

"What's that mean?" Tucker asked.

"I'm thinking maybe she's going to cook some strange food or something. Or maybe show me scrapbooks from Haiti. Or make me watch some foreign film."

Tucker had looked skeptical at the mention of strange food, and by the time Travis got to foreign film Tucker was

207

outright grimacing.

"Sounds like fun."

Travis knew that it did not sound like fun.

"Sushi won't kill me."

"She's making you sushi?"

He had no idea. "Well, she's not making me pot roast." That he was sure of.

"You won't like sushi."

"How do you know?" No way had Tucker ever eaten sushi.

"Sushi isn't steak," Tucker said. Then he paused. "Is it?"

Travis shook his head. "No."

"What is it?"

He was pretty sure it was fish. And some other things. "Not steak." That was kind of the important part.

"Or chicken?" Tucker asked.

"I don't think so."

"Well, good luck with that."

Yeah. Luck. *That* was what he needed.

৽৽৻ঽ

"Sasha, it's me."

Lauren had a list in hand of all the ingredients she needed her assistant to gather and overnight ship to Sapphire Falls for the big, exotic dinner she had planned for Travis the next night.

Tonight she'd have to come up with something else to give him a taste of her world, but…

"Oh, thank *God*!" Sasha exclaimed. "Where have you been? No, never mind. No time. I put you down for a plus one. Your flight leaves Omaha at four. That gets you here in time to dress and get to the dinner at eight. Michael is working up the talking points and Carrie thinks she can get you at the vice president's table. But we're debating about if that's really where you should be. Joe mentioned that getting you with Senator Andrews might be better."

Lauren knew her mouth was hanging open. She was staring at the daisies embroidered on the corner of Travis's dish towel without really seeing them. Sasha hadn't even paused for a breath.

"Mason and the team are back in Port-au-Prince. Stephen is in the hospital but isn't critical. Nadia's already been released and Mason refused treatment. Big surprise," Sasha muttered. "You need to talk to him on the way to the airport. He's been trying to reach you as well."

Lauren's mind was whirling. "Sasha!" she said loudly. "What the hell are you talking about?"

There was a long pause on Sasha's end of the phone.

"Sasha? Are you there? What's going on?" Lauren's adrenaline had started pumping even before she fully made sense out of Sasha's words. Something big was happening. Hospitals were involved. *Mason* was involved. And she had a flight and a dinner in her near future.

"Did you get *any* of my messages?" Sasha finally asked.

"No." Lauren had noticed that she had several missed calls and voice mails but she'd intended to return them after she'd given Sasha her shopping instructions. "Start at the beginning."

"A group of farmers from another village stormed Plaines Paisible this morning. They are demanding more aid in *their* village and aren't leaving Plaines Paisible until someone accompanies them back to their village with equipment and supplies. They came in with weapons and staked out in the primary field and took our equipment hostage."

"Oh, my God." Lauren made it to the kitchen table and plopped into a chair.

"Most of the villagers and our team escaped. Stephen tried to save some of our stuff and ended up shot in the leg.

Nadia got into it with one of their leaders and got hit in the face. They broke her nose but she's okay. Mason has a least a couple of broken ribs but apparently managed to get one of their weapons away."

Lauren closed her eyes as her stomach roiled. Her team, her *best friend*, had been in danger. They could have been killed. One of them had been *shot*. And Mason had wrestled with someone with a gun? All while she'd been fucking around in the back of Travis's truck.

She rubbed her forehead. She had to keep it together. "Now what?"

"Our team is refusing to leave Haiti."

Lauren wasn't surprised to hear that.

"Mason is working with the leaders of the aid organizations to give these people what they want and to get our stuff back, but Outreach America is demanding help and protection from the government before they're willing to go back in. The Haitian leaders are hesitant so Outreach America has contacted the White House."

Well, this was a fucking mess. Outreach American was the primary organization at work in Haiti with Mason and Lauren's company. They were responsible for getting IAS involved and into Haiti in the first place. The White House, however, had been involved from the beginning. They'd worked with the Haitian government to get Outreach America into the poorer villages and had helped with translators and local liaisons. It was mostly for the good PR the project brought to the White House, but it had been beneficial having their backing. If Outreach America was spooked, the White House would listen. And would very likely overreact.

"What's in the works?" Lauren asked.

Whether she had been reachable or not, she knew her team would have been putting a plan together. She would have to give final approval, but she was sure many pieces were already in place. It was ten in the morning in Sapphire

Falls, eleven a.m. in Haiti. She was sure balls were rolling.

"I've talked to Joe several times," Sasha said. "He told me to give you another hour and then he'd come and find you."

Lauren sighed. Joe could have tried, but he probably wouldn't have found her and Travis and the truck. Which was good. She was embarrassed enough just in her own mind when she thought about what she'd been doing while her best friend and team members were under attack.

She felt like an idiot.

She needed to be on call, available, twenty-four-seven. It wasn't like local village invasions happened a lot or that there were team members in the hospital on a regular basis. It wasn't like her phone rang non-stop. But she and Mason needed to be reachable at any time. Everyone who worked for them believed in what IAS was doing, everyone would pull together, do their part, make it work. But Lauren and Mason were the heart and soul. They had to be there.

"What does Joe want to do?" Lauren asked. When it came to PR and government relationships, she trusted Joe completely.

"You and him at the dinner tonight, doing some damage control, calming things down. We can't have anyone sending troops in. That would be a disaster."

Lauren agreed one hundred percent. Troops marching in where people had already acted desperately would not end well.

"What's the dinner?"

"Senator Atkin's birthday party. Black tie. Eight o'clock. Joe will be your plus one. I emailed you the flight information. I'll meet you at the airport and I'll send Jen out to get a dress."

Lauren really, really loved Sasha. She and Mason had long ago made the decision to keep a condo in DC for their frequent trips and stays. Sasha kept the place stocked with anything they needed, when they needed it. Including evening gowns, when the occasion called for it.

"We'll have to send Phoebe more chocolate-covered strawberries for borrowing Joe again," Lauren said lightly.

Phoebe occasionally accompanied Joe to the black tie DC events. She loved flying first class and staying in the high-rent condo and playing dress-up for a night here and there. But more often she told Joe to go ahead and she'd see him when he got back to Sapphire Falls. Joe was there for work and spent most of his evening in boring-to-Phoebe political discussions or talking to the media or giving interviews about IAS and their work.

Phoebe liked to pout and act put out about Lauren always being by Joe's side in photographs. Mostly because she liked the don't-worry-I-don't-want-your-fiancé gifts Lauren sent.

"I'll put that on the to-do list," Sasha said.

"So I need to talk Senator Andrews and or the vice president *out of* helping Outreach America with military support," Lauren summarized.

"Basically."

"And then I'm guessing I need to get my butt down to Haiti."

"I don't think we should leave the situation in Mason's hands," Sasha agreed. "You'll need to meet with Outreach America and then with the village leadership."

And very possibly with the leadership of the group that had taken over Plaines Paisible.

That was what she did, that was what she primarily brought to the table for IAS. She was fantastic with people, a skilled negotiator, and she had a way of smoothing almost any situation over.

The fog that had filled her head with the rapid-fire news of that morning's events began to fade and her focus returned. She knew what she had to do.

She had to get to Omaha, a two-hour drive from Sapphire Falls, get on a plane to DC and to the dinner. That was her first step.

"Try to get something in green," she told Sasha. "Floor length. And I'll need a hair appointment."

"I'll see if Heather can meet us at the condo," Sasha said.

"Thanks. See you soon."

They disconnected and Lauren took a deep breath. Possibly her first since dialing Sasha's number.

As the haziness faded, she became aware of her surroundings again. She was in Travis's kitchen. Travis Bennett. The man she'd been having sex with in the bed of his truck while her best friend and their employees had been shot at and essentially robbed.

Mason had put up a fight, but at least he was smart enough to get out without more damage. The loss of their supplies sucked, but everyone was alive. And once Lauren got over there, she could get their stuff back. If she could keep the vice president from getting involved and get there in time to talk to the heads of the organizations and come to some kind of agreement that would help everyone…

She looked around again. She was getting distracted. She had to pack her stuff here. And get to her car. And tell everyone what was going on. Clearly Phoebe knew. Adrianne would too. Lauren sucked in a quick breath at the thought of Mason's pregnant wife. Adrianne was her friend too. Was Adrianne okay? Obviously she'd be worried. Was she keeping calm? She couldn't let this get her all worked up with the baby and her history of heart issues. Lauren stood and started pacing. She would need to be sure Adrianne was all right. It was good Phoebe was staying here. She could keep track of Adrianne. But Lauren needed to get Mason back here to Sapphire Falls ASAP. He needed to be with his wife. And no doubt he was pissed. Pissed that someone would interrupt his work. Pissed that someone would take his stuff. Pissed that someone would threaten any member of his team.

And when Mason Riley got pissed, he said unfortunate things that pissed everyone else off.

He could easily turn this into a major international incident.

Lauren really needed to get to Haiti. Even more, she needed to get Mason *out* of Haiti. For his safety…and the safety of the whole project.

She lifted her phone to dial just as it rang.

It was Mason.

"Mason."

"Where the hell have you been?"

Apparently, some of her missed voice messages were from him. "Out. Sorry."

"All night?"

She couldn't help but raise an eyebrow at that—Mason was rarely protective or parental toward her. "Yes, all night."

"With Travis?"

"Ye—hey, how did you know that?"

"Adrianne."

Of course. "You've talked to her. Did you tell her about your broken ribs and that you refused treatment?"

"They're not broken. Bruised. I'm fine."

And he probably was. Mason knew things about things that astonished Lauren even after all of these years. He'd probably self-examined and determined the proper diagnosis within minutes.

"What *does* she know?"

"That we've evacuated Plaines Paisible and that this is fucking everything up."

Yep, he was pissed. Not scared, not worried, not stressed. Just pissed. That was Mason.

"And nice deflection, by the way," he said.

She sighed. "Okay. Yes, I was out all night with Travis," she said. "I'm sorry. I didn't realize that the one night I left my phone behind would be the night all hell would break loose."

She heard his deep breath. Dammit. She was trying really hard not to feel guilty and to not freak out. Once she was on the plane to DC, she'd feel better. She'd be *doing* something. But right now she felt pretty helpless.

And guilty.

It figured that the night she let herself get distracted by a hot country boy would be the night her friend and her team needed her.

"I need you here," Mason said.

And to think she'd been considering talking to him about her cutting her trip short next month. "I know."

"Sooner versus later."

She had to admit that it was endearing how aware Mason was of his weaknesses. He knew he wasn't the best at negotiations or keeping his temper in check. He had a single-minded focus when it came to work, and when things got in his way, especially things he felt were superficial—like politics and looking good for the media— he lost his cool.

This village invasion by a local group of farmers who simply wanted some of the help for *their* families—not militia, not an environmental or social group protesting their work—would make him crazy. All the farmers would have had to have done was calmly asked if Outreach America or IAS could help them. Mason would have likely hiked to their village and started planting their fields himself. But because they'd come in with guns blazing— literally—now Mason was pissed.

And probably on the verge of making things worse.

"I have a dinner tonight. The VP and Senator Andrews."

Mason would know what that meant.

"Okay. We'll stay in Port-au-Prince until you get here."

"You should come home," she told him.

"Don't overreact. If we can get back in there in the next

few days, we can salvage the project. I've got stuff to finish."

"Seriously, Mason. If things are volatile, we shouldn't both be there."

They'd made that morose decision together a few years ago. They couldn't both be somewhere if there was a risk. One of them had to survive for the company.

"I'm not leaving until you're here. We'll talk about it then," he said firmly.

She knew it was pointless to argue with him over the phone. She was a much better debater in person.

"Fine. I'll be there tomorrow."

"What about Travis? Ad says—"

"It's nothing," Lauren said quickly.

Lord. Travis. What was she going to do about him? Nothing. There was nothing to do. They'd been hanging out and screwing for two days. Big deal.

Yes, it had been fun. Yes, she'd started to fall under the Sapphire Falls spell. Yes, she felt closer to Travis than she had to anyone in a long time.

But it had been two days.

And now she had to go to DC. And Haiti. And save her best friend and their biggest international project.

"You're sure?" Mason asked, his tone telling her that *he* wasn't so sure.

"It was a…diversion…a few days of fun while I was stuck here."

"Travis is a good guy."

"The world is full of good guys."

"Uh huh."

Mason knew her too well.

"Okay, it was a little more than fun. But really, Mason, it's been two days. And it's me and *Travis*. How serious could it be?"

"And you're not even going to try to find that out?"

"I have to be on a plane in a few hours, Mason."

"You're not *moving* here," he said. "You'll come, you'll fix it all up and then you can go back to Sapphire Falls and your knock-off Uggs."

She rolled her eyes. "Adrianne told you about the boots?"

"She sent me a picture," Mason said. "It looked suspiciously like you were sitting on that patio at the Come Again watching a sand volleyball game."

"I was...coerced."

Mason snorted. "She also told me about your plan to hate Sapphire Falls."

"I don't want to *hate* Sapphire Falls!" she snapped. "I wish everyone would stop saying that."

"Well, that's a good thing," he said agreeably. "Because no one expected to dislike Sapphire Falls more than I did, and look at me now."

Mason was in the running for Citizen of the Year. He was neck and neck with Joe Spencer, as a matter a fact, another big-city transplant to the tiny town with the hooks that sank deep and pulled unsuspecting visitors in fast.

"Yeah, yeah." Mason would love the idea of Lauren going to Bennett family dinners and serving on the festival board and tending a bunch of chickens.

Well, maybe not the chickens. But the rest, definitely. He would also love to know that Travis had pegged her already—she wanted a home, a family, a more stable place to belong. But she was afraid of what she had to do, or give up, to have it.

Travis was fine. Happy. Settled. Just like Shawn had been. There was no risk for him. If she didn't work out, didn't stay, didn't go along with whatever he wanted, there was always another girl, another option able to fit into her spot.

He wouldn't be giving anything up. He wouldn't be making any kind of sacrifice for them to be together. There was nothing for him to regret if things fell apart. He'd move on no problem, because his life wouldn't have really changed.

Suddenly, frantic barking erupted from the front yard. She swung in that direction and started for the living room. "I have to go. I'll call you from the plane. Don't do anything stupid." And she hung up.

She looked out the windows but didn't see Travis's truck. Or anything else that might have excited the dogs.

But they were still barking. And growling.

Lauren stepped out onto the front porch. She immediately saw Luna and Nellie, but Tank wasn't with them.

The girls were focused on something around the corner of the house. The fur on the backs of their necks was standing up and they looked equally angry and nervous.

The hair on the back of Lauren's neck stood up too.

Dammit. This wasn't good. She could feel it.

She inched to the edge of the porch and leaned on the wooden railing, peering around the side of the house.

Fuck.

Tank was there. Crowded up against the house, growling...and being stalked by a mountain lion.

A mountain lion.

Holy shit.

Lauren knew that it wasn't uncommon for people in this part of the state to see the big cats. They'd been reproducing steadily after being extinct from the area for decades. But dammit.

Poor Tank.

She glanced at Luna and Nellie.

Dammit again. They were definitely getting ready for a fight. The cat was several feet from Tank but the dog didn't have much of an escape route. Lauren knew the girls would try to help their friend. They were hunting dogs. They were tough.

She was going to have to intervene. And there was

really only one way to do that.

She spun and headed into the house. Like all good farm boys who liked to hunt, Travis had a gun rack in the back mud room off the kitchen. On the rack hung four shotguns.

But, since Travis was a responsible gun owner, none of them were loaded and the case with the ammunition was locked.

Dammit.

She went back into the kitchen, her heart pumping hard. She was already on adrenaline overload after the phone call from Sasha and the conversation with Mason. She had enough to worry about. She couldn't have one of Travis or Tucker's dogs getting hurt or killed, and she couldn't just let the wild cat roam the farm. There were other animals to think about too.

She looked around, trying to figure out where Travis might keep the key for the case. Her gaze swept past and then came back to rest on the four hooks hanging on the side of the fridge. They held keys. Lots of them. But she quickly located two that were small enough to belong to the lock on the case. She grabbed them and was back in the mud room within a minute. The first key she tried worked.

It had been years, but loading a shotgun was, evidently, like riding a bike.

Shotgun loaded, adrenaline coursing, she made herself walk calmly back to the front of the house. She did, however, kick the door open and stride out onto the porch like a badass.

She'd always liked guns.

She stepped onto the grass. "Luna, Nellie, come," she said firmly.

The dogs did not want to obey. They hesitated and growled deeper. Nellie bared her teeth. Luna took a step forward toward the cat, who was inching closer to Tank.

Lauren took a deep breath. "Luna, Nellie, *come*," she repeated.

She needed them out of the way. She'd been a good shot at one point, but it had been a long time.

The girls obeyed but were clearly not happy about it.

Once she was between them and the cat, she called to Tank. "Tank, come." The dog was about twenty feet from her. He whimpered but didn't move.

Tank was not a badass.

Fine.

Lauren pointed the gun skyward and shot into the air, hoping to run the cat off.

Both animals jumped, but rather than running away from the sound, the cat suddenly lunged at Tank.

"No!" Lauren shouted and, purely by instinct, pointed the gun and shot.

The bullet hit the dirt just two inches from the cat's paw. Lauren couldn't have made that shot if she'd tried.

The cat turned and fled.

And Tank ran to Lauren like his tail was on fire.

She knelt and laid the gun beside her, pulling the dog into her body.

"Jesus, I don't know if I'm more pissed off or turned on."

Lauren spun and fell over onto her butt as Travis bent and retrieved the gun from the dirt.

Tank took the opportunity to give her a big thank-you kiss right across the mouth and Luna and Nellie came running for reassurance and love as well.

Patting and cooing to the dogs, Lauren got back on her feet. But she was covered in dirt and dog slobber now.

"Pissed off or turned on?" she finally repeated.

"Yes. You know how to shoot a shotgun?" Travis asked.

"Yes."

"And you loaded it yourself."

"Yes."

"Seriously."

"Yes."

"And you did it to save the dogs."

"Yes."

He just looked at her.

She tucked her hair behind her ear and looked back at him.

"I'm seriously torn between wanting to shake you and wanting to fuck you."

Heat flooded through her. Lord, between the endorphins and the adrenaline she might never sleep again.

"I'm only going to let you do one of those things, you know," she said. She knew that his urge to shake her came from concern though, and she appreciated that.

He didn't say anything to that. Several seconds ticked by.

"You could have shot my dog. Or my living room window. Or *yourself.*"

"Hey, I know what I'm doing."

He pushed a hand through his hair and muttered, "Jesus," again.

Finally, he asked, "I suppose you know how to use a calf puller too?"

She laughed and shook her head. "I have only a very faint idea what that even is."

"I have a pregnant cow that's having some trouble. I need to get out and help her."

"You were out in the pasture?"

He wasn't covered in mud so she assumed he'd been to the river with his friends. A part of her wished she could go float on an inner tube in the river after all. Her job was more exciting…but sometimes it was *too* exciting.

"I drove through to check on her on the way back."

"You need my help?"

He looked her up and down. She was still dressed in her clothes from last night…and that morning. She hadn't showered or changed or even looked in a mirror.

She wasn't so sure she wanted to look in a mirror at this point.

"If you don't mind gettin' a little dirty."

She gave him a little smile. "I seem to be getting better at it."

And in a few hours she was going to be as *un*-dirty as she could get. In heels and an evening gown, full hair and makeup, the whole nine yards.

Suddenly, getting dirty one more time with Travis—whatever that entailed—was strangely appealing.

"Okay, City, let's go."

He unloaded the shotgun and tucked the shells in his front pocket before propping the gun on his shoulder. "Come on," he said to the dogs and got them safely into the garage with water and food so that they didn't have to worry about the cat coming back while they were gone. Then he stored the gun on the rack in his truck and slid in behind the wheel.

On the way out to the pasture, he called someone and told them about the mountain lion at his place.

"DNR," he told her as he disconnected. "They'll come out and try to find and trap him. Take him away from the farm."

Department of Natural Resources. The same people who would have probably been mad at her if she'd actually shot the thing. There was a hunting season in Nebraska, but June wasn't it.

"Great."

They pulled up in the north pasture a few minutes later.

Sure enough, there was a very pregnant cow, lying on her side.

She didn't look good.

"So I don't really *love* cows," Lauren said.

"You don't have to love her."

"I *do* really love filet mignon."

Travis chuckled and opened his door. "I won't tell her."

Lauren followed. Trepidation. That was absolutely what she was feeling. The cow was *big*. And not just the pregnant part of her. But when she lifted her head and lowed at them, Lauren's gut tightened. The cow had big round eyes that were filled with fear and hope. Though *that* was probably really stupid. A cow couldn't feel hope. Could she?

The cow made another mournful mooing sound and Lauren sighed.

She was well on her way to never eating red meat again.

Dammit.

"So, pulling a calf..." Lauren said, trailing off so Travis would fill her in.

"The calf is breach," he said. "They're supposed to come out front legs first and then the head. This one's head is first and the legs are tucked under. We're going to have to fix the position and then do some pulling."

Lauren looked at the cow, then at Travis, then down at her clothes, including her Duggs.

A week ago, she never would have believed any of this was even a tiny possibility. But now, all of sudden, she really liked these boots and realized that she was never going to be able to wear them again.

"Okay, tell me what to do."

"Well, you can help me get gloved and lubed."

"You country boys are sure into some weird stuff," she said, paraphrasing the words he'd said to her only a few days ago. Even though it felt like years in some ways.

She took the gloves from him.

"And we're just gettin' started," he said with a wink.

She held them as he slipped his hands into them. Then she squeezed a generous amount of lubricating gel onto his hands.

"Okay, you'll need gloves too," he said, indicating another pair on the tailgate.

Lauren was again struck by the incredible contrast between this and what she was going to be doing in a few hours. She was going to be shaking hands with senators, and hopefully, the Vice President of the United States with these hands. They'd never believe what she'd been up to prior to the dinner. She grinned and pulled the gloves on. She turned to find Travis kneeling behind the cow, about to slide his hand into places Lauren never wanted to *think* about, not to mention see.

"Seriously?'

"How did you think we were going to do this?" he asked.

He started to probe the area and the cow gave a low moo.

"I know but…this could ruin our sex life."

Of course, her being in Haiti was going to ruin their sex life anyway.

"Nah, I'm going to bring new life into the world. I'm gonna be a damned hero," he said. He slid his hand into the cow. "You're gonna want me even more."

Lauren swallowed hard. She could never un-see this.

"Okay, I have to push him back a bit," Travis said, almost as if he was talking to himself. "Then I need to get the legs up in front of the head. Come here."

Oh, hell no.

"I don't really think—"

The cow gave a long low moo that sounded downright desperate.

"Oh, all right," she muttered. The poor thing was giving birth and things weren't going well. She was hurting. She needed help. The least Lauren could do was try.

She knelt next to Travis. "What do I do?"

"Reach in here."

As much as she would have liked to think he was kidding, it was clear he wasn't. He had both of his hands in position and he indicated that she should reach in between his hands.

She closed her eyes and did it.

She grimaced, but she did it.

"Now what?"

"Feel for the hooves."

Sure. She'd just feel around for... "Oh, hooves! I've got them." There wasn't anything else that could be.

"Okay, grab them tightly and pull them forward."

She did it. It was slippery and the mama cow didn't sound thrilled, but Lauren did it.

"Nice," Travis praised when he saw the hooves for himself. "Okay, now when she strains, we pull. When she rests, we rest."

Lauren still hadn't opened her eyes, but she could feel what he was talking about. He took hold of one of the legs and she put both of her hands around the other.

"Be sure you hold right there at that joint," he said. "We don't want to hurt it. Pull hard when she strains but don't put your body weight behind it or anything. I don't think this will be too bad now that we're coming feet first."

She nodded.

When she felt the cow strain, she pulled. She felt the calf moving toward them and felt a little thrill shoot through her.

"There we go," Travis said.

The next time the animal strained and they pulled there was even more movement.

The front hooves, the legs and the snout were now visible.

"Okay, I think we're good," Travis said. "We should move ba—"

Suddenly the cow gave a hard push and the calf slipped forward quickly, sliding out into the world...and into Lauren's lap.

CHAPTER TEN

There was probably something really wrong with him, but seeing Dr. Lauren Davis holding a slimy newborn calf in her lap, blood, mud and worse on her crazy fake Uggs, made Travis fall a little more in love with her.

He was, however, a little concerned about her mental state at the moment.

She looked frozen, her mouth in a little O, her hands up in the air, as she stared at the calf lying across her thighs.

The calf was probably about seventy pounds and had immediately started squirming, so Travis quickly scooped it up and laid it on the grass.

Lauren scrambled to her feet, looking a bit shell-shocked.

"You okay?" he asked, stripping his gloves off.

Lauren continued to stare at the calf as the newborn began struggling to get his legs under him to stand. It would take him a few tries, but amazingly, he'd accomplish it.

Travis peeled Lauren's gloves off her hands as well. "Lauren?" He squeezed her hands and moved in front of her, blocking her view of the baby cow.

She blinked up at him.

"You okay?" he repeated. He didn't think she was actually hurt, though that was no baby kitten that had landed on her. Still, it was more likely she was processing the blood, guts and other stuff. Because it wasn't just on her boots.

"This is…"

He braced himself as she trailed off. Her help really had been valuable. He probably could have repositioned and pulled the calf himself, but having two people made it easier on everyone, including the baby and mamma cow. But it was messy business. Perhaps the calving might have just been too much.

Hell, he should have started with this a few days ago rather than river parties and sex in a truck. This would have scared her off right away.

He was damned glad he hadn't started with this.

He took her upper arms in his hands and bent to look her in the eye. "Thank you for doing this with me. I know this is…a lot. This is something some girls who've grown up around here wouldn't be able to handle."

She seemed to shake herself at that. She took a deep breath and shrugged out of his grasp.

"I'm handling it just fine."

"You look a little…dazed."

"I've never seen anything be born before." Her gaze flickered past him to where the calf and his mother were.

Her eyes widened and Travis turned to find the baby on his feet. He was wobbly, but he was up. His mother was licking him, cleaning him up and getting to know him.

Travis glanced back at Lauren. "Kind of cool, isn't it?" he asked.

She didn't have to think it was cool. She didn't have to ever help with it again. But for some stupid reason, he hoped she'd agree.

"It's…"

Again he felt himself brace for her answer.

"It's a big problem."

Dammit.

He sighed. "Okay. No more blood and guts."

She frowned at him. "The blood and guts aren't the problem."

"The ruined boots?"

She looked down. "Dammit," she muttered. Then she looked back up at Travis. "It's a big problem because this is the dirtiest I've ever been, that was the *grossest* thing I've ever done, and I will now never be able to eat beef again. And I *like* filet mignon. And a good cheeseburger once in a while. I've even eaten, and enjoyed, veal. And I *still* love it here!"

Travis wasn't going to smile. He couldn't.

But she still loved it here. She wanted to stay.

He felt like crowing like a damned rooster.

"Lauren, I—"

"And," she went on, her voice still higher pitched than usual. "This all completely distracted me from the fact that I need to get on a plane in a couple of hours and go save my best friend and my company."

She turned and stomped toward the truck.

Travis frowned, glanced back at the cows and then started after her.

The calf seemed to be doing fine. He'd come back out and move them to the barn in a little bit.

"What are you talking about?"

Her hand was on the door handle of his truck, but she turned. "I have to go to DC tonight."

Travis felt his frown deepen. "I thought you were here for a month."

She nodded. "I did too. But…" She shrugged. "Things happen. I'm on call for issues and problems twenty-four-seven. Things often change quickly."

Travis couldn't completely identify the thoughts going through his head, but he definitely wasn't happy. Things had changed all right. She was getting close, feeling things she didn't want to feel. For him.

And now she was talking about leaving.

"My brother Ty is coming home this weekend," he said. "I was hoping you could meet him. Actually, meet my whole family." He couldn't ask her to stay. Exactly. She was going to come and go. That was how it was going to be if he was involved with her. He couldn't expect different and he couldn't be pissed when she couldn't stay. But he could be disappointed and wish she was here. Right? "Can you come back?"

Hell, she flew all over the world all the time. It wasn't impossible to think that she could make a trip to DC tonight—and he ignored the way his chest tightened at that thought—and be back here for Sunday dinner.

She shook her head. "No. I'll be in Haiti until the end of July."

"Haiti?" What the hell? So now this wasn't a quick trip to DC. "You're going to *Haiti*? When?"

"I leave tomorrow morning."

Now she was frowning too.

"You weren't supposed to leave until the first of July."

She crossed her arms. "Things changed."

"What things?"

"Several things, actually. But it's for the better. Honestly, I don't know what you people put in the water around here, but I've been here for only a few days and I'm already sucked in. Staying much longer would be bad."

"Bad how?" he asked sharply. "Bad because you'd feel at home and be even more settled, and maybe you would have finally had to admit that you love…being here."

Jesus, he'd almost slipped there. He knew he was falling for her and hoped she felt the same, but he couldn't just blurt it out like that. He couldn't just say, "You're falling in love with me". He couldn't just dump, "By the end of this month, I'm pretty sure I'll be totally in love with you" on her either.

But she was willing and able to pack up and leave with only a few hours' notice to be gone to another country for weeks at a time.

That could mean one of two things. Either she was not feeling all the complicated, crazy stuff he was feeling. Or she was feeling it just as strongly or more so.

"I've already admitted that I love being here," she said. "But that doesn't mean I can forget about everything else."

Travis moved in closer, forcing her to look up at him on purpose. He was in her space. Just like he wanted to be in her...*everything.* Her life, her thoughts, her heart.

"You don't strike me as a runner, City."

She narrowed her eyes. "What does that mean?"

"It means that you're tough. You do what has to be done. You face things. I get that you're scared here, but running isn't going to fix it. You're going to miss me. You're going to miss Sapphire Falls."

"What is it that you think I'm scared of?"

"That you want to give things up. That you *don't* want to go to DC. That you *don't* want to go to Haiti. That you want to stay right here. With me."

She stared at him. She took a deep breath. Then another.

He could see that her fingers were digging into her arms and could read the tension on her face.

"So," she finally said, quietly and coolly. Too coolly. "You think that I'm all worked up and tense and worried because of you. You think that I'm struggling because suddenly nothing is more important to me than you and that I'm feeling...what? Guilty about it? Or that I'm worried about how to tell my partner that I want out of our company and business because of *you?* Or that I'm trying to figure out how to break it to the villagers in Haiti who are depending on me to improve their lives that my plans have changed because of *you?* Or maybe that I'm rehearsing what I'm going to say to the President of Outreach America, oh, and the President of the *United States,* when I have to tell them that I've decided to give it all up and raise chickens instead with *you?*"

He opened his mouth.

She went on anyway. "This isn't about you, Travis. My trip to DC, my decision to go to Haiti...it's not about you or my feelings for Sapphire Falls or being *scared* of anything. It's what I have to do and, believe it or not, what I *want* to do."

Yeah, well, maybe that was all true. And, yes, her work

was important. And, yes, he was sure that she did need and want to go to DC and Haiti. Sometimes. From time to time. Here and there.

But he was more concerned that she was always *going* somewhere. She was always leaving. And when she did come back there was always a reason—Mason, IAS, Adrianne's pregnancy. It was never just because it was something *she* wanted. Did Lauren Davis ever do anything for herself? Just because?

He wanted her to come back to him and he wanted it to be because she *wanted* to do that too.

"I want to see you on August 1st," he said.

Her cheeks were flushed and she was clearly wound tight. "What?"

"I want to see you the minute you get back. You can come here or I'll come to you. Whatever. But Haiti isn't your home. And DC isn't your home and Chicago isn't your home."

"You think Sapphire Falls should be," she said.

"I think *I* should be."

Her eyes widened. "What does that mean?"

"I want to be something you *want* too, Lauren," he said. He moved in a little closer but didn't touch her. "I want to be as big of a deal as Haiti is. I want to be what you come back to. You come back to the US because you don't *belong* in Haiti. But you don't stay in DC because you don't belong there either. You also don't stay in Chicago because that's not home. You need something to come back to, something that you want. Just that you want. It doesn't have to be something that will save the world, or something you have to do, or something that is counting on you, or something that is a huge humanitarian or political effort. You need something that's just for you."

She swallowed hard. "You're complicating things."

He *wanted* to complicate things. Because that meant that he *could* complicate things. That he could make her feel and want things that complicated things.

Yeah, he wanted that a lot.

"I know. If it's any consolation, my life was easier before you became hot and charming and funny and sexy too."

She cocked her head to one side. "I've always been hot and charming and funny and sexy."

He nodded, looked into her eyes and said with sincerity. "Then I never stood a chance, did I?"

Her eyes flickered with emotions. She pressed her lips together and pulled in a long breath. Finally, she said, "I know what I would be getting into here. But I'm not sure you know what you're asking to be a part of."

"Then tell me. Show me."

"We did talk about giving you a taste of my life."

"We did."

"What are you doing for dinner tonight?"

Did that mean she was staying and not jetting off to DC tonight?

"Whatever you want."

"Great. Dinner's at eight." She stepped around him and got into the truck.

His heart pounding, Travis rounded the front bumper and slid behind the wheel.

As he started the truck, she looked over. "I don't suppose you have a tux?"

♋

The details of everything between *I don't suppose you own a tux* and him standing in a posh ballroom in Washington, DC, with a scotch in one hand and Senator Thompson's hand in the other were a little hazy.

But here he was.

"Ms. Davis says you're involved with IAS's growing project out in Nebraska," the senator said.

Thompson was a democrat from Kansas, new to the Senate and eager to learn.

"Dr.," Travis said.

"Excuse me?"

"It's Dr. Davis." And she'd sent the senator over to Travis to keep him busy. Dammit.

"Oh, of course," Senator Thompson said. "Anyway, she said to ask you about how local farmers can get involved with IAS. There are some family farms in my district that I'd really like to get a spotlight on. Family farms are disappearing."

Travis knew that. Of course he knew that. He was part of a family farm. But he had to respect the guy. Family farms needed more advocates. Especially policy-making advocates.

But he was also aware that Lauren had put him to work. Not just to keep him out of her way while she charmed and persuaded the senator she'd come to see and the VP—Travis still couldn't believe he was in the same room with the Vice President of the United States—but also because involving the farmers who worked with IAS in the PR around what the company was doing was very effective in delivering their message. Lauren had given him, his brothers and the other Sapphire Falls farmers that very speech about a year ago when they'd hosted a weekend in Sapphire Falls for various media outlets interested in seeing IAS at work.

Travis chatted with the senator for several minutes, telling him how the Bennett farms had gotten involved and the benefits they'd personally seen as well as the fact that they truly believed in IAS and what they were doing for agriculture around the world. Yes, Lauren and Mason's pet project was in Haiti, but IAS was doing a lot for family farms, self-sustaining communities and agricultural research all over the US and in other countries.

As the senator went on about climate change and the

recent drought in Kansas, Travis glanced around the room and located Lauren by the huge floor-to-ceiling windows that were draped in red velvet and looked out onto the lights of Capitol Hill.

It was really unfucking believable.

The woman in the emerald-green floor-length evening gown looking sexy and cool and composed, charming all the men in the room and making him hard just in the way she sipped her champagne, had shot at a mountain lion just a few hours ago. And, more than that, had been covered in cow.

Literally.

Travis grinned and lifted his glass of scotch.

Not beer. Oh, no. A party like this called for scotch.

Or so Joe Spencer had told him.

Travis also couldn't believe that six hours after the calf had charmed Lauren into a near-vegetarian lifestyle, he had flown first class, put on a tux and ridden in a limo, all for the first time in his life.

So far, a lot of this rocked.

The only drawback was that he hadn't spoken to, or even made eye contact, with Lauren in over an hour.

And the snails at dinner. All he could think as he'd tried to choke them down was *why?* Why eat snails when there were chickens and pigs and cows and, if they had to stick with things that lived in the water, good old fish of all kinds? The crabmeat cheesecake with portabella sauce hadn't been horrible, but if you were going to put gravy on something, what was wrong with a mashed-up potato?

And then there had been the asshole senator from Nevada he'd sat next to who could only talk about his golf game and bitch about some teachers' organization that was bugging him about sponsoring an education bill.

And the fact that there wasn't a beer in sight.

Seriously? Once you made six figures you couldn't drink beer anymore?

But the biggest drawback was that he hadn't been able to talk to Lauren, or touch her or hear her laugh or even tell her she looked gorgeous.

After the calving, he'd driven her to the farm, they'd both showered—separately, changed clothes, packed quickly and headed to the airport. But she'd been on her phone for much of the drive and typing on her laptop when she wasn't. They'd boarded the plane almost immediately, but she'd been on her phone again until she'd had to shut it down and had been on her laptop the rest of the time. A car had picked them up at the airport. A woman named Sasha, apparently Lauren's assistant of some kind, had already been in the back seat and they'd talked about the party and who would be there and Lauren's best shot for getting a chance to talk to the vice president. When they'd arrived at the condo he'd heard about from Phoebe, Lauren had swept upstairs and Sasha had handed him a tux.

When he'd next seen Lauren, an hour and a half later, she'd been dressed in the evening gown, her hair upswept, her makeup done...and she'd been on the phone again.

He'd leaned in to kiss her, but she'd turned so he only got her cheek as she continued to talk.

He'd heard the name Mason at least twelve times and had gritted his teeth harder each time.

They'd gotten into the limo, arrived at the party, and he still hadn't had a chance to talk to her, or kiss her, or run his hands over the silky dress or tell her any of the things that were starting to rumble and roil in his chest and gut.

She looked amazing in the evening gown and heels. She'd looked sophisticated and cool and sexy and in charge.

But he wanted to strip her right out of it and take down her hair. Not because he wanted her naked. Because he didn't want her sophisticated and cool. He wanted her rumpled and real and...dirty.

He liked the mouthy Lauren who bought Duggs just to

annoy him, who knew how to load a shotgun, who had developed a taste for Booze in only two days. She might not play sand volleyball or go for mud runs—yet—but she looked damned good in his truck, front or back, and she could sing along to country radio.

Sure, it'd be easier for him to be in love with a hometown Sapphire Falls girl who actually did want to raise chickens. But that wasn't going to happen now. He was in love, or well on his way, with Lauren Davis.

He'd accused her of being scared. The truth was *he* was scared. The spontaneous flight to DC, the dress, the limo, the snails—there couldn't be two places more different than her world in DC and his world in Sapphire Falls.

Watching her now, Travis realized he was losing her. Or that he hadn't really fully had her to start with.

"Senator," Travis interrupted whatever Thompson had been saying. "I don't suppose you hunt or fish."

Thompson grinned. He was in his late forties, graying at the temples, but Travis saw a spark in the other man's eyes that he liked. Thompson was truly interested and was down to earth enough that Travis could tolerate him.

"I love both," Thompson told him. "I'm a country boy at heart."

"Then tell you what," Travis said. "You should come out to Sapphire Falls. I'll show you the fields and our operations and then I'll take you fishing at the prettiest little pond you've ever seen, and we can talk all day about what to do to save family farms in the Midwest."

Thompson nodded, regarding Travis intently. "You have some good ideas about that?"

"I live it every day."

Thompson nodded again. "You know how to cook anything we catch?"

"I'll make you a meal that will make you never want to leave Sapphire Falls."

"What if I bring a couple of friends? Like maybe

Senator Willis."

Senator Willis was the senator from Oklahoma who had been a big proponent of large farming operations run by corporations. Travis knew it was all about lobbyists and money, but having a chance to have Senator Willis on his farm and in his kitchen? Hell, yeah. He'd show the guy what it was really all about.

"Absolutely. Open invitation."

"I'll call you." Thompson took Travis's cell number down on a napkin, shook his hand and headed for another group.

"You gunning for my job, Bennett?"

Travis turned to find Joe next to him.

"Just trying to help the cause," Travis said with a smile. It was nice to see a familiar face.

"Well, Lauren will be impressed. She's gone head to head with Willis a number of times without much luck."

Travis shrugged. "She's Wonder Woman, but no one can do it all."

"Don't say that to her face. She'll decide to prove you wrong and run for president or something."

Travis laughed, but he didn't feel particularly amused. Joe was right, and Travis had to wonder if she'd ever stop feeling like she had to always do more and be more.

"You have no idea what I'd do for a beer," Travis admitted to Joe.

Joe laughed. "I suspect that most of these guys feel the same way, but scotch makes them look more refined. But I have connections. Come on."

He led Travis out to the patio off the ballroom beyond the huge glass doors. The evening had cooled off and there was a nice soft breeze, but it was humid in DC. A waiter appeared with two bottles of imported beer. Joe handed one to Travis and tipped the waiter.

"It's not Budweiser," Joe said, lifting his bottle in salute.

"But it's not scotch," Travis said, clinking his bottle against Joe's and then sipping.

It wasn't Budweiser. It was better.

Travis sighed with pleasure. He leaned forward onto the stone wall that ran the length of the balcony and looked down on the city lights. It wasn't a dark sky with a billion stars twinkling, but it was pretty in its own right.

Joe mimicked his pose and they lapsed into a comfortable silence.

"So how would you like to make me your best friend?" Joe asked after a few quiet minutes.

Travis looked over. "I gotta warn you, I've got guys who've lied to the high school principal and the cops for me, who've loaned me big chunks of money, and who've helped me build a *house*. I've also got three guys I share blood and parents with. So it's gonna have to be something big."

Joe chuckled. "But that's not a no."

Travis shrugged. "I'm open-minded."

Travis knew Joe wasn't serious. He and Joe had shared enough beer and barbecues for Travis to know that Joe had a brother too. He understood the brotherly bond and he knew that Travis and his buddies in Sapphire Falls were tight. But Travis was very interested in hearing why Joe thought he was in the running to be one of Travis's best buds.

"Well, are any of those guys willing to spend two weeks in a third-world country for you?" Joe asked.

Travis looked over with eyebrows up. "T.J. once camped out with me for Garth Brooks tickets."

"For how long?"

"Twenty-six hours."

"Not quite the same thing."

No, it wasn't. So why was Joe doing this? Whatever it was.

"I'm not sure I'm following here. You want a bromance

with me? There are easier ways."

Joe nodded and looked back over the city. "Probably. But the truth is, I'm doing it for Lauren."

"Okay." Travis liked anyone who cared about Lauren.

"She needs more time in Sapphire Falls. She needs more time with you."

Travis pivoted slowly to face the other man. His heart was hammering. Lauren had asked Joe to step in for her? That was big. Huge even. Lauren didn't ask for help. She honestly didn't think anyone else could do what she did. Except maybe Mason. But definitely not Joe. But if she'd asked Joe... "Seriously? She wants to stay longer?"

Joe cleared his throat and straightened from the railing. "I didn't say it was *her* idea."

Travis frowned. His heart thumped again, but it didn't feel nearly as good now. "What wasn't her idea?"

"Me going to Haiti. And handling things with Senator Andrews. And keeping Mason from getting shot at again."

Travis's mind was whirling. None of this was Lauren's idea. But Joe was talking about going to Haiti so Lauren wouldn't have to. And Mason had been *shot at*? "What?" Travis demanded. "Mason was shot at?"

"Well, the whole team was. Only Stephen got hit."

"Someone on the team got *shot*?"

"Yes, but it's only a superficial wound."

"Joe, I think you need to give me a few more details here."

A flash of green appeared in his peripheral vision. Joe must have seen it too. He sighed. "I think you're about to hear a whole lot of details. Some of which may include me getting fired."

Travis turned to look. Lauren was stalking toward them, her heels clicking hard against the stone of the balcony.

"She's going to fire you?" Travis asked.

She did, indeed, look pissed.

"She can't actually fire me. Mason would have to

agree, and he's on board with all of this. But she's probably going to try," Joe admitted.

Travis tipped back the rest of his beer.

Joe did the same.

"Oh, by the way," Joe said. "She's going to be pissed at you too."

"Me? What'd I do?" Travis asked.

"You're the main reason we all think she should spend more time in Sapphire Falls," Joe said, drawing himself up tall as his boss approached.

Well, okay, Travis would shoulder that particular burden because, dammit, he was a good reason for her to stay in Sapphire Falls. He also straightened and squared his shoulders.

ဆင်္ကြ

Lauren was furious. People were messing in her life. She didn't let people do that.

"What the hell is going on?" she demanded as soon as she was close enough to Joe that she could chew him out without anyone else hearing it.

She'd love to yell. She'd like to swear. But none of that would happen here, and Joe had known that. Like a little kid who chose the middle of a public place to throw a tantrum because his mother wouldn't be able to discipline him the way he deserved, Joe had chosen the birthday party to go behind her back and screw everything up.

Thankfully, he was out on the balcony, so that there was at least some semblance of privacy. And thankfully, Travis was with him. That just proved what she'd suspected. Travis was involved in this somehow.

"I assume you finally had a chance to talk to Senator Andrews," Joe said.

"I did. And I'm guessing you know what he said."

"That he and I had already had a conversation and

everything is a go."

"Almost word for word." She crossed her arms. She glanced at Travis and then back to Joe. She'd been avoiding looking at Travis a lot tonight. He was distracting as hell. He looked completely gorgeous and completely out of place in the tux. He'd also been wearing an expression all night that alternated between bewildered and annoyed.

Well, this definitely wasn't Sapphire Falls. Which had been the whole point.

Okay, *some* of the whole point.

He was also here because she hadn't been ready to say goodbye.

Seeing him in her world, choking down snails and making small talk with people he had nothing in common with was supposed to turn her off and drive home the point, to both of them, that this was not going to work.

Instead, seeing him choking down snails and making small talk had endeared him to her. If a big, hard, cocky farmer could be endearing.

Dammit.

He was really trying. He had to hate all of this. He'd already loosened his tie and it now hung around his neck as a simple piece of black silk. She assumed Sasha or Joe had tied it for him. No way did Travis know how to tie a bow tie. But he'd looked suave and handsome with it tied. And now he looked devastatingly sexy with it loose.

Dammit.

"Senator Andrews was very helpful. He understood our situation and said he'd do whatever he could to help. He and the vice president do feel strongly about you and the team having an armed escort back to Plaines Paisible."

She forced herself to focus on Joe and the fact that things were coming apart.

"That's not—"

"I told him we would agree to two guards, but they would need to be dressed as civilians and conceal the weapons. Going in there obviously armed isn't going to help a thing."

He was right, of course. It was what she would have negotiated herself. But *she* should have been the one to negotiate it.

She glared at him. "We don't need guards at all." Probably. Maybe. If they went in peacefully and reached out to the people who so obviously wanted their attention—

"Bullshit."

This came from Travis. She looked at him. Ignoring him had been impossible when he *wasn't* talking. Now that he apparently had something to say, she wasn't going to be able to keep from looking at him—and probably yelling at him.

"Excuse me?"

"If there are people with guns that are obviously willing to use them, then you need guards with you."

"I'm pretty good with a gun myself."

He snorted. *Snorted.*

"I shot that—" She took a deep breath. "Never mind." She looked back to Joe. "I don't appreciate you getting involved without my knowledge."

"Government relations and PR is part of my job," Joe said with a shrug. "There was an issue, I was in a position to take care of it, so I did. In fact," he said, pushing away from the short stone wall that ran the perimeter of the balcony. "I'm also in the position to go to Haiti and stay for the next three weeks. You can go back to Sapphire Falls."

His words hit her like punches. *He* was going to go to Haiti? She didn't have to? She could go back to Sapphire Falls?

Uh huh.

She frowned at Travis. "Is that right?"

He frowned back. "So you *didn't* ask Joe to take care of all of this so you could stay in Sapphire Falls with me a while longer? Even though he's obviously capable of taking care of all of this?" Travis asked.

Lauren met his gaze straight on. "No, I didn't."

"Because…"

"Because I want to take care of it."

"But it doesn't have to be you."

She pressed her arms tighter against her stomach. She could feel the sequins on the bodice of her gown pressing into her skin.

"My best friend and my company need *me* to be there."

"Joe said that Mason knows about this. And he's fine with it."

Those words stabbed into her. Mason was fine with it? Fine with her staying back in Sapphire Falls? Hanging out at the river? Having sex on kitchen tables? Well, great. She was so glad that Mason was fine with that.

"Maybe *I'm* not fine with it."

"I'm going to get another drink," Joe said.

Neither Lauren or Travis responded or even glanced at him.

"Don't you get it?" Travis asked, his tone full of frustration and tension. "Joe can go to Haiti. You can stay. For a change."

Her chin lifted at that, almost without her being conscious of it. *For a change* seemed to hang in the air between them. He thought she was scared. He thought she kept leaving because she was looking for something. And he thought that she'd found what she'd been looking for in Sapphire Falls. With him.

He was asking her—practically challenging her—to stay. He was asking her to choose.

This felt far too familiar.

"I don't want to stay." What she really didn't want was to take a risk with her heart. They'd only been doing…whatever it was they were doing…for a few days. That was hardly enough to gamble on. What if she stayed and something happened to Mason or to their relationship with Outreach America or they didn't get the crops in the ground?

Travis took another step, looking down at her with an intensity that made her want to cry.

"I'm in love with you."

Her chest and gut tightened. Love. He'd used the word love.

There was no way he could mean that. No way could that already be true.

But she felt it too.

She was falling for him too.

She'd been in love before. In fact, she liked being in love. But it hadn't felt like this before.

Travis made her want to stay. He made her want to turn it all over to Joe. He made her wish for the first time in forever that she had a nine-to-five gig.

"Stay. Give us a chance, Lauren."

But what if she stayed and Travis changed his mind? What if she stayed and *she* changed her mind? What if the starry skies and gorgeous sunsets and new baby calves and lovable dogs and friends who would do anything for you got old? What if she missed her Gucci pumps—because God knew, there would be very little call for them in Sapphire Falls—and sushi and skinny soy caramel macchiatos? What if she started to *like* beer?

He reached out, ran his hand up and down her arm. "I know you feel it too."

She did. But there were too many what ifs. And she really did like sushi. And she liked martinis, not beer. And she liked…her life. She didn't want to give it up. But no one had tempted her like Travis. Not since Shawn. And that meant she needed to get on that plane to Haiti.

Maybe Joe could handle things in DC and Haiti. But Lauren couldn't handle things in Sapphire Falls.

"I have to go," she said.

Then she turned and walked calmly and steadily from

the balcony, through the big doors, across the ballroom, out of the hotel and down the grand marble stairs to the waiting limo.

It wasn't until the long car pulled away from the curb that Lauren glanced back. Travis and Joe both knew where the condo was. They could come after her if they wanted to.

But they wouldn't.

She'd made her decision.

Cinderella had made a mistake in running from the ball and losing her shoe. If she had left calmly and coolly, she wouldn't have left anything behind and she wouldn't have ever seen her Prince Charming again.

Lauren hadn't left anything behind.

At least, she hadn't left anything behind that anyone could return to her.

She was afraid Travis would always have her heart.

CHAPTER ELEVEN

"So you're miserable."

"Yep." Miserable was absolutely the right word for how Travis felt. It had been three weeks since Lauren had walked away from him in DC, and miserable was how he'd been feeling every minute since. But the moment he'd blurted out, "I'm in love with you," he'd known he'd messed up.

"Because she left or because she hasn't been in contact?" Ty, Travis's youngest brother, was sitting across from him at the Come Again, munching on French fries. Ty was a triathlete—an Olympic silver medal triathlete to be exact—so French fries were a rare treat for him, and he waited until he visited Sapphire Falls to indulge.

"Both." Well, both of those things *and* the fact that she'd left immediately after he'd told her how he felt.

"Explain to me again how telling her you love her was a bad idea?"

Ty had been refusing to tell his brothers why he was in Sapphire Falls for an extended visit. He came home from Colorado every few months, but never for more than a few days at a time. This time he was staying for a while. But he wasn't saying why. "Some stuff to take care of," was all he would tell them. And he'd quickly picked up on Tucker's questions to Travis about Lauren.

Inevitably, Travis had told him the entire story about Lauren's stay in Sapphire Falls and their joint mission to cure her of her infatuation.

Which had apparently worked perfectly.

He'd called it back when Lauren had first proposed the idea of becoming immune to Sapphire Falls. He'd known she'd make some nice guy fall in love with her—he just hadn't known it would be him.

He'd also known that she'd eventually realize Sapphire

Falls wasn't big enough or fancy enough or fast-paced enough and she'd leave—he just hadn't known that a lot of that would be bullshit she was telling herself to avoid getting hurt.

He'd known she'd break the poor sucker's heart. But he hadn't known that she'd be breaking her own heart as well.

"I tried to use her feelings for me to get her to stay instead of going and doing what she wanted to do." The words had tumbled out. Yes, he'd meant them. He was in love with her. And, yes, he'd thought maybe that would matter. He wanted her to stay. He didn't intend for her to *never* leave again, but he didn't want her to leave right now. They were just getting started, and looking at her in that green dress with her hair up, the lipstick, the earrings— looking so different from the woman that he'd been with in Sapphire Falls—he'd panicked. And it had been a crappy thing to do. "But I do love her."

"So go tell her that," Ty said, taking a bite of a French fry.

"What do you mean?"

"Go there and tell her you love her. Then she'll know it's not an either-or thing."

Travis frowned. "Just go there? To Haiti."

"Why not?"

Tucker, who was sitting to Travis's left, making his way through a huge Reuben, chuckled. "Because DC was the first time Trav has ever even flown. If it weren't for Husker football games in Lincoln, he'd never leave home."

Travis frowned harder at the brother who was only twenty months younger than him. "Hey, you've never flown either."

Tucker nodded. "Don't need to fly to get what I want."

And up until Lauren Davis had come into his life, Travis had shared that sentiment. He wasn't looking for anything else or anything more because he'd had everything he wanted and needed. He hadn't needed to leave home. His work didn't require travel and he'd never been bitten by the travel bug, never longed to see faraway places.

But that didn't mean he *wouldn't*. The trip to DC had had a few high points. Not the snails, of course, but he'd definitely thought about asking the driver to stop at a few of the national monuments when they'd driven past.

"It's not about the flying," Ty said. He'd flown all over the world to participate in major triathlon events. He was sponsored by a men's shaving-cream company and a company that made swimming equipment, so he flew first class and attended parties a lot like Lauren did. "It's about being willing to do something new and strange."

"I'm not *opposed* to new things," Travis said.

His brothers both chuckled again.

"You were the first one down in Hailey's office at City Hall when they wanted to repaint all of the street light poles but wanted to use a new color," Tucker said.

"It's *Sapphire* Falls. The street light poles should be blue," Travis said. That wasn't opposition to new things. That was just common sense.

"You were pissed at Dad for days after he chopped the old apple tree down," Ty reminded him.

Travis sighed. He had been. He'd known, even then, that it was irrational. The tree had been hit by lightning and had needed to be taken down. But his being upset hadn't been about not liking change. He was nostalgic. He'd always imagined his own kids climbing up in that tree to pick apples.

"And you hung on to your last truck *way* past the time you should've let her go," Tucker said.

"It's crazy to get something new just because the odometer hits a certain number." Besides, his butt had fit just right in that seat. He'd known every quirk and eccentricity of that truck. He'd had a lot of good times in that truck. And, yeah, okay, it had taken a couple of weeks for him to get used to all the buttons and automatic features on the new truck. But he was good now.

His brothers laughed. "You tell yourself whatever you need to," Tucker said. "But you don't like new things. You're happy. Things are just how you like 'em and you're not interested in changing that up."

Travis couldn't exactly argue with that. He'd spent twenty-nine great years here doing just what he was doing. It seemed a little crazy to think about changing that up.

He almost laughed out loud at that.

Even if Lauren had agreed to give up her travels, her job, her interests and move full-time to Sapphire Falls to raise chickens, *nothing* about his life would have been the same.

"I'm *not* opposed to change," he said again. In fact, he'd very much like each and every one of the changes Lauren would bring to his house and his life to start *tomorrow*.

"What about traveling? Leaving Sapphire Falls once in a while? Sleeping in a bed that isn't covered with a quilt your grandmother made?" Ty asked.

Sure, why not? The only thing he needed in or on his bed was Lauren. "Seeing the Grand Canyon would be cool," he said.

Tucker laughed and Ty grinned.

"What?"

"The Grand Canyon isn't exactly..." Ty started.

"Exciting," Tucker filled in.

"You've never been," Travis said. "How do you know?"

"I have been. And the Grand Canyon is safe," Ty said.

Travis frowned. "What's that mean?"

"It means," Ty said, "that it wouldn't be much of a risk or take you very far outside of your comfort zone. It's a big hole in the ground. It's amazing, and beautiful, but it's not like it would change your life."

"It could," Travis argued. "I've read about people who go out there and feel something change inside of them and suddenly they give up their big corporate jobs and move to Arizona."

Ty rolled his eyes. "You don't have a big corporate job to give up."

"But I have a job I could give up to move to Arizona."

"You're missing my point," Ty said, pointing at him with the end of a French fry.

Travis gritted his teeth. "Maybe you're not doing a very good job of making it."

"My point is that when we talk about traveling away from home, your first suggestion is the Grand Canyon. A very outdoorsy, big, beautiful place where people camp and hike and fish and canoe on a river. A lot like around here. You didn't say New York City or LA. You definitely didn't say Rome or Paris. Because those places would require you to do something really new and different."

Travis thought maybe he should be offended. Or mad. But he wasn't either. Ty and Tucker knew him. "I'm boring."

Ty shook his head. "You know who you are and you have what you want. People spend lifetimes looking for those two things and never finding them. You're...lucky."

He didn't feel very damned lucky.

Tucker had said essentially the same thing about Travis knowing what he wanted. But now Travis felt the untruth of that statement hit him in the gut. He had some of what he wanted, but a lot of what he wanted was in Haiti right now.

"And that means," Ty went on, "you've never been motivated to try anything new."

Travis thought about that too. It made sense. To change, a person needed a reason. He'd never had a reason to do anything other than what he'd always done. His life had provided money, happiness and reward.

Until Lauren had come along.

Lauren had said he was stuck. But that probably wasn't totally accurate. Being stuck implied being someplace involuntarily and unable to get out. Travis had been exactly where he wanted to be with no desire to change it. But he *could* change things up if he wanted to.

His not wanting to do new things was partly why he'd been the perfect guy to help her *not* like Sapphire Falls.

Fuck.

Maybe she had come to like Sapphire Falls in spite of that, and maybe she had even developed feelings for Travis in spite of all of that. But his apparent rut, his lack of motivation for something else, had made it possible for her to turn and walk away from him in spite of his declaration of love.

"Being content is okay," Tucker said, as he had the day before. He bit into his burger and chewed for a moment. "Of course," he went on after he'd swallowed, "content isn't the same thing as excited."

No, it wasn't.

"Being excited is good," Ty said, nodding.

Being excited *was* good.

And Travis got excited. Not about snails and bow ties, but he got excited about his farm and his family and his friends and his hometown.

He also got excited about Lauren.

Not only in the physical or sexual sense, but in the she's-amazing-and-I-want-to-be-with-her-no-matter-what sense.

Excitement to make a difference and change the world and to do more than her small hometown expected had driven Lauren to leave her home and family.

Maybe his excitement for her could get him unstuck.

He'd never leave Sapphire Falls completely, of course. But a quick trip to Haiti wasn't out of the question.

And maybe her excitement for *him* would help *her* get unstuck from the crazy idea that she couldn't have it all.

Ty must have seen something in Travis's face. The man who had not only left home and everything he'd grown up with to move to Colorado to train seriously and compete in triathlons, but had also gone to London to compete in the Olympics—and win—said, "If you have a chance, try legim. It's pretty good."

"You've had Haitian food?" Travis remembered Lauren mentioning that exact dish.

"Of course."

Of course. Ty said it as if it wasn't at all strange.

"How's it compare to Mom's meatloaf?" Travis asked.

"Nothing will ever compare to Mom's meatloaf," Ty said. "But that doesn't mean I haven't discovered some other pretty awesome things. And some other pretty horrible things." He shuddered.

"Do I want to know?" Travis asked.

Ty shook his head. "The point is, man cannot live on meatloaf alone. I know what's out there. I know what I like, don't like, want and don't want because I've tried a lot of things."

"Now we're talking about women, right?" Tucker asked. "Tell us more about the women you've tried and what you like and don't like."

Ty laughed. "You read about a lot of it in the tabloids, didn't you?"

Ty had hooked up with a fellow Olympian briefly during and after London, catching the media's attention with his brash romantic gestures and their public—very public—displays of...affection was a gentle word for it. The media had really gone crazy though, when he'd had a crystal statue thrown at his head in the middle of a swanky LA jewelry store by said fellow Olympian. Fortunately, she was a skier, not a thrower of any kind, so just the edge of the statue had caught his jaw and he'd only needed six simple stitches. But the coverage had continued as the story of his cheating with an up-and-coming actress had surfaced. And led to the crystal-statue incident.

Travis chuckled, feeling lighter than he had since Lauren's assistant had tightened the bow tie around his neck.

"Hey, Travis."

Suddenly the table was surrounded.

Phoebe, Adrianne, Hailey and Matt Phillips circled the table. They were all smiling. Which he didn't trust for a second. He'd known three of these people for most of his life. If Phoebe, Matt and Hailey were all smiling at him at the same time, something was up.

"Hey, guys."

Hailey pulled a chair away from another table and slid it in between Travis and Tucker. "When you talk to Lauren next, tell her that we love the idea she sent about the Christmas tour of homes."

Travis couldn't hide his surprise. "She sent you an idea about the Christmas tour of homes?"

"Yes. And I also liked her idea about the moonlight margaritas, but we're going to have to talk about that some more."

He knew he was staring, but he couldn't help it. "Lauren Davis has been sending you ideas for Sapphire Falls?"

"Yes. Almost daily."

That made his chest ache. He'd told her she would think about Sapphire Falls even when she was jetting around the world. She was missing it.

The idea that she might be sad or lonely made his chest ache too. He wanted her to be happy. To feel some of the contentment he'd taken for granted until she'd come along.

It was interesting now that she'd come along he felt less content and more restless than ever.

"She called you?" Travis asked Hailey.

"Email. Though we are going to Skype the day after tomorrow."

"Skype?"

"Video chatting," Phoebe said, pulling up another chair between Ty and Tucker. "Like you and she have been doing since she left."

He shook his head. "I haven't talked to her."

"At all?" Adrianne said, propping a hand on her hip.

"No."

"You've been texting then?" Matt asked.

Travis frowned up at the other man. Matt was married to one of Lauren and Mason's scientists, Nadia. Who was currently in Haiti. "No. No texting either. Nothing."

"You haven't been in touch with Lauren at all since she left?" Phoebe clarified.

"Right."

"Why the hell not?" Hailey asked. "These three all have people over in Haiti. They all have people who travel away from Sapphire Falls on a regular basis. But they make it work. They're all happy and in love and doing just fine. So what's wrong with *you*?"

Ty chuckled. "You're going to give relationship advice, Madam Mayor?" he asked.

Hailey gave him a bored glance. "I guess we could ask you. You've been madly in love with yourself for what? Twenty-two years or so?"

Ty gave her a grin. "Well, surely *you* can understand my infatuation."

Hailey rolled her eyes and turned back to Travis. "I'm pointing out that you don't have to mope and be miserable. Nothing's perfect, but *grownups* work things out. Rationally. Reasonably."

"Aren't rationally and reasonably kind of the same thing?" Ty asked.

Travis frowned at his brother. He didn't know what was going on with Hailey and Ty, but it was clear that Ty was trying to antagonize her. And that it was working.

"*Adults* can admit how they feel," Hailey went on.

"*Grownups* have *relationships*. Things go two ways, there's give and take, communication. That kind of stuff." She was looking at Travis, but he had a feeling she wasn't really talking to him.

Ty settled back in his seat. "Tell us more. Sounds like those self-help books are starting to really pay off."

Hailey looked over at Ty calmly. Then she flicked her wrist and knocked over the glass of ice water in front of him, dumping it into his lap.

Ty shot back from the table with a curse.

"I haven't read the chapter on self-restraint yet," she said. She looked at Travis again. "You need to realize something."

Travis didn't know what Ty had done to get on Hailey's bad side, but she was riled up and Travis wasn't about to make it worse.

He gave her a solemn nod. "Go on."

"You fell in love with a woman that you have to share with the world. Quit being a baby and pouting about it," Hailey told him bluntly. "Work it out. Having her for part of the time is better than not having her at all."

"Oh, really," Ty said, looking up from blotting his crotch with a napkin.

Hailey ignored him. "I know you think you know what you want. But you'd be bored with a Sapphire Falls girl who just wants to raise chickens."

"You're absolutely right," Travis said.

"People in the military are deployed for a lot longer than anyone from IAS spends in Haiti," Phoebe said.

"That's true. I'm sure we can handle a few weeks at a time," Travis said.

"If you really love her, you want her to do this work," Adrianne said. "This is important to her."

"I agree. I believe that she needs to keep doing her work," Travis said.

"And Haiti is a great place to visit," Matt added. "I was

hesitant the first time too, but Nadia was worth it. And I've never regretted going. And Nadia is only part of the reason."

"I'm looking forward to it."

Apparently, they'd all finally recited their parts of the script, because Hailey leaned in and narrowed her eyes. "You agree with all of that?"

"I do," Travis said. "I have to be willing to go to her if I want her to come back to me."

And he was willing. Completely. It was just Haiti, after all. A completely different world than he was used to.

But even his world was completely different now. There was no escaping change. And he was ready.

Hailey sat back and crossed her arms. "Okay, so as I said before, the next time you talk to her, tell her I love her ideas about the Christmas tour of homes."

"I'll tell her," Travis said. And he would. But that wasn't going to be the first thing he said—or did—to Lauren when he saw her in person again.

✦✦✦

"You're being ridiculous, you know," Mason said.

Lauren frowned at him as they washed the worst of the caked mud off their hands in the big trough outside the makeshift headquarters building. They put the buildings up and took them down as they moved to various planting sites, and they'd be taking this one down in a few hours. The last of the seeds were going in the ground in this section today.

"Okay, so what if I stay? What if I cut back, change my role in the company, go to DC less? I stay and then he decides I'm not what he wants? What if what he wants has been next door all along? Then I'm screwed."

They washed quietly for a moment. Then Mason said, "Not every person you love is going to be like Shawn."

She took a deep breath. "I gave up everything for him, Mason."

"I know."

"And it didn't matter. He didn't give anything up."

"I know."

"And neither will Travis."

Mason shook his head. "You don't know that."

"I've never met someone happier," Lauren said. "And the crazy thing is, that's one of the things that makes me love him. He's...happy. Fulfilled with basic stuff. Roots, family, a future that looks a lot like the past."

"So why don't you want to be there with him?"

"I do," she protested. But when Mason gave a snort, she amended it to, "Part of me does. But that's stupid right? I mean, I was hanging out with him and *not* arguing for two days."

"Sometimes it happens like that," Mason said, reaching for a bottle of water. "It did for me and Adrianne."

And Lauren had thought that was crazy...until she'd seen them together.

"Adrianne gets you. She understands all of this."

"Travis does too," Mason said.

She really wanted to believe that. "How do you know?"

"He's just as driven," Mason said. "He farms. That takes guts and determination. He helps hold his family together, he helps support his town. He's there whenever someone needs him, even if someone else could do the same job. He's there because he wants to be, because he believes in what he's built and what he's part of." Mason gave her a little grin. "Sound familiar?"

"Oh sure, Travis and I are two peas in a pod," she said dryly. If only...

"You are. Different focuses, but the same drive and the same passion."

For some reason, that made her heart thump.

"But if our focuses take us in different directions—"

"Then you'll have to find a midway point to meet once in a while."

God, he made it sound so easy.

"He'd have to be willing to come partway."

"He went to DC."

"He hated it."

"But he went. For you."

"He was seduced by my ability to shoot a gun."

Mason chuckled. "Whatever works for you two."

"Seriously," Lauren said, shaking her head. "I just surprised him. And the sex is good. Really good."

"So keep surprising him and keep the sex really good. And maybe let him surprise you."

But Travis didn't need to surprise her. She liked him exactly as he was. Which was leading to the biggest heartache of her life.

"Don't tell me you weren't a little surprised he got his project going so quickly," Mason went on.

"His project?" Lauren asked.

"The one he and Senator Thompson brainstormed while they were fishing."

Lauren tripped over a rock. She caught herself and swung to face Mason. "Travis and Senator Thompson went *fishing*?"

"You introduced them in DC, right?" Mason asked.

"Well, yes." Sort of. She'd sent Thompson over to talk to Travis about his part in the IAS growing project to keep Travis busy while she talked to the people she needed to see at the party.

"As you know, Travis is a pretty charming guy," Mason said. "He invited Thompson to Sapphire Falls to fish. Thompson showed up a week later."

Lauren was stunned. Of course, she found Travis charming. But more in the how-did-my-panties-end-up-on-the-floor-of-your-truck way than in the political-lobbyist way.

"And they brainstormed a *project*?" Lauren asked. She thought back over the night of the party. She'd left Travis alone for an hour. Maybe an hour and a half.

Maybe she should hire him.

"Yes, they're going to take some inner-city kids in Kansas City to Sapphire Falls and have them stay on Travis's farm for a few days. Show them life in the small town, on the farm, things they haven't experienced before. They hope it will give the kids an appreciation for life outside of their world, tune them in to nature in a way they can't get in the city, and show them what it's like to have real neighbors and a community. And help them find ways of bringing some of that back to where they live."

Lauren was completely dumbfounded.

"It worked on you," Mason said with a little smirk.

"What did?" she asked. "I've always thought real neighbors and community were important."

"But staying with Travis in Sapphire Falls softened you up and made you think about things differently than you had in a long time."

She frowned. "I didn't need softening up. I'm sweet even. And open-minded."

Mason chuckled. "Sure you are. Completely open-minded. Willing to entertain all kinds of new ideas."

"I am." At the moment, she was entertaining the idea that Travis Bennett had come up with an amazing project and that she was very impressed.

She should definitely hire him.

And she should definitely tell him she was in love with him. Because she'd fallen for him somewhere between the grape slushy and pulling the calf together, but the fact that he was going to bring city kids to his farm and show them his compost pile—because she was sure he was going to teach them to compost—made her want him with an intensity that…made as little sense as all the rest of it but felt so right she thought she was going to burst.

"Are you open-minded enough to admit that Joe is ready to take over some of your responsibilities?" Mason asked as they headed for the fields again.

Lauren couldn't help but grin at that. Mr. Joe Spencer, the rich playboy who'd grown up in the lap of luxury was, as a matter of fact, currently filthy and sweaty in that very field. He thought he wanted to do her job in DC at the fancy parties with the free liquor? Then he could learn all about this part of her job too. Firsthand. Up close and personal.

And Mason was right. Joe was doing a great job. He was throwing himself into it all.

"Nadia's ready to help me out more too," Mason went on. "She loves her time in Haiti."

"Does Matt agree?" Lauren asked of Nadia's husband, Sapphire Falls golden boy himself, Matt Phillips. "Does *Phoebe* agree?" she added, thinking of Joe's wife.

"They do," Mason said. "They agreed that two-week stints at a time would work. Though Matt is interested in doing another year of teaching over here, in which case he and Nadia could stay more permanently."

"Is two weeks enough?"

"More than," Mason said. "And we certainly don't need a constant presence here anymore. This is our third season."

Lauren thought about all of that. There were people in place who could take some of the load. Who *wanted* to take some of the load. And IAS didn't need to be in Haiti as much at this point anyway.

She felt her heart pounding and wasn't sure if it was in anticipation of all the things this could mean...or in panic.

If she didn't have Haiti and IAS demanding her time and energy and concentration...what was she going to do? If Hailey would let her work on the Christmas tour of homes or something, that would be one thing, but the mayor hadn't gotten back to her on that. Or her other six ideas.

"And, yes, that will mean downtime," Mason said, reading her easily.

"But I—"

"Will have plenty of time to raise some chickens."

"I do *not* want chickens."

Mason chuckled. Someone approached to ask him about some numbers. He steered the man in Nadia's direction.

Lauren watched the exchange with happiness and trepidation.

Their company was successful. Brilliant people like Nadia wanted to work for them. And Lauren and Mason had done a hell of a job choosing and training their team. Things would likely run perfectly whether she and Mason were at the helm or not.

Not that she'd admit it to him, but Joe had handled the entire situation with Senator Andrews beautifully.

Damn him.

"Well, there is an area in West Africa I've been thinking about," she told Mason.

"No."

She looked up at him. "What?"

"No more areas right now," Mason said. "Give Joe the lead for down the road. But not now."

She started to argue but took a deep breath instead and found herself nodding. "Okay. Time for a change."

Mason grinned. "Things have already changed, babe. You're just slow admitting it."

Lauren opened her mouth to reply to that. But she was interrupted by a deep voice.

"Well, hell, City, if you'd told me it was gonna be like this, I woulda been here a long time ago."

Lauren froze. She felt her boots sinking down into the mud at the edge of the field, but she couldn't move. She was staring.

At Travis.

She'd imagined him in her dreams every night she'd been in Haiti, but she hadn't conjured him during the day until now.

He continued toward her. "Now I don't know much about bowties and limos. But this is just farming. I know all about farming." He stopped in front of her.

She snorted at that. Travis farmed with tractors and spreaders and combines. Huge expensive machines that saved a lot of manual work. Here it was all old-fashioned. They worked by hand. They used tools and animals when they had them. But this was *not* farming the way Travis was used to.

Still, he stood right in front of her, big and broad and hard. And looking completely happy.

"I loved the green dress on you, but you look best ankle deep in mud."

She wore black rubber work boots that were, indeed, ankle deep in the mud. She wore long linen pants and a light cotton shirt, a wide-brimmed hat and about six hours' worth of dust.

She absolutely didn't look her best at all.

But when Travis lifted one hand to cup her face and looked at her with all of the love and humor and tenderness and longing that she saw in his eyes, she felt gorgeous.

"You're really here?" she asked.

"For two weeks. Then I'm hoping to take you home with me for a little while."

Home. The word took her breath away.

"What about...everything in Sapphire Falls?" She almost teared up saying the name. She missed it. She missed the town square and the dogs and the Come Again and even the coffee.

"Well, the thing about corn is that it grows even when I'm not there," Travis said with a little smile.

"The corn isn't the only thing that keeps you from

leaving," she said softly.

He gave her the slow grin that made her insides turn to goo. "Turns out that I've just never had a good reason to leave."

"And now you do?" He'd said he loved her. But she sure wouldn't mind hearing it again. And then throwing herself into his arms, ripping off his clothes and telling him she felt the same way.

He nodded. "And I hope it's the same reason you finally have for *not* leaving. At least some of the time."

Lauren lifted her hand to press his more firmly against her face. He was really here. In Haiti. For her.

"Well, someone once told me that home isn't a place you never leave. It's the place you go back to."

His smile faded and his gaze burned into her. "That same person has discovered that home is actually the place where you're who you most want to be."

"And that's Sapphire Falls for you?"

"It's wherever you are, Lauren."

God, she loved when he said her name like that—gruff and intense. She pressed her lips together. This was a dumb time to cry.

"Oh, and I brought you these."

She looked down at the box he'd been carrying in his other hand. The top said *Duggs* in simple black letters. He'd brought her new boots. Roses, candy, jewelry—there wasn't a single thing that he could have gotten her that would have meant more.

She shook her head and swallowed. "I think you should know," she told him. "I *really* don't want to raise chickens."

He grinned. "I can handle the chickens."

"But I might like a pig. One of the villagers has piglets."

"Oh, no, did you…"

She grinned and nodded. "I saw them being born."

He groaned but laughed. "You're going to end up a vegetarian. Then what am I going to do with you?"

She moved in and wrapped her arms around him. "I'll still be able to eat snails."

He shuddered and then hugged her close. "And I'll be sitting across the table eating my bacon cheeseburger."

She laughed. So they weren't always going to be on exactly the same page. That was no problem at all.

Because it turned out that a good-looking, suntanned, slow-talking, cheap-beer-guzzling small-town *farmer* had, indeed, changed her mind about almost everything.

"I love you," she told him, leaning back to look up into his eyes.

"I love you too. More than anything."

He kissed her. Sweet, hot and full of promise.

Then Lauren took his hand and tugged him toward the field in Haiti where *some* of her dreams were coming true. "Come on, Farmer Boy. I think it's my turn to get *you* dirty."

ABOUT THE AUTHOR

Erin Nicholas is the author of sexy contemporary romances. Her stories have been described as toe-curling, enchanting, steamy and fun. She loves to write about reluctant heroes, imperfect heroines and happily ever afters. She lives in the Midwest with her husband, who only wants to read the sex scenes in her books; her kids, who will never read the sex scenes in her books; and family and friends, who say they're shocked by the sex scenes in her books (yeah, right!).

You can find Erin on the Web at www.ErinNicholas.com, on Twitter (http://twitter.com/ErinNicholas) and on Facebook (https://www.facebook.com/ErinNicholasBooks)

Look for these titles by Erin Nicholas

Now Available at all book retailers!

Sapphire Falls
Getting Out of Hand (book 1)
Getting Worked Up (book 2)
Getting Dirty (book 3)

The Bradfords
Just Right (book 1)
Just Like That (book 2)
Just My Type (book 3)
Just the Way I Like It (short story, 3.5)
Just for Fun (book 4)
Just a Kiss (book 5)
Just What I Need: The Epilogue (novella, book 6)

Anything & Everything
Anything You Want
Everything You've Got

Counting On Love
Just Count on Me (prequel)
She's the One
It Takes Two
Best of Three
Going for Four
Up by Five

The Billionaire Bargains
No Matter What
What Matters Most
All That Matters

Single titles
Hotblooded

Promise Harbor Wedding
Hitched
(book 4 in the series)

Enjoy this Excerpt from
Just Right

The Bradfords, book one

by Erin Nicholas

If only he wasn't so good at being bad...

Dr. Ben Torres, better-than-a-Boy-Scout, surgeon extraordinaire, has been interested in ER nurse Jessica Bradford-and her bright red peek-a-boo thong-for a long time now. But punching a patient in the nose-and the subsequent suspension-is probably not the best way to get on her good side.

Or is it?

Jessica is one step away from the big promotion she's worked for all her professional life, and now everything rides on her ability to keep Dr. Perfect-aka handsome, heroic Ben-on a short leash until the potential lawsuit blows over. And to keep her raging crush on him under wraps.
First order of business is to pry her knight in shining scrubs' perfect ass off a bar stool. Except he refuses to move until she agrees to-and then loses-a bet for 48 hours of her undivided attention.

It's all downhill from there. And despite herself, Jessica can't help but give in to the temptation to go down with him.

Warning: Contains hot love in a store dressing room and in the front seat of a car-at the expense of a very nice strawberry patch, unfortunately-oh, and hooker boots. Can't forget the hooker boots.

Excerpt

It was not a good day to go low-carb.

Not that any day was a good day to go low-carb. But as she struggled to hold the bloody, pissed-off drunk down on the trauma room table, Jessica Bradford really missed the double-chocolate jumbo muffin that was a part of her usual Wednesday morning routine.

"Get off me! Let me go! Get off me, you bitch!"

She didn't think she'd been called a derogatory term this early in the morning before. Great, a new record.

It was going to be a long day.

She sighed. As the first nurse into the room as the gurney rolled in, Jessica got the questionable privilege of getting to hold the guy's hand. Kind of. She somehow wrestled the man's arm down again, thumping it against the examining table with more force than was strictly necessary. Dan, another of the ER nurses, got a firm grip on his wrist.

"Okay, Linda, now," Dan said to another nurse. "Get it in now."

Linda's hands were admirably steady as she inserted the needle to deliver a potent sedative into the man's forearm.

"Ow! You bitch!" The man attempted to bring his hand up alongside Linda's head.

His arm rose only a couple of inches as Jessica and Dan held strong, but Jessica's arms burned with the effort and she knew she couldn't hold him much longer.

Amazing. The man looked like he'd been in a minor scuffle—and had come out the winner—instead of a head-on collision on the expressway. Not to mention that he had been acting like a pain in the ass since he'd been brought in. That had to use up some energy.

Linda focused on her task and managed to get the needle taped down securely before the man could rip it free with his thrashing. Fortunately, his other arm was broken in at least three places and he was unable to use it to do more damage to himself or the staff working to help him.

"Please let it work quickly," Jessica, prayed.

The crash of metal against the hard tile floor was earsplitting as the man's right foot kicked over the tray near the bed and the array of instruments hit and scattered. But he'd been aiming for the nurse who was cutting open the leg of his blue jeans.

"Get off of me!" the man bellowed. "Goddamn it!"

"Not quickly enough," Dan replied dourly.

Jessica had to put all one hundred and twenty pounds of her body weight against the man's arm to keep him from yanking the IV out before the sedative could work.

"Turn the drip up," Jessica muttered.

The man tried to thrash his other arm, but instead moaned loudly. Of course, the alcohol content of his blood likely dulled the intensity of the pain somewhat. Including the pain from the gash on the top of his head that was spurting blood even as the ER physician, Matt Taylor, labored to stitch it shut. The man's head jerked from side to side and he continued to swear at everyone who came into his line of vision.

Nearly three minutes later, he finally began wearing out, or the medication was kicking in, or both, because he started to calm. Jessica slowly released her hold on him, then carefully stepped away from the table, rolled her head and rubbed the back of her arm. Wrestling a man with three times her muscle mass and ten times her adrenaline levels had definitely created some knots.

Just then, the exam room doors banged open.

And Ben Torres walked in.

Jessica froze mid-knead.

The genes Ben had inherited from his half-Hispanic father were gloriously evident in his tanned skin, dark hair and deep brown eyes. But even without the eyes, he took up space in a confident, graceful, solid way that made Jessica think about things she hadn't thought about in years. Things like large hands and proportionate other body parts. And other thoughts entirely inappropriate in a place where things truly were life and death.

It wasn't her fault she got distracted. Dr. Ben Torres was magnificent. Even when he was upset. As he obviously was now.

He was scowling as he stalked into the room.

"How are the kids?" someone asked.

"Dead in the ambulance," Ben said flatly without looking at anyone but the man on the table.

A nurse automatically handed Ben gloves, which he pulled on as he came toward the man.

"What about the mother?" Dan asked.

"In a coma. Bleeding profusely," Ben said shortly, stopping at the foot of the table the man lay on. "She won't make it."

No one responded for a moment and all sexual thoughts fled Jessica's mind as she stared at Ben. It wasn't just the news he'd delivered. It was tragic, but unfortunately not an uncommon report for an emergency room. It was the way Ben said the words. There was a coldness in his voice that Jessica had never heard from him. The rest of the staff responded similarly, shrinking away as he passed them. Ben was always serious in the ER, intent on his work but calm and composed. Now he looked furious, barely holding on to his anger.

Then the relative silence was interrupted by, "Son of a bitch!"

The man on the table suddenly tried to sit upright. Matt's hands still held the end of the thread that was partially keeping the man's scalp together. The man howled in pain as the thread in his head pulled and his mangled arm shifted.

People around the table lunged to restrain him again and someone yelled, "Give him more!" Someone went for a syringe and Jessica went for the wrist with the IV. But as she leaned in, the man grabbed the front of her shirt and jerked her forward.

"Damn it! Get me out of here! Get them off of me!"

She wrapped her hands around the man's arm and opened her mouth, but before she could respond, Ben pushed in next to her and grabbed the man's wrist. He twisted and the man yelped and let go. Jessica stumbled back as Dan came forward too and pushed against the man's chest, forcing him back down on the table.

"Calm down," Ben ordered the man.

"Screw you."

"These people are trying to help you," Ben said, through gritted teeth.

Jess was close enough to see the tension in his face.

"Screw them!" the man shouted. "I don't want their help."

He pulled hard against the arm Ben held, then grimaced in pain as Ben squeezed his wrist.

"Don't you remember me, Ted?" Ben asked, his jaw tight. "I put your sorry ass back together two months ago when you plowed your car into that tree."

The man didn't look any happier, but his struggling slowed a bit as he stared at Ben. "That's right," Ben went on. "Thanks to me you were able to get up this morning and appreciate the beautiful sunrise and get ready for work at a rewarding job where you help people and contribute to society. Oh, wait."

He leaned in closer to Ted, his expression dark, his tone cold. "That was the woman lying on that table in the next room. But the breakfast she made and the hugs she gave her kids and the latte she bought today were all her last. Because of you."

Jessica wasn't breathing and she knew no one else in the room was either. She couldn't tear her eyes away from Ben and the intensity of the emotions on his face.

Ted squirmed on the table and tried to turn his head away from Ben's stare of contempt, but Ben caught Ted's chin in his hand and forced the man to look at him.

"Look at you." Ben's voice was low and angry. "You're barely scratched up compared to those kids, but these people still have to stay and help you. But I know you're wasting their time, just like you wasted mine. I spent four hours in that operating room making sure you would live. But when you got in your car this afternoon you were basically telling me to fuck off, weren't you? And this time you took three people with you."

Ben looked like he'd like to take the man's head off. "That woman and her kids would still be alive if I hadn't done my job so well. It's probably a good thing you don't need surgery today. I might not be having as good a day."

Jessica wanted to gasp at Ben's implication, but she couldn't force any air into her lungs. And she couldn't look away to see what how the rest of the staff was reacting.

"You're a waste of time. And you are going to jail for this."

Ted's eyes went wide and he struggled in Ben's hold, thrashing his head side to side.

"This is crap! Get me out of here! Goddamn assholes!"

The man's bellowing jerked Jessica out of her daze. Thank goodness, because she was close enough to Ben that she found herself flinching away as he pulled his arm back. She jumped when his fist came forward quickly and connected with Ted's face.

Ted howled and struggled to lift a hand to where blood was now running from his nose. But the staff stood frozen for several seconds.

Dan reacted first, pivoting and putting his shoulder into Ben's chest. "Back up, Torres."

Dan had to let up on the pressure he was exerting to keep Ted down and the man thrashed, rolling side to side. Dan gritted his teeth and turned back to subdue the patient, unable to deal with both men at once.

Jess recovered, sort of, and stepped in front of Ben. "I've got him," she said to Dan, putting both hands on Ben's chest.

She pushed him back, aware of the pounding of his heart under her palm and, inappropriately, aware that she'd never touched Ben other than brushing against his arm or hand while they were working.

"Dr. Torres," she said, willing him to look at her when he resisted the pressure on his chest.

His six foot two inches to her five foot six was a significant difference, not to mention his solid two hundred pounds of muscle to her slim build, which was mostly from good genes versus good exercise habits.

She pushed harder. "Ben!"

He looked down at her and backed up a step. She followed him as she glanced over her shoulder at the man who continued to moan and complain.

"You could have broken his nose," she said for Ben's ears only.

"I did."

She looked up quickly. His tone was so flat she could only assume that cracked cartilage had been his intention. She swallowed, not sure what to say to that. And completely unable to fully pull her attention from the body heat soaking into her palms.

§◦✍

Ben stared down into the eyes of the woman he'd

purposely been not touching since he'd come to Omaha. She looked so damn good. She smelled delicious. And her hands were on him. Finally.

Ben glared at the man writhing on the table and the rage tightened his chest again. He wanted to concentrate on something good, something pleasurable and sweet, like the woman in front of him.

But Ted Blake had to get into his car this morning instead of sleeping off his drinking binge.

Ben wasn't sorry he'd hit Ted. He wanted the selfish, stupid bastard to feel at least a measure of the pain he'd caused. The blood from Ted's nose couldn't come close to equaling the amount of blood the five-year-old and two-year-old in the next room had lost because of him. But the feel of his fist connecting with the cartilage in Ted's nose had been at least slightly satisfying. Ben knew it meant he'd stooped to Ted's level, that two wrongs don't make a right and all that bullshit. But hitting Ted had definitely felt good.

And damn, Ben wanted to feel good. It had been a long time since things had been that simple.

He especially wanted to kick his obsession with fixing things—things that didn't stay fixed in particular.

Ben focused again on Jessica, who still had her hands braced on his chest and who was still looking at him like…he was a successful, respected surgeon who'd punched a patient in the face.

He just wanted to feel good. And he had an excellent idea about how to make that happen at the moment.

He grabbed her by the upper arms, pulled her up onto her tiptoes and kissed her, eliciting as many gasps from the ER staff as when he'd hit Ted.

This felt so much better.

Hell, he was going to get suspended anyway. Might as well add sexual harassment to the list while he was at it.

Not that Jessica was responding like a woman being

harassed. Her hands gripped his shoulders and she tipped her head to the right, making the fit of their mouths more absolute. She pressed her chest and hips against him, parting her lips for his tongue to invade the silky heat of her mouth.

In fact, the only reason Ben didn't back her up against the nearest wall and make things really interesting was the security guards who showed up.

One cleared his throat. "Dr. Torres, we've been asked to escort you off of St. Anthony's campus."

Ben released Jessica, finally feeling some of the long-sought satisfaction when he saw her lift her hand and press her fingers against her lips, her green eyes wide, a long strand of her dark hair slipping from the ponytail she always wore neat and tight.

"Okay." He had no intention of resisting.

"The patient is finally under sedation," he heard a nurse report to Dan.

Perfect.

"Let's go." Ben turned and led the way out of the trauma room, more than ready to leave.

The truth was, he should have walked out of the ER and not come back a long time ago.

21919687R00167

Made in the USA
Middletown, DE
14 July 2015